Robert Williams Buchanan

David Gray

And Other Essays, Chiefly on Poetry

Robert Williams Buchanan

David Gray
And Other Essays, Chiefly on Poetry

ISBN/EAN: 9783337275457

Printed in Europe, USA, Canada, Australia, Japan

Cover: Foto ©Andreas Hilbeck / pixelio.de

More available books at **www.hansebooks.com**

DAVID GRAY,

AND

OTHER ESSAYS, CHIEFLY ON

POETRY.

BY

ROBERT BUCHANAN.

David Gray.

LONDON:

SAMPSON LOW, SON, AND MARSTON,

MILTON HOUSE, LUDGATE HILL.

1868.

FIRST WORD.

IT is from no desire to appear in a new character that I publish the present volume. The following Essays, indeed, are prose additions and notes to my publications in verse, rather than mere attempts at general criticism, for which, indeed, I have little aptitude. They are my Confession of Faith. I have here briefly touched on several great and magnificent questions immediately affecting the poetic personality :—on the nature and character of the Poet *par excellence*, on the Student's Vocation, on what is and what is not moral in the Student's Utterance, slightly on religious light and truth; illustrating my matter by such sketches as that of Whitman, and such notes as that on Herrick's Hesperides. More would have been added, and particularly an Essay on "The Poetry of David Gray," had not my health suddenly broken down just as the volume was going to press.   The book, however, is complete as it stands,—an epitome of what may be said hereafter in different ways.

The biography of David Gray is another matter.   A large portion of it appeared some years ago in the " Cornhill Magazine," but the additions, now first published, are very important. It is a story known and told as only one could know and tell it; and will, I trust, send still more readers to Gray's wonderful poems.   The little green-bound duodecimo, " The Luggie and other Poems, by the late David Gray," was wafted out unto the great world, heralded by a kindly preface and a brief memoir.   It excited little or no comment.   The exquisite music was too low and tender to attract crowds, or to entice coteries delighted with the scream of the whipper-snapper.   Nevertheless, a few rare spirits heard and welcomed the truest, purest, tenderest lyrical note that has floated to English ears this half-century.

Robert Buchanan.

Sligachan, Isle of Skye,
    Dec. 1, 1867.

CONTENTS.

I.

THE POET, OR SEER:

A DEFINITION.

He keeps, where there is lack of light,
The loveliness of perfect sight.
Hark! how his human heart anon
Leaps with the bliss he looks upon!—
Go forth, O perfect Heart and Eyes,
Stand in the crowd, and melodise!

He keeps, where there is lack of light,
The loveliness of perfect sight.
Hark! how his human heart anon
Leaps with the bliss he looks upon!—
Go forth, O perfect Heart and Eyes,
Stand in the crowd, and melodise!

THE POET, OR SEER.

WHAT then is the Poet, or Seer, as distinguished from the philosopher, the man of science, the politician, the tale-teller, and others with whom he has many points in common? He is, indeed, a student as other students are, but he is emphatically the student who sees, who feels, who sings. The Poet, briefly described, is he whose existence constitutes a new experience—who sees life *newly*, assimilates it *emotionally*, and contrives to utter it *musically*. His qualities, therefore, are triune. His sight must be individual, his reception of impressions must be emotional, and his utterance must be musical. Deficiency in any one of the three qualities is fatal to his claims for office.

I. And first, as to the Glamour, the rarest

and most important of all gifts; so rare, indeed, and so powerful, that it occasionally creates, in very despite of nature, the other poetic qualities. Yet that individual sight may exist in a character essentially unpoetic, in a temperament purely intellectual, might be proven by reference to more than one writer—notably, to a leading novelist. That proof, however, is immaterial. The point is, how to detect this individual sight, this Glamour, how to describe it,—how, in fact, to find a criterion which will prove this or that person to be or not to be a Seer.

The criterion is easily found and readily applied. We find it in the special intensity, the daring reiteration, the unwearisome tautology, of the utterance. The Seer is so occupied with his vision, so devoted in the contemplation of the new things which nature reserved for his special seeing, that he can only describe over and over again—in numberless ways—in infinite moods of grief, ecstasy, awe—the character of his sight. He has discovered a new link, and his business is to trace it to its uttermost consequences. He beholds the world as it has been, but under a new colouring. While small men are wandering up and down the world, proclaiming a thousand discoveries, turning up countless moss-grown truths, the Seer is standing still and wrapt, gazing at the apparition, invisible to all eyes save his, holding his hand upon his heart in the exquisite trouble of perfect perception. And behold! in due time, his inspiration becomes godlike, insomuch as the invisible relation is incorporated in actual types, takes shape and being, and breathes and moves, and mingles in tangible glory into the approven culture of the world.

For, let it be noted, Nature is greedy of her truths, and generally ordains that the perception of one link in the chain of her relations is enough to make man great and sacerdotal; only twice, in supreme moments, she creates a Plato and a Shakespeare, proving the possibility, twice in time, of a sight imperfect but demi-godlike. " Life is a stream of awful passions, yet grandeur of character is attainable if we dare the fatal fury of the torrent." Thus said the Greek tragedians, but how variously! The hopelessness of the struggle, yet the grandeur of struggling at all, is uttered by all three—each in his own 'fashion. In despite of madness, adultery, murder, incest, —in connection with all that is horrible,—in defiance of the very gods, Œdipus, Ajax, Medea, Orestes, Antigone, agonize divinely, and, perishing, attain the repose of antique sculpture. The same undertone pervades all this antique music, but is never so obtruded as to be wearisome. Never was the tyranny of circumstance, the inexorable penalties enforced even on the innocent when laws are broken, represented in such wondrous forms. Under such penalties the innocent may perish, but their reward is their very innocence. Even when they lament aloud, when they exclaim against the direness of their doom, these figures lose none of their nobility. In the *Philoctetes,* the very cries of physical pain are dignified; in the *Œdipus,* the bitterness of the blind sufferer is noble; in the *Prometheus,* the shriek of triumphant agony is sublime.

These three dramatists uttered the truth as they beheld it; nor do they interfere in any wise with higher interpretations of the same conditions. They used the light of their generation; and the value of their revelation lies in the sincerity and splendour of the contemporary utterance. The same thing is not to be said again. It was a cry heard early in time; it is an echo haunting the temple of extinct gods. But its truth to humanity is eternal. We have the same agonies to this day, but we regard them differently. All that can be said on the heathen side has been said supremely.

While the dramatist depicts the fortunes and questionings of small groups and individuals, the epic poet chronicles the history of the world. It is not every day we can have an epic; for only twice or thrice in time are there materials for an epic. Homer is the historian of the gods, and of the social life under Jove and his peers; through his page blows the fresh breeze of morning, the white tents glimmer on Troy plain, horses neigh and heroes buckle on armour,—while aloft the heavens open, showing the glittering gods on the snowy shoulder of Olympus, Iris darting on the rainbow, whose lower end reddens the grim features of Poseidon, driving his chariot through the foam of the Trojan sea. The passion of the *Iliad* is anger, the action, war; in the *Odyssey*, we have the domestic side of the same life, the softer touches of superstition, the milder influences of gods and goddesses, heroes and their queens. But the life is the same in both—large, primitive, colossal—absorbing all the social and religious significance of a period.

What Homer is to the polytheism of the early Greeks, the Old Testament is to the monotheism of the Hebrews. It is the epic of that life—the wilder, weirder, more spiritual poem of a wilder, weirder, more spiritual period. It is the utterance of many mouths, the poem of many episodes, but the theme is unique, pre-eminent—the spirit of the one God, breathing on His chosen peoples, and steadily moving on to fixed consummations foreshadowed in the prophets. We have had no such wondrous epic as this since, and can have none such again. It is the poem of the one God, when yet He was merely a voice in the thunder-cloud, a breath between the coming and going of the winds.

Where else, in Virgil's time, subsisted the matter for an epic? To sing of Æneas and his fortunes was certainly patriotic, but the subject, at the best, was merely local—a contemporary, not an eternal, theme. The two great forms of early European life had been phrased in the two great early epics; and till Christ taught, the time for the third great poem of masses had not come. In point of fact, the third great poem has not yet been written. The *New Testament*, of course, is didactic, not poetic; and the *Paradise Regained* of Milton is purely modern and academic.

The fourth European epic is the *Divine Comedy* of Dante; the fifth and last is the *Paradise Lost* of Milton. It is scarcely necessary to describe in detail the character of the vision in each of these cases. Dante saw Roman Catholicism as no eye ever saw it before, watched it to its uttermost results, made of it an image enduring by the very intensity of its outlines,—framed of it the epic of the early church. Milton's perfect sight pictured, under latter lights, the wonders of the primeval world. The theme was old, but the light was new; and no man had *seen* angels till Milton saw them, having been first blinded, that his spiritual sight might be unimpeded.

Thus, all these men,—Homer, the framers of

the biblical epos, Æschylus, Sophocles, Euripides, Dante, Milton,—were poets by virtue of having seen some side of truth as no others saw it. If some were greater than others, their materials were perhaps greater. Not every one is so situated in time as to see the subject of a new epos, waiting to be sung. But the Seer " shines in his place, and is content." Even Goethe had his truth to utter, and was so far a Seer. He was great in literature, by virtue of his spiritual littleness. It needed such a man to see nature in the cold light of self-worship, to betoken the futility of pure artistic striving. Yet this, at the best, was negative teaching, and so far, inferior.

But, it may be objected, these men surely expressed more than one truth in their generation. In no wise, for each had but one point of view; there was no hovering, no doubting; their gaze was fixed as the gaze of stars. The object is eternal, it is the point of view which changes. Take Milton, for example; the peculiarity of Milton as a Seer is the angelic spirituality of his sight, its rejection of all but perfectly noble types for poetic contemplation. It would seem that, from having once walked with angels, he sees even common things in a divine white light. He breathes the thin serene air of the mountain-top. He seems calm and passionless; his heart beats in great glorified throbs, with no tremor; his speech is stately and crystal·clear; he is for ever referring man to his Maker; for ever comparing our stature with that of angels. Mark, further, that his spiritual creatures are profoundly intellectual creatures, strangely subtle and lofty reasoners. He holds pure intellect so divine a thing that, in spite of himself, he makes the devil his hero. "The end of man," he says in effect, "is to contemplate God, and enjoy Him for ever." But he says this in a way which is not final; there may be truth beyond Milton's truth, but one does not belie the other; this blind man saw as with the eye, and spake as with the tongue, of angels.

Utterances such as these once attained, perceptions so peculiar once welded into the culture of the world, it behoves no man to re-utter them in the reiterative spirit of their first discoverers. He who looks at life exactly as Milton, or Keats, or Dante did, may be an excellent being, but he is certainly too late to be a Seer. Yet each new Seer is, of necessity, familiar with the discoveries of his predecessors; the white light of Milton's purity chastens and solemnizes Wordsworth's diction; while the glow of Elizabethan colour tinges the pale cheek of Keats the lover. The Seer is not the person of Goethe's epigram,—

> Ein Quidam sagt: " Ich bin von keiner Schule;
> Kein Meister lebt mit dem ich buhle;
> Auch bin ich weit davon entfernt,
> Dass ich von Todten was gelernt."
> Das heisst, wenn ich ihn recht verstand—
> " Ich bin ein Narr auf eigne Hand !"

Nay, as each great Poet sings, we again and again catch tones struck by his predecessors— Homer, Æschylus, Dante, Job, Solomon, Milton, Goethe, and the rest,—but deeper, stronger, more permanent than all, we catch the broken voice of the man himself, saying a mystic thing that we have never heard before. The later we come down in time, the frequenter are the echoes; they are the penalty the modern pays for his privileges. Æschylus and the rest echo Homer and the minstrels. The Hebrew prophets, the heathen poets, the Italian minstrels,—Homer, Moses, Tasso, Dante,—reverberate in every page of Milton; yet they only add volume to the English voice. Shakespeare catches cries from all the poetic voices of Europe,* daringly translating into his own phraseology the visions of other and smaller singers, and mellowing his blank verse by the study even of contemporaries. In Chaucer's breezy song come odours from the Greek Ægean, and whispers from Tuscany and Provence. Aristophanes, again and again, inspires the poetically humorous twinkle in the eyes of Molière. But the plagiarism of such writers is kingly plagiarism; the poets ennoble the captives they take in conquest; refusing instruction from no voice, however humble; accepting the matter as divinely sent by nature, but never imitating the tones of the medium which transmits the matter.

There is no better sign of unfitness for the high

---

* Note how he spiritualises still further what is already spiritual in the poetic prose of Plutarch; as an example, compare with the original passage in the Life of Antony the Speech of Enobarbus, descriptive of Cleopatra in her barge.

poetic ministry than a too tricksy delight in imitating other *voices*, however admirable. Racine caught the Greek stateliness so well that he has scarcely an accent of his own, save, of course, the mere general accentuation of his people. In reading him, therefore, we have constantly before our mind's eye the picture of a Frenchman on the stage of the great amphitheatre; we see the masks, the fixed lineaments expressive of single passions; and we hear the high-pitched soliloquies of Greece translated into a modern tongue. Racine, indeed, is better reading than any translator of the tragedians, but he is no Seer. On the other hand, Molière was nearly as much under influence as Racine, but the splendour of his individual vision lifted him high into the ranks of poetic teachers. He was an arrant thief, robbing the playwrights of all countries without mercy, but the roguish gleam of the thief's eyes is never lost under the load of stolen raiment. We think of *him*, not of what he is stealing; the dress makes plainer, instead of hiding, the natural peculiarities of the wearer.

There is, then, no danger in echoes, where

they do not drown the voice; when they are too audible, that is the case. The greatest artists utter old truths with all the force of novelty; not in philosophy only, but in poetry also, are the worn cries repeated over and over again. These cries are common to all the race of Seers, and may be described as the poetic " terminology."

According to the dignity of the revelation will be the rank of the Seer in the Temple. The epic poet is great, because his matter is great in the first place, and because he has not fallen below the level of his matter. The dramatist is great by his truth to individual character not his own, and his power of presenting that truth while spiritual-izing into definite form and meaning some vague situation in the sphere of actual or ideal life. The lyric poet owes his might to the personal character of the emotion aroused by his vision. Then, there are ranks within ranks. Not an eye in the throng, however, but has some object of its own, and some peculiar sensitiveness to light, form, colour. To . Milton, a prospect of heavenly vistas, where stately figures walk and cast no shade; but to Pope (a seer, though low down in the ranks) the pattern of tea-cups, and the peeping of clocked stockings under farthingales. While the rouge on the cheek of modern love betrays itself to the languid yet keen eyes of Alfred de Musset, Robert Browning is proclaiming the depths of tender beauty underlying modern love and its rouge; each is a Seer, and each is true, only one sees a truth beyond the other's truth. After Wordsworth has penetrated with solemn-sounding footfall into the aisle of the Temple, David Gray follows, and utters a faint cry of beautiful yearning as he dies upon the threshold.

One word, in this place, as to the *end* of Art— poetic art particularly, and the mistaken ideas concerning that end. That end has been described from time immemorial as " pleasure." Now, art is doubtless pleasant to the taste. It may be said, further, that art, even when it uses the most painful machinery, when it chronicles human agony and pictures tears and despair, does so in such a way as to cause a certain enjoyment. But the pleasure thus produced is not the aim, but an accompaniment of the aim, proportioned and regulated by qualities existing in materials extracted from life itself. The aim of all life is accompanied by pleasure, includes pleasure, in the highest sense of that word. The specific aim of art, in its definite purity, is *spiritualization;* and pleasure results from that aim, because the spiritualization of the materials of life renders them, for subtle reasons connected with the soul, more beautifully and deliciously acceptable to the inner consciousness. Even in very low art we find spiritualization of a kind. But pleasure, as mere pleasure, is produced on every side of us by the simplest and least intricate experiences of existence itself. The woe and hopelessness of the popular creed is that it thoroughly separates art from utility. Pleasure, merely as pleasure, is worthless to beings sent down on earth to seek that euphrasy which purges the vision of the inner eye — beings to whom art was. given, not a mere musical accompaniment to a dull drama, but as the toucher of the mysterious chords of inquiry which invest that drama with a grand and divine signification. Nor must we confound the purifying spirit of art with didactic sermonizing and direct moral teaching. The spirit who seizes the forms of life, and passes their spiritual equivalents into the minds of men on chords of exquisite sensation, wears no academic gown, writes no formal treatises in verse. The exquisite sensation is a means, and not an end. It is a consequence of the divine system on which she works, and she produces it as much for its own sake as Nature creates a butterfly for the sake of the down on its wings.

The lower condition of the aim of art, if I have stated that aim properly, places fresh obstacles in the way of the construction of an exact science of pleasure. What is one man's delight is another man's aversion. One lady enjoys the method of Miss Braddon, while her neighbour even gets beyond George Eliot. Scores of people absorb as much pleasure out of Longfellow as a solitary idealist extracts from Richter. But though pleasure emanates from all works properly called artistic, ranks are apportioned in the Temple of Worthies according to the amount of spiritualization, not according to the amount of pleasure involved. The higher the spiritualization the less the need of direct teaching; the smaller the artist, the more his need to sermonize.

We admit "Lear" to be great art, because it absorbs, in one perfect spiritual form, picturesque, emotional, musical, the amplest and most dramatic elements of human existence. We call the *Cenci* smaller art, because it spiritualizes elements in themselves horrible and narrow as representing humanity. And we call the amusing "Ingoldsby Legends" no art at all, because their direct aim is pleasure, and they spiritualize no form of life whatever.

Contemporary critics are fond of affirming that art, so far from having any moral purpose, has nothing to do with morality. This is saying in effect that nature has nothing to do with morality. For art is the spiritual representation, the *alter ego*, of nature ; and nothing that is true in nature is false in art. Astronomy as much as morality, concrete experiences as well as abstract ideas, have their place in nature and in art; they are a part of the whole, which has two lives, the lower and the higher, the real and the artistic. An essentially immoral form, a bestiality, a lie, an insincerity, is an outrage in life ;* but it has no

---

* See *après*, the paper on " Literary Immortality." We

permanent place in art, because spiritualization is fatal to its very perceptibility. The basest things have their spiritual significance, but their baseness has evaporated when the significance is apparent. The puddle becomes part of the rainbow.

It is necessary to understand these points clearly; for if pleasure were the end of art, and art had nothing to do with morality, the purport of this volume would be unintelligible.

II. The second essential peculiarity of the Poet is that of emotional assimilation of impressions. Where intellect coerces emotion, by however faint an effort, the result is criticism of life, however exquisite. Where emotion coerces intellect, the result is poetry.

It is not enough, observe, to *see* vividly. Sir Walter Scott could see as vividly as Keats,— but he was incapable of such emotion. Scott, indeed, is the greatest modern writer who may unhesitatingly be described as unpoetic. He was

---

have modern instances of subjects chosen for artistic treatment, which are abominable and false in *nature—e. g.* the Sapphic passion.

true both to human types and to society. He
was able to clothe the bare outline of history with
vivid form and colour. Writing at a time when
individualism was at its height in England, ere
Whig and Tory had merged into one vacuous
nonentity, he could not fail to shadow forth those
higher aspirations which are the exclusive property of individual men of genius. Yet no man
ever laboured to depict trifles with a more lofty
devotion to general truth. There was no finicism
in the author of "Waverley." He depicted in
faithful æsthetic photography the manners and
qualities of ordinary or extraordinary men and
women. He was not always profound, nor always
noble. But over all his works lies the brilliant
radiance of the artistic sympathies, giving, to what
might otherwise have been simply a colourless
likeness, the marvellous beauty of an exquisite
literary painting. Scott, however, was no poet.
His very success in prose fiction, as well as the
failure of his metrical productions, betokens his
unpoetic nature. He *saw*, but was not *moved*
enough to *sing*. For there is this marked difference between poetic and all other utterance: it

owes everything to concentration. Deep emotion is invariably rapid in its manifestation, as we may mark in the case of the ordinary cries of grief; and the temperament of the poet is so intense, so keen, that nought but concentrated utterance suffices him. Whereas, the true secret of novel-writing is the power of expanding.

The *apparence* of pure coercive intellect varies, of course, according to the nature of the singer. In Sappho and Catullus, and all purely lyrical Seers, the intellectual note is hardly heard at all; in Ovid and Chaucer, it is heard faintly; in the subjective school of writers, such as Shelley, it is painfully audible. But even in Shelley, where he writes poetry, emotion prevails. " Queen Mab " has justly been styled a pamphlet in verse, and the " Revolt of Islam " is only occasionally poetic.

It follows that we are, on the whole, more powerfully moved by purely lyrical utterance than by utterances of higher portent. Sappho *troubles* us more than Sophocles, Keats more than Words-worth. The personal cry, so sharp, so rapid, so genuine, can never fail to find an echo in our hearts. The manly exclamation of Burns,—

> For pity's sake, sweet bird, nae mair,
>   Or my puir heart is broken!

the fetid breath of Sappho, screaming,—

> Cold shiverings o'er me pass,
>   Chill sweats across me fly!
> I am greener than grass,
>   And breathless seem to die!

the passionate voice of Catullus,—

> Cœli, Lesbia nostra, Lesbia illa,
> Illa Lesbia, quam Catullus unam
> Plus quam se, atque suos amavit omnes!

the tender lament of Spenser over Sidney, the scream of Shelley, the warm sigh of Keats, all move deeply in the region of melancholy and tears. But the happy calls move us deliciously, although truly " our sweetest songs are those that tell of saddest thought." The lighter strains of Burns, the songs of Tannahill, some verses of Horace, others of Ovid, the lyrics of Drayton and George Wither, and many other glad poems which will occur rapidly to every student, possess the lyrical light in great intensity and sweetness.

But not only in poems professedly lyrical is this lyrical light to be found; it is noticeable in poetry

of any form, wherever there is extreme emotion,
and may invariably be looked for as the characteristic of the true singer.   Œdipus piteously exclaiming in his blindness,—

> τί γὰρ ἔδει μ' ὁρᾶν,
> ὅτῳ γ' ὁρῶντι μηδὲν ἦν ἰδεῖν γλυκύ;

Dante, in the great joy of his divinely beloved
one, feeling his pale studious lips and cheeks turn
into rose-leaves.*   Samson Agonistes groaning,—

> O dark, dark, dark, amid the blaze of noon,
> Irrevocably dark, total eclipse,
> Without all hope of day.

Macbeth's last twilight murmur,—

> I have lived long enough ; my way of life
> Is fallen into the sear, the yellow leaf ;
> And that which should accompany old age,
> As honour, love, obedience, troops of friends,
> I must not look to have !

Cleopatra in the heyday of her bliss ; the sad
shepherd, chasing the footsteps of his love, and
warbling in tuneful ecstasy,—

---

* Purgatory, xxx.

Here she was wont to go! and here! and here!
Just where those daisies, pinks, and violets grow:
The world may find the spring by following her,
For other print her airy steps ne'er left;
Her treading would not bend a blade of grass,
Or shake the downy blow-ball from his stalk;
But like the soft west wind she shot along,
And where she went the flowers took thickest root,
As she had sow'd them with her odorous foot.

And Bernardo Cenci, in the horror and anguish
of that last parting, screaming,---

                O life! O world!
Cover me! let me be no more! To see
That perfect mirror of pure innocence
Wherein I gazed, and grew happy and good,
Shiver'd to dust! To see thee, Beatrice,
Who made all lovely thou didst look upon—
Thee, light of life, dead, dark! While I say "sister,"
To hear I have no sister; and thou, mother,
Whose love was a bond to all our loves,---
Dead! the sweet bond broken!

These utterances, one and all, sad or glad, are
essentially lyrical, only differing from the first
class of lyric utterances in belonging to fictitious
personages, not to the writer. Romeo and Juliet
swarms with lyrics; every great play of Shakespeare is more or less full of them. They betoken

the true dramatic force, and are less distinct in the lesser dramatist. They are plentiful in Beaumont and Fletcher, in Ford, in Webster; less plentiful in Massinger; scarcely audible at all in Shirley and Ben Jonson. Where they should appear in the bombastic tragedies of Dryden, rhetoric and rhodomontade appear instead; and to come down to modern times, where shall we look for the lyrical light in the pretentious tentatives of Sheridan Knowles and Johanna Baillie? If these tentatives sometimes rise to dignity of movement, that is the most which can be said of them. We have powerful emotional situations, and no emotion.

It is here that all professed " imitations " of the classics fail. They reproduce the *repose* so admirably, as in many cases to send the reader to sleep. But we search in vain in them for the representation of the great fires, the burning passions, of the originals.* Insensibly, as has been

---

* The " Philoctetes " of Mr. William Lancaster is to my mind a fine attempt at classic reproduction. It is very noble in parts. Mr. Swinburne's " Atalanta " is also fine, but it seems, on the whole, less sincere.

shrewdly remarked, we derive our notions of Greek art from Greek sculpture, and forget that although calm evolution was rendered necessary by the requirements of the great amphitheatre, it was no calm life, no dainty passion, no subdued woe, that was thus evolved. The lineaments of the actor's mask were fixed, but what sort of expression did each mask wear?——the glazed hopeless stare of Œdipus, the white horror-stricken look of Agamemnon, the stony glitter of the eyes of Clytemnestra, the horridly distorted glare of the Promethean furies, the sick, suffering, and ghastly pale features of Philoctetes. Where was the calm here? The movement of the drama was simple and slow, yet there was no calm in the heart of the actors, each of whom must fit to his mask a monotone—the sneer of Ulysses, the blunted groan of Cassandra, the fierce shriek of Orestes. The passion and power have made these plays immortal; not the slow evolution, the necessity of the early stage. They are full of the lyrical light.

But though lyrical emotion is the intensest of all written forms of emotion, and must invariably be attained wherever poetry interprets the keenest human feeling and passion, there are forms of emotion wherein intellect is not coerced so strongly. Two forms may be mentioned, and briefly illustrated here—emotional meditation, and emotional ratiocination.   Either of these forms is of subtler and more mixed quality than the purely lyrical form.

We have numberless examples of emotional meditation in Wordsworth; the thought is strong, solemn, unmistakably intellectual, but it is spiritualized withal by profound feeling.   Observe, as an example of this, the following portion of the "Lines composed a few miles above Tintern Abbey:"—

O sylvan Wye! thou wanderer through the woods,
How often has my spirit turned to thee,
And now, with gleams of half-extinguished thought,
With many recognitions dim and faint,
And somewhat of a sad perplexity,
The picture of the mind revives again:
While here I stand, not only with the sense
Of present pleasure, but with pleasing thoughts,
That in this moment there is life and food
For future years.   And so I dare to hope,
'Though changed, no doubt, from what I was when first

I came among these hills; when like a roe
I bounded o'er the mountains, by the sides
Of the deep rivers, and the lonely streams,
Wherever nature led; more like a man
Flying from something that he dreads, than one
Who sought the thing he loved.   For Nature then
(The coarser pleasures of my boyish days,
And their glad animal movements all gone by,)
To me was all in all.   I cannot paint
What then I was.   The sounding cataract
Haunted me like a passion: the tall rock,
The mountain, and the deep and gloomy wood,
Their colours and their forms were then to me
An appetite; a feeling and a love
That had no need of a remoter charm,
By thought supplied, or any interest
Unborrowed from the eye.   That time is past,
And all its aching joys are now no more,
And all its dizzy raptures.   Not for this
Faint I, nor mourn, nor murmur; other gifts
Have followed, for such loss, I would believe,
Abundant recompense.   For I have learned
To look on Nature, not as in the hour
Of thoughtless youth; but hearing oftentimes
The still, sad music of humanity,
Not harsh nor grating, though of ample power
To chasten and subdue.   And I have felt
A presence that disturbs me with the joy
Of elevated thoughts: a sense sublime
Of something far more deeply interfused,
Whose dwelling is the light of setting suns,

And the round ocean, and the living air,
And the blue sky, and in the mind of man,
A motion and a spirit, that impels
All thinking things, all objects of all thought,
And rolls through all things.

By the side of this exquisite passage, let me place another by the same great reflective writer,—

When, as becomes a man who would prepare
For such an arduous work, I through myself
Make rigorous inquisition, the report
Is often cheering; for I neither seem
To lack that first great gift, the vital soul,
Nor general truths, which are themselves a sort
Of elements and agents, under-powers,
Subordinate helpers of the living mind.
Nor am I naked of external things,
Forms, images, nor numerous other aids
Of less regard, though won perhaps with toil,
And needful to build up a poet's praise.
Time, place, and manners do I seek, and these
Are found in plenteous store, but nowhere such
As may be singled out with steady choice;
No little band of yet remembered names
Whom I, in perfect confidence, might hope
To summon back from lonesome banishment,
And make them dwellers in the hearts of men
Now living, or to live in future years.

Sometimes the ambitious power of choice, mistaking
Proud spring-tide swellings for a regular sea,
Will settle on some British theme, some old
Romantic tale by Milton left unsung;
More often turning to some gentle place
Within the groves of chivalry, I pipe
To shepherd swains, or seated, harp in hand,
Amid reposing knights, by a river side
Or fountain, listen to the grave reports
Of dire enchantments faced and overcome
By the strong mind, and tales of warlike feats,
Where spear encountered spear, and sword with sword
Fought, as if conscious of the blazonry
That the shield bore, so glorious was the strife,
Whence inspiration for a song that winds
Through ever-changing scenes of votive quest;
Wrongs to redress, harmonious tribute paid
To patient courage and umblemished truth,
To firm devotion, zeal unquenchable,
And Christian meekness hallowing faithful loves.

There can be no mistaking the qualities of these
two passages.   The first is poetry, the second is
the merest prose ; the emotion in the first extract
so breathes on the thought as to fill it with exquisite music and subtle pleasure not to be coerced
by meditation.   Yet the mood of both is a meditative mood. In the " Prelude," from which the above
extract is taken, and in the " Excursion," prose and

poetry alternate most significantly.   Where the
feeling is vivid and intense, the lines lose all
that cumbrousness and pamphletude which have
blinded so many readers to the real merits of
these two compositions.

Wordsworth, too, has passages of emotional
ratiocination; so also has Milton.   But I can
better illustrate that mood of poetry by two extracts from Mr. Browning.   The first is from the
" Epistle of Karsheesh," a poem wherein an Arab
leech details his encounter, during his travels,
with the case of Lazarus :—

> He holds on firmly to'some thread of life,
> (It is the life to lead perforcedly,)
> Which runs across some vast distracting orb
> Of glory on either side that meagre thread
> Which, conscious of, he must not enter yet,—
> The spiritual life around the earthly life.
> The law of that is known to him as this,
> His heart and brain move there, his feet stay here.
> So is the man perplext with impulses,
> Sudden to start off crosswise, not straight on,
> Proclaiming what is Right and Wrong across,
> And not along this black thread through the blaze.
> " It should be" balked by " here it cannot be,"
> And oft the man's soul springs into his face,
> As if he saw again and heard again

His sage, that bade him " Rise," and he did rise.
Something, a word, a tick of the blood within
Admonishes; then back he sinks at once
To ashes, that was very fire before,
In sedulous recurrence to his trade
Whereby he earneth him the daily bread;
And studiously the humbler for that pride,
Professedly the faultier that he knows
God's secret, while he holds the thread of life.
Indeed the especial marking of the man
Is prone submission to the Heavenly will,—
Seeing it, what is it, and why is it?
Sayeth, he will wait patient to the last,
For that same death which must restore his being
To equilibrium, body loosening soul,
Divorced even now by premature full.growth.

The second extract is from " A Death in the
Desert," in which John the Evangelist is supposed
to detail his opinions of his contemporaries, and, in
a spirit impossibly prophetic, to review the arguments, in the " Leben Jesu," against miracles :—

I say that man was made to grow, not stop;
That help, he needed once, and needs no more,
Having grown up but an inch by, is withdrawn :
For he hath new needs, and new helps to these.
This imports solely, man should mount on each
New height in view; the help whereby he mounts,
The ladder rung his foot has left, may fall,
Since all things suffer change save God the Truth.

Man apprehends Him newly at each stage
Whereat earth's ladder drops, its service done ;
And nothing shall prove twice what once was proved.
You stick a garden plot with ordered twigs
To show inside lie germs of herbs unborn,
And check the careless step would spoil their birth ;
But when herbs wave, the guardian twigs may go,
Since should ye doubt of virtues, question kinds,
It is no longer for old twigs ye look,
Which proved once underneath lay store of seed,
But to the herb's self, by what light ye boast,
For what fruit's signs are.   This book's fruit is plain,
Nor miracles need prove it any more.
Doth the fruit show ?   Then miracles bade ware
At first of root and stem, saved both till now
From trampling ox, rough boar, and wanton goat.
What ?   Was man made a wheel work to wind up,
And be discharged, and straight wound up anew ?
No !—grown, his growth lasts ; taught, he ne'er forgets:
May learn a thousand things, not twice the same.

This might be pagan hearing : now hear mine.

I say, that as the babe you feed awhile
Becomes a boy and fit to feed himself,
So minds at first must be spoon-fed with truth :
When they can eat, babe's nurture is withdrawn.
I fed the babe whether it would or no :
I bid the boy or feed himself or starve.
I cried once, " That ye may believe in Christ,
Behold this blind man shall receive his sight !"

I cry now, " Urgest thou, *for I am shrewd*
And smile at stories how John's word could cure—
Repeat that miracle and take my faith ?
I say, that miracle was duly wrought
When, save for it, no faith was possible.
Whether a change were wrought i' the shows o' the world,
Whether the change came from our minds which see
Of the shows of the world so much as and no more
Than God wills for His purpose,—(what do I
See now, suppose you, there where you see rock
Round us ?)—I know not; such was the effect,
So faith grew, making void more miracles
Because too much ; they would compel, not help.
I say, the acknowledgment of God in Christ
Accepted by thy reason, solves for thee
All questions in the earth and out of it,
And has so far advanced thee to be wise.
Wouldst thou unprove this to reprove the proved ?
In life's mere minute, with power to use that proof,
Leave knowledge and revert to how it sprung ?
Thou hast it; use it and forthwith, or die!

Both these passages are ratiocinative; yet one is a poem, the other not even art. There is a flash of ecstasy through the strangely cautious description of Karsheesh; every syllable is weighed and thoughtful, yet everywhere the lines swell into perfect feeling. What shall be said, however, to St. John on Strauss? The violence of the imaginative effort to reach St. John's views on miracles precludes all emotion; and because there is no emotion, false notes occur in every page of the poem. The mind has forced itself into a certain attitude, instead of suffering itself to be coerced by powerful feeling.

All these moods, indeed, are but the consequence of that first mood, wherein the Seer receives his impression. If that first mood be too purely intellectual, if the Seer be not stirred extremely in the process of assimilation, there is a certainty that, in spite of clear vision, he will produce prose,—as Milton did occasionally, as Wordsworth did very often; as Shakespeare seldom or never does, and as Keats never did.

It is certain, then, that clear vision can exist independently of emotion; that, however, emotion is generally dependent on clear vision; and that, in short, he who sees vividly will in most cases feel deeply, but not in all cases.

Let me mention one more notable case in point. I mean Crabbe,—the writer to whom modern writers are fondest of alluding, and whom, to judge from their blunders concerning him, they appear to have been least fond of reading. A careful study of his works has revealed to me abundant knowledge of life, considerable sympathy, little or no insight, and no emotion. The poems are photographs, not pictures. There is no spiritualization, none of that fine selective instinct which invariably accompanies deep artistic feeling. There is too constant a consciousness of the "reader," too painful an attempt to gain force by means of vivid details. Now, these are not the poetic characteristique. The poet derives his force from the vividness of the feeling awakened by his subject or by his meditation; he does not betray himself by clumsy efforts to gain attention. A thought—a touch—a gleam of colour—often suffice for him. Whereas Crabbe betrays his purely intellectual attitude at every step. He describes every cranny of a cottage, every gable, every crack in the wall, every kitchen utensil,—when his story concerns the soul of the inmate. He pieces out a churchyard like so much grocery, into so many lives and graves. There is no glamour in his eyes when he looks on death;—he is noting the bedroom furniture and the dirty sheets. There is no weird music in his ears when he stands in a churchyard;—he is recording the quality of the coffin-wood, sliding off into an account of the history of the parish beadle, and observing whose sheep they are that browse inside the stone wall of the holy place.

III. I am now led directly to the discussion of the third poetic gift,—that of music; for metrical speech is the most concentrated of all speech, and proportions itself to the quality of the poetic emotion. The most powerful form of emotion is lyrical emotion, and the sweetest music is lyrical music.

Poetic vision culminates in sweet sound,— always inadequate, perhaps, to represent the whole of sight, but interpenetrating through the medium of emotion with the entire mystery of . life. Nothing, indeed, so distinguishes the variety of Seers as their melody. It is the soul's perfect speech. A break in the harmony not seldom betrays a dizziness of the eyes, an inactivity of the heart. A false note betrays the false maestro. A cold or forced expression indicates insincerity.

This music, this last wondrous gift, carries with it its own significance and wisdom ; it has a wondrous glamour of its own, like the dim light that is in falling snow. What exquisite sound is this, —where the thought and the emotion die away into a murmur like the wash of a summer sea ?—

> Thou wast not born for death, immortal bird !
>   No hungry generations tread thee down ;
> The voice I hear this passing night was heard
>   In ancient days by emperor and clown.
> Perhaps the self-same song that found a path
>   Through the sad heart of Ruth, when, sick for home,
>   She stood in tears among the alien corn ;
>   The same that oft-times hath
> Charmed magic casements, opening on the foam
>   Of perilous seas, in faery lands forlorn.

Or this,—so perfect in its fleeting rapture : —

> Sound of vernal showers,
>   On the twinkling grass,
> Rain-awakened flowers,
>   All that ever was
> Joyous, and clear, and sweet, thy music doth surpass.
>
> Teach us, sprite or bird,
>   What sweet thoughts are thine :
> I have never heard
>   Praise of love or wine
> That panted forth a rapture so divine !

Teach me half the gladness
That thy brain must know,
Such harmonious madness
From my lips would flow,—
The world should listen then, as I am listening now.

Or these lines from the "Willow, Willow," of Alfred de Musset:—

Mes chers amis, quand je mourrai,
Plantez un saule au cimetière.
J'aime son feuillage éploré,
La pâleur m'en est douce et chère,
Et son ombre sera légère
A la terre où je dormirai.

I might fill pages with such quotations.

The examples just given are examples of purely lyrical music,—from its personal nature, the most concentrated of all music. For the sake of contrast, now, let me turn to the least concentrated form of all, as it is represented in particular writers.

At a first view, it would seem that epic poetry is most apt to be unmelodious, on account of the diffuse character of its materials as generally conceived. But this is an error *à priori*. The materials are not diffuse—they are only large and various; and the music is emotional and concentrated, though not to the extent noticeable in less dignified forms of writing. Like dramatic poetry, it is all-embracing, and includes in its compass all elements, from lyrical feeling to emotional meditation. The stateliness and constancy of its movement do not preclude the sharp lyrical cry or the deep meditative pause. Homer is the most various of singers. His successors are less various, precisely because they are less great. Again and again in the sharp solemn progress of Dante through Hell are we startled by bursts of wilder melody. Even in " Paradise Lost" there are some occasions when the deep organ bass changes into a scream.

This is but saying what has been already said of lyrical emotion. In brief, lyrical emotion and lyrical music as its expression intersect all great poetry, whatever its nature; and the reason need not be further explained. Lyric music is the *ideal* speech of intense personal feeling; and that is why the exquisite music of Greek tragedy is not confined to the choruses.

But just as all emotion is not markedly personal, all music is not lyrical. No music is so exquisite, so profoundly interesting to men; but there are more complex kinds of expression, sounds more variegated and diffuse. Take the following passage from the "Paradise Lost" of Milton:—

> For now, and since first break of dawn, the Fiend,
> Mere serpent in appearance, forth was come,
> And on his quest, where likeliest he might find
> The only two of mankind, but in them
> The whole included race, his purpos'd prey.
> In bower and field he sought where any kind
> Of grove or garden plot more pleasant lay,
> Their tendence or plantation for delight;
> By fountain or by shady rivulet
> He sought them both, but wish'd his hap might find
> Eve separate; he wish'd but not with hope
> Of what so seldom chanc'd, when to his wish,
> Beyond his hope, *Eve separate he spies,*
> *Veil'd in a cloud of fragrance, where she stood,*
> *Half spy'd, so thick the roses blushing round*
> *About her glow'd, oft stooping to support*
> *Each flower of slender stalk, whose head, though gay*
> *Carnation, purple, azure, or speck'd with gold,*
> *Hung drooping, unsustain'd;* them she upstays
> Gently with myrtle band, mindless the while
> Herself, tho' fairest unsupported flower,
> From her best prop so far, and storm so nigh.
> Nearer he drew, and many a walk travers'd

Of stateliest covert, cedar, pine, or palm,
Then voluble and bold, now hid, now seen
Among thick-woven arborets and flowers
Imborder'd on each bank, the hand of Eve:
Spot more delicious than those gardens feign'd,
Or of reviv'd Adonis, or renown'd
Alcinous, host of old Laertes' son,
Or that, not mystic, where the sapient king
Held dalliance with his fair Egyptian spouse.

*   *   *   *   *

So spake the enemy of mankind, enclos'd
In serpent, inmate bad, and toward Eve
Address'd his way, not with indented wave,
Prone on the ground, as since, but on his rear,
Circular base of rising folds, that tower'd
Fold above fold, a surging maze, his head
Crested aloft, and carbuncle his eyes;
With burnish'd neck of verdant gold, erect
Amidst his circling spires, that on the grass
Floated redundant; pleasing was his shape
And lovely; never since of serpent kind
Lovelier, not those that in Illyria chang'd
Hermione and Cadmus, or the God
In Epidaurus; nor to which transform'd
Ammonian Jove, or Capitoline was seen
He with Olympias, this with her who bore
Scipio the height of Rome.   With tract oblique
At first, as one who sought access, but fear'd
To interrupt, side-long he works his way:
As when a ship, by skilful steersman wrought
Nigh river's mouth, or foreland, where the wind

Veers oft, as oft so steers and shifts her sail:
So varied he, and of his tortuous train
Curl'd many a wanton wreath in sight of Eve,
To lure her eye; she, busied, heard the sound
Of rustling leaves, but minded not, as us'd
To such disport before her through the field,
From every beast, more duteous at her call
Than at Circean call the herd disguis'd.
He bolder now, uncall'd before her stood,
But as in gaze admiring: oft he bow'd
His turret crest, and sleek enamel'd neck,
Fawning, and lick'd the ground whereon she trod.

In these exquisite passages of pure description, the music perfectly represents the subdued emotion of the artist; there is no excitement, but vivid presentment;—and we hear the very movement of the snake in the involution and picturesqueness of the lines. I cannot do better than place by the side of the above a passage from the same great poet, which seems to me especially false and inharmonious. It is very brief:—

The Most High

Eternal Father, from his secret cloud,
Amidst in thunder utter'd thus his voice:
Assembled angels, and ye powers return'd
From unsuccessful charge, be not dismay'd,
Nor troubled at these tidings from the earth,

Which your sincerest care could not prevent,
Foretold so lately what would come to pass,
When first this Tempter cross'd the gulf from Hell.
I told ye then he should prevail and speed
On his bad errand, man should be seduc'd
And flatter'd out of all, believing lies
Against his Maker ; no decree of mine
Concurring to necessitate his fall,
Or touch with lightest moment of impulse
His free will, to her own inclining left
In even scale.   But fall'n he is, and now
What rests but that the mortal sentence pass
On his transgression, death denounc'd that day ?
Which he presumes already vain and void,
Because not yet inflicted, as he fear'd,
By some immediate stroke ; but soon shall find
Forbearance no acquittance ere day end.
Justice shall not return as bounty scorn'd.
But whom send I to judge them ? whom but thee
Vicegerent Son ? to thee I have transferr'd
All judgment, whether in Heaven, or Earth, or Hell.
Easy it may be seen that I intend
Mercy colleague with justice, sending thee
Man's friend, his mediator, his design'd
Both ransome and redeemer voluntary,
And destin'd man himself to judge men fall'n.

Where is the thunder here ? Where is the solemn
music ? Instead of awe-inspiring sound, we have
bald and turgid prose, pieced out clumsily into

ten-syllable lines, every one of which limps like Vulcan. And why? Precisely because Milton had no spiritual glamour of the Highest, such as he had of Satan, for example,—felt no real emotion in recording His utterances, not even the cold meditative emotion which just redeems many other parts of " Paradise Lost " from sheer prose. He was forcing his mind to hear a voice, attempting to represent the utterance of a personality ungrasped by his imagination.

Mere rhetorical music is the least poetic of all, although sometimes it has an exceeding charm, as in Virgil's famous lines on Marcellus, and much of the poetry of rhetorical periods in England.

Akin to such rhetorical music is the melody of the ornate school of writers, singers who mar expression by too elaborate effort. Melody, indeed, as represented in our true singers, may be divided into three kinds, just as the singers themselves may be divided into three classes,—the simple, the ornate, and the grotesque. The first kind is the sweetest and best ; we find it in the great lyrists, from Sappho to Burns. Wherever Shelley sings perfectly, as in the " Ode to the Skylark," his music loses all its insincerities and affectations. Ornate and grotesque music have common faults,—the first sacrifices the emotion and meaning by thinning and straining them too carefully ; the second loses in portent what it gains in mannerism ; and both, therefore, betray that dangerous intellectual self-consciousness which is a barrier to the production of true poetry. A thing cannot be uttered too briefly and simply if it is to reach the soul. Music that conceals, instead of expressing, thought, music that is nothing but sweet sounds and luscious alliterations, is not poetry. We have the sweet sounds everywhere, in fact : in the wash of the sea, in the rustle of leaves, in the song of birds, in the murmur of happy living things. The world is full of them, its heart aches with them ; they are mystical and they are homeless. It is the office of poetry not barely to imitate them, but to link them with the Soul, and by so doing to use them as symbols of definite form and meaning. They issue from the soul's voice with a new wonder in their tones, and are then ready to be used as man's perfect language and speech to God.

I need delay little more on this branch of poetic power, which, indeed, contains matter for a whole volume.   It is clear that there is no poetry without music, but that music varies extremely, according to the quality and intensity of the emotion. It may safely be affirmed that no subject is unfit for poetic treatment which can be spiritualized to this uttermost form of harmonious and natural numbers. So closely is melody woven in with and representative of emotion and of sight, that it has been called the characteristique of the true Seer. But let us never lose sight of the fact that music *is* representative, and valuable, not for the sole sake of its own sweetness, not for the sole sake of the emotion it represents, but mainly and clearly valuable for the sake of the poetic thought and vision which it brings to completion.   There may be melodious sound without meaning, fine versification without thought; but the most exquisite melody and versification are those which convey the most exquisite forms of poetic vision.

The tongue must be guided by the eye, if the heart is to be reached by the ear; a series of sighs is not a poem.

Thus, then, have been briefly described the qualities of the Poet. He is cardinally the Seer, the man who beholds what others behold not, and the consequence of his vision is deep emotion finding its expression in beautiful music. None of the gifts may be dispensed with; how many a pretender, how many a laurel-wearer, must truth dethrone, because he lacks eyes. How many must be set aside because, in spite of nearly perfect sight, they are too cold and impassive. A number, too, must be rejected solely because they cannot sing. Southey and Bowles are examples of defective vision; Scott and Crabbe are examples of defective emotion; Bacon and Walt Whitman are examples of defective music.

Nor let it be conceived that vision can exist in its highest splendour in other men than the born Seers. The vision which moves so deeply as to turn the very breath of the soul into music is equalled by no other vision : its discoveries are the most supreme, its significance the most divine. The proof of perfect sight is perfect song ; other men may see clearly, but the Poets are the discoverers and watchmen of the world ; they stand

on an eminence and see far into the happy valleys.
There is, indeed, a growing tendency in modern
life to separate poetry from the poet; but how
much is the effect of true song enhanced by the
solitary singer on the headland, his white robes
blowing in the wind. On such a headland the
poet should stand; his face must shine—bright,
individual, beautiful—in the midst of his creations.
It is not entirely by the character of the vision
that we intuitively recognize a genuine "bit" by
Milton, or by Dante, or by Burns; we recognize
them chiefly by the temper of the emotion, as expressed in the music; and thus, through all great
and genuine poetry, runs that personal note which
we call the characteristique of the singer. He who
is wholly sunk in his art dies with his art. Arts do
die; but the true history of literature is the life of
men.

The perfectly approven Seer is a *sacer vates*, a
priest in the great Temple of Poesy. What are his
priestly functions? Is he merely a chaunter in the
great choirs of nature,—an intoner of responses,—
a swinger of incense before the altar. Nay; his
office is white and ministerial, fulfilling daily

functions of divine significance. He is a justifier of the ways of God to men. Without that perfect sight of his, why should God have selected him? Had not very God selected him, how should he be so moved? Were his voice unmusical, how should men heark to his news? But once invested, once clearly persuaded that he is a *vates*, he finds his task become easy to him. He has only to sing aloud, and his heart is eased, and he is glad. Whether his tidings be sad or merry, he is glad; for he is serving an exquisitely beautiful Master. "It is," says Emerson, "dislocation and detachment from God that makes things ugly." He should have said *seeming* dislocation; no things are quite separated from God, and it is the poet's office to see the faint lines of communication. Those lines detected, the ugly thing is ugly no more, but is glorified in the strange and tender sweetness issuing from God's eyes.

And here we have the clue to all these Proteustricks in which the Seers, from Shakespeare downwards, delight. Everything, everybody, illustrates the poetic discovery. What the Seer beholds as an idea he rushes to corroborate in life,

and so creates ideals.   He is certain of his truth,
but he is never tired of fresh verification.   Again
and again he approaches us in disguise,—now he
is one man, then another man, now one woman,
then another woman; but the same revelation is
heard, albeit qualified by the character of the personage.   By one mouth or another he is bent on
reaching our souls.   That is the dramatic forti-
tude, the *vivida vis* of song.   But where one Seer
illustrates his truth by human beings, his brother
Seer seeks verification in nature, finds sermons
in stones, and corroborate wisdom in all things.
While Shakespeare plays Proteus, Wordsworth
calls hills and woods and streams to witness.
Seers there are also who gaze at one aspect of
nature, so lost in looking that they can only cry,
" See ! see ! " The light streams straight into their
eyes; they will not stir, lest it die away;—they
desire no verification beyond the tears on their
own cheeks, the ache in their own hearts.   Such
an one was David Gray.

If Hamlet and the great voices cannot reach
us, cannot stir us, tongues have been given to the
very hills.   If the hills and great forces cannot

move us, there are Seers translating the voice of the running brook. If the running brook and gentle powers have no spell upon us, the cry of a departing voice shall warn us of our souls. Blessings even on the childish voices, which utter tiny truths in tender syllables, dulcet to ears not over keen to the hearing of sounds from the world of spirits.

Let this, moreover, be said,—the Seer never *lies*. He is the man of truth, who cannot disturb the order and inferences of things, however much he may upset the order and inferences of idealists. He will admit no prevarications, no tawdry insincerities; he is largely sane and beautiful, and need not imitate the devices of the eyeless.

Is it objected that there have been great Poets who have sung things which modern culture admits to be false, not true ? But eternal truth is one matter, and contemporary truth is another. We may not believe now in the terror and vengefulness of the Lord God Avatar of the Hebrews, although that belief dwelt in the thunder-cloud of Ezekiel's life, and issued from it in a lightning flash of prophecy. We may not believe in Dante's

Inferno, nor in Mahomet's Paradise, nor in the seventy angels of a Mussulman, nor in Milton's devil,—but these are great, either as contemporary or poetic facts, true spiritually. For it is doubtless the business of the Seers to mark the great epochs in the march of man; and on each occasion of chronicling, the Seer (being *not* God, but the finite priest) deems in all sincerity that the mystery of things is solved, and bursts into rapturous song. The voice of Job, in eternal wail, sounds over the tracts of time, sounding the weariness of human speculation. The spirit of Æschylus darkly commemorates supernaturalism at strife with intellect. Plato is an awful rumour of all that the unassisted mind of man can conceive of immortality. All these and such things were new, and true; and the intensity of the contemporary revelation, acting through the splendour of the eternal truth, has made them endure for ever. I pin my faith on the Incarnation, but I can admit the spiritual truth of other men who deny the Incarnation,—Plotinus, Proclus, Voltaire, Rousseau, and all others.

For the Temple of Nature, where the poet ministers, is a wondrous prism, in shining through which the perfect whiteness of God's truth is merely turned into its constituent colours. None of these colours are false, and none are quite true; here, then, before the prism, all creeds may join the Poet. He may enter in, who knows any one of the thousand names of God, which are scattered for mysterious sounds up and down the earth. Within the temple no blasphemy is heard. The prismatic radiance of God strikes across the altar. A medley of strange tongues is heard on every side,—tongues of all lands, from China to Cana of Galilee, crying together Πατὴρ Ἀνδρῶν τε Θεῶν τε! One understands as much of the white light as the other understands. The fact that each can see, is stirred, and sings exquisitely, is at least a sign that their contradictions are countenanced by the oracle.

It is in the weird pale circle of the moral law that the Seers are bound to have a definite terminology. No modern Seer, for example, can possibly despise the poor,—or sympathize with the scholastic views of Socrates' love for Alcibiades,—or deny the equality of natural rights.

His predecessors have not worked for nought.
Burns has at least taught that the poor are God's
creatures, full of noble qualities. Wordsworth has
at least shown wherein the lowly are approven by
the great combined forces of nature and the
human heart. Not to carry on these illustrations,
it is clear that no modern Poet dare lie against
the accumulated testimony of his predecessors.
He cannot without gross insincerity (which he
may call "culture" if he please) write precisely
as Sophocles wrote, much as he may recognize
the spiritual truth of such writing; for he could
not do so without first believing as Sophocles believed,—in which case he would be behind his
age, and therefore unfit for priestly office at all.
Nor may he write as Chaucer, or as Milton, or as
Shelley wrote. We are beyond that. So far
from being behind his age, he is far in advance of
his age.* He is a torch-holder, peering forward
into the dark To-come ; he is a singer, chaunting
his new discovery therein. The task, a special

---

* It might be curious to note in detail how far Browning's
orthodoxy is in advance even of our most liberal orthodoxy.

task, of circulating the old truths, showing them in new lights, belong to quite another person,—to the reproducer, not to the creator.

The class of reproducers is very large and very useful, consisting of men deficient only in one poetic quality, that of perfect individual vision. The reproducer feels acutely, sings exquisitely, but he is feeling and singing what has been discovered for him by predecessors. His delicate and sensitive eye at once appreciates the beauty pointed out to him (provided it be not contemporary or prospective beauty, which it is the nature of his vision not to see at all); his exquisite voice has been known to phrase the discovery even more charmingly than the Seer himself. The mere artist may frequently outvie the Seer in technical work. The following little poem by an American poet illustrates this point clearly:—

> The morning comes, but brings no sun;
> The sky with storm is overrun;
> And here I sit in my room alone,
> And feel, as I hear the tempest moan,
> Like one who hath lost the last and best,
> The dearest dweller from his breast!
> For every pleasant sight and sound,
> The sorrows of the sky have drowned;

> The bell within the neighbouring tower,
> Falls blurred and distant through the shower;
> Look where I will, hear what I may,
> All, all the world seems far away!
> The dreary shutters creak and swing,
> The windy willows sway and fling
> A double portion of the rain
> Over the weeping window pane.
> But I, with gusty sorrow swayed,
> Sit hidden here, like one afraid,
> And would not on another throw
> One drop of all this weight of woe!

All that is exquisite,—more exquisite than Wordsworth often is,—yet how instantly do we feel that the poem could never have been written save under Wordsworth's direct influence. A volume might be filled with such examples. A notable contemporary work of reproduction is Mr. Morris's "Life and Death of Jason," where Homeric force and Chaucerian piteousness are mingled into truly beautiful music. This is a case of veritable reproduction, really good and notable work, as distinguished from those insincere imitations which now abound in literature.

Let me not be understood to imply that the functions of the Seer do not include artistic and reproductive functions; but in his case, the smaller quality is lost in the greater,— the artist in the maker.

It is necessary, in conclusion, to say a few words on the training of the Seer. He must, as has been frequently insisted upon, have all the culture of his time :—no one-sided culture,— none of that elaborate intellectuality which rejects all food but what nourishes self-consciousness; but a truer culture, implying simply familiarity with what has been done by his predecessors, and absorption of the truths which they have introduced into poetic terminology. Philosophy, history, science, must all be familiar in their general bearings. Otherwise, how shall the Seer know that he is better than a tinkling cymbal, echoing what men have said in the world's morning? Want of culture, properly so called, is at the bottom of many poetic failures. In a word, the Seer is made as well as born. He must know, as well as see. Else he will be taking every cockchafer for an unknown species, or rushing into the senate breathless with the discovery that the sun is risen.

Perfect culture is perfect character,—the amplest development of natural gift and inspiration. It means life and strife, and probationary years of silence, and love of true literatures, and a creed of some sort. In these modern days, it must mean, above all,—Charity. "Though I speak with tongues of men and of angels, and have not charity, I am become as sounding brass or a tinkling cymbal. And though I have the gift of prophecy, and understand all mysteries, and all knowledge; and though I have all faith, so that I could remove mountains, and have not charity, I am nothing." With these words written in his heart, the Seer need fear no world, even if he is compelled to look at souls through the dark glass of his university.

II.

DAVID GRAY.

Two friends, in interchange of heart and soul;
But suddenly Death changed his countenance,
And graved him in the darkness, far from me.
                    The Luggie, by DAVID GRAY.

Quem Di diligunt, adolescens moritur.

DAVID GRAY.

ITUATED in a by-road, about a mile from the small town of Kirkintilloch, and eight miles from the city of Glasgow, stands a cottage one storey high, roofed with slate, and surrounded by a little kitchen-garden. A whitewashed lobby, leading from the front to the back-door, divides this cottage into two sections; to the right, is a roof fitted up as a hand-loom weaver's workshop; to the left is a kitchen paved with stone, and opening into a tiny carpeted bedroom.

In the workshop, a father, daughter, and sons worked all day at the loom. In the kitchen, a handsome cheery Scottish matron busied herself like a thrifty housewife, and brought the rest of the family about her at meals. All day long the soft hum of the loom was heard in the workshop; but when night came, mysterious doors were thrown open, and the family retired to sleep in extraordinary mural recesses.

In this humble home, David Gray, a hand-loom weaver, resided for upwards of twenty years, and managed to rear a family of eight children—five boys and three girls. His eldest son, David, author of "The Luggie and other Poems," is the hero of the present true history.

David was born on the 29th of January, 1838. He alone, of all the little household, was destined to receive a decent education. From early childhood, the dark-eyed little fellow was noted for his wit and cleverness; and it was the dream of his father's life that he should become a scholar. At the parish-school of Kirkintilloch he learned to read, write, and cast up accounts, and was, moreover, instructed in the Latin rudiments. Partly through the hard struggles of his parents, and partly through his own severe labours as a pupil-teacher and private tutor, he was afterwards enabled to attend the classes at the Glasgow University. In common with other rough country lads, who live up dark alleys, subsist chiefly on oatmeal and butter forwarded from home, and eventually distinguish themselves in the class-room, he had to fight his way onward amid poverty and privation; but in his brave pursuit of knowledge nothing daunted him. It had been settled at home that he should become a minister of the Free Church of Scotland. Unfortunately, however, he had no love for the pulpit. Early in life he had begun to hanker after the delights of poetical composition. He had devoured the poets from Chaucer to Wordsworth. The yearnings thus awakened in him had begun to express themselves in many wild fragments—contributions, for the most part, to the poet's-corner of a local news-paper—"The Glasgow Citizen."

Up to this point there was nothing extraordinary in the career or character of David Gray. Taken at his best, he was an average specimen of the persevering young Scottish student. But his soul contained wells of emotion which had not yet been stirred to their depths. When, at fourteen years of age, he began to study in Glasgow, it was his custom to go home every Saturday night in order to pass the Sunday with his parents. These Sundays at home were chiefly occupied with rambles in the neighbourhood of Kirkintulloch; wanderings on the sylvan banks of the Luggie, the beloved little river which flowed close to his father's door. On Luggieside awakened one day the dream which developed all the hidden beauty of his character, and eventually kindled all the faculties of his intellect. Had he been asked to explain the nature of this dream, David would have answered vaguely enough, but he would have said something to the following effect: "I'm thinking none of us are quite contented; there's a climbing impulse to heaven in us all that won't let us rest for a moment. Just now I would be happy if I *knew* a little more. I'd give ten years of life to see Rome, and Florence, and Venice, and the grand places of old; and to feel that I wasn't a burden on the old folks. I'll be a great man yet! and the old home, the Luggie and Gartshore wood, shall be *famous* for my sake." He could only measure his ambition by the love he bore his home. "I was born, bred, and cared for here, and my folk are buried here. I know every nook and dell for miles around, and they are all dear to me. My own mother and father dwell here, and in my own *wee* room " (the tiny carpeted bedroom above alluded to) " I first learned to read poetry. I love my home; and it is for my home's sake that I love fame."

Nor were that home and its surroundings unworthy of such love. Tiny and unpretending as is Luggie stream, upon its banks lie many nooks of beauty, bowery glimpses of woodland, shady solitudes, places of nestling green for poets made. Not far off stretch the Campsie fells, with dusky nooks between, where the waterfall and the cascade make a silver pleasure in the heart of shadow; and beyond, there are dreamy glimpses of the misty blue mountains themselves. Away to the south-west, lies Glasgow in its smoke, most hideous of cities, wherein the very clangour of church-bells is associated with abominations. Into the heart of that city David was to be slowly drawn, subject to a fascination only death could dispel,—the desire to make deathless music, and the dream of moving therewith the mysterious heart of man.

At twenty-one years of age, when this dream was strong within him, David was a tall young man, slightly but firmly built, and with a stoop at the shoulders. His head was small, fringed with black curly hair. Want of candour was not his fault, though he seldom looked one in the face; his eyes, however, were large and dark, full of intelligence and humour, harmonizing well with the long thin nose and nervous lips. The great black eyes and woman's mouth betrayed the creature of impulse; one whose reasoning faculties were small, but whose temperament was like red-hot coal. He sympathized with much that was lofty, noble, and true in poetry, and with much that was absurd and suicidal in the poet. He carried sympathy to the highest pitch of enthusiasm; he shed tears over the memories of Keats and Burns, and he was corybantic in his execution of a Scotch "reel." A fine phrase filled him with the rapture of a lover. He admired extremes—from Rabelais to Tom Sayers. Thirsting for human sympathy, which lured him in the semblance of notoriety, he perpetrated all sorts of extravagancies, innocent enough in themselves,

but calculated to blind him to the very first principles of art. Yet this enthusiasm, as I have
suggested, was his safeguard in at least one
respect. Though he believed himself to be a
genius, he loved the parental roof of the hand-loom
weaver.

And what thought the weaver and his wife of
this wonderful son of theirs? They were proud
of him, proud in a silent undemonstrative fashion;
for among the Scottish poor concealment of the
emotions is held a virtue. During his weekly
visits home, David was not overwhelmed with
caresses; but he was the subject of conversation
night after night, when the old couple talked in
bed. Between him and his father there had arisen
a strange barrier of reserve. They seldom ex-
changed with each other more than a passing
word; but to one friend's bosom David would
often confide the love and tenderness he bore for
his over-worked, upright parent. When the boy
first began to write verses the old man affected
perfect contempt and indifference, but his eyes
gloated in secret over the poet's-corners of the
Glasgow newspapers. The poor weaver, though

an uneducated man, had a profound respect for education and cultivation in others.   He felt his heart bound with hope and joy when strangers praised the boy, but he hid the tenderness of his pride under a cold indifference. Although proud of David's talent for writing verses, he was afraid to encourage a pursuit which practical common sense assured him was mere trifling. At a later date he might have spoken out, had not his tongue been frozen by the belief that advice from him would be held in no esteem by his better educated and more gifted son. Thus, the more David's indications of cleverness and scholarship increased, the more afraid was the old man to express his gratification and give his advice. Equally touching was the point of view taken by David's mother, whose cry was, " The kirk, the free kirk, and nothing but the kirk ! " She neither appreciated nor underrated the abilities of her boy, but her proudest wish was that he should become a real live minister, with home and " haudin' " of his own. To see David,—" our David,"—in a pulpit, preaching the Gospel out of a big book, and dwelling in a good house to the end of his days !

But meantime the boy was swiftly undermining all such cherished plans. He had saturated his heart and mind with the intoxicating wines of poesy,—drunken deep of such syrups as only very strong heads indeed can carry calmly. He differed from older and harder poets in this only,—that he had not the trick of disguising his vanity, knew not how to ape humility. The poor lad was moved, maddened by the strange divine light in his eyes, and he cried aloud: "The beauty of the cloudland I have visited! the ideal love of my soul!" Thus he expressed himself, much to the amusement of his hearers. "Solitude," he exclaimed on another occasion, "and an utter want of all physical exercise, are working deplorable ravages in my nervous system; the crows'-feet are blackening about my eyes, and I cannot think to face the sunlight. When I ponder over my own inability to move the world, to move one heart in it, no wonder that my face gathers blackness. Tennyson beautifully and (so far) truly says, that the face is ' the form and colour of the mind and life.' If you saw *me!*" His verses written at that period, although abounding with echoes of his two pet poets, show great intensity and the sweetness of perfect feeling. Some of the lyrics in his volume, printed among the Poems Named and without Names, belong to this period. His productions, however, were for the most part close reproductions of the manner of Keats; and so conscious was he of this fact, that in one of these pieces he expressly styled himself, "a foster son of Keats, the dreamily divine." Wordsworth he did not reproduce so much until a later and a purer period. One of these unpublished pieces I shall quote here, to show that David, even at the crude assimilate period, showed "brains" and vision noticeable in a youth of twenty.

EMPEDOCLES.

"He who to be deem'd
A god, leap'd fondly into Ætna flames,—
Empedocles."—MILTON.

How, in the crystal smooth and azure sky,
Droop the clear, living sapphires, tremulous
And inextinguishably beautiful!
How the calm irridescence of their soft
Ethereal fire contrasts with the wild flame
Rising from this doomed mountain like the noise

Of ocean whirlwinds through the murky air!
Alone, alone! yearning, ambitious ever!
Hope's agony! O, ye immortal gods!
Regally sphered in your keen-silvered orbs,
Eternal, where fled that authentic fire,
Stolen by Prometheus ere the pregnant clouds
Rose from the sea, full of the deluge! Where
Art thou, white lady of the morning; white
Aurora, charioted by the fair Hours
Through amethystine mists weeping soft dews
Upon the meadow, as Apollo heaves
His constellation through the liquid dawn?
Give me Tithonus' gift, thou orient
Undying Beauty! and my love shall be
Cherubic worship, and my star shall walk
The plains of heaven, thy punctual harbinger!
O with thy ancient power prolong my days
For ever; tear this flesh-thick cursed life
Enlinking me to this foul earth, the home
Of cold mortality, this nether hell!

   Rise, mighty conflagrations! and scare wild
These crowding shadows! *Far on the dim sea
Pale mariners behold thee, and the sails
Shine purpled by thy glare, and the slow oars
Drop ruby, and the trembling human souls
Wonder affrighted as their pitchy barks,
Guided by Syrian pilots, ripple by
Hailing for craggy Calpe;* O, ye frail
Weak human souls, I, lone Empedocles,
Stand here unshivered as a steadfast god,
Scorning thy puny destinies.

                              I float
To cloud-enrobed Olympus on the wings
Of a rich dream, swift as the light of stars,
Swifter than Zophiel or Mercury
Upon his throne of adamantine gold.—
Jove sits superior, while the deities
Tread delicate the smooth cerulean floors.
Hebe, (with twin breasts, like twin roes that feed
Among the lilies), in her taper hand
Bears the bright goblet, rough with gems and gold,
Filled with ambrosia to the lipping brim.
O, love and beauty and immortal life!
O, light divine, ethereal effluence
Of purity! O, fragrancy of air,
Spikenard and calamus, cassia and balm,
With all the frankincense that ever fumed
From temple censers swung from pictured roofs,
Float warmly through the corridors of heaven.

Hiss! moan! shriek! wreath thy livid serpentine
Volutions, O ye earth-born flames! and flout
The silent skies with strange fire, like a dawn
Rubific, terrible, a lurid glare!
Olympus shrinks beside thee! I, alone,
Like deity ignipotent, behold
Thy playful whirls and thy weird melody
Hear undismayed. O gods! shall I go near
And in the molten horror headlong plunge
Deathward, and that serene immortal life
Discover? Shriek your hellish discord out
Into the smoky firmament! Down roll

Your fat bituminous torrents to the sea,
Hot hissing! Far away in element
Untroubled rise the crystal battlements
Of the celestial mansion, where to be
Is my ambition; and O far away
From this dull earth in azure atmospheres
My star shall pant its silvery lustre, bright
With sempiternal radiance, voyaging
On blissful errands the pure marble air.

O, dominations and life-yielding powers,
Listen my yearning prayer: To be of ye—
Of thy grand hierarchy and old race
Plenipotent, I do a deed that dares
The draff of men to equal. You have given
Immortal life to common human men
Who common deeds achieved; nay, even for love
Some goddesses voluptuous have raised
Weak whiners from this curst sublunar world,
Pillowed them on snow bosoms in the bowers
Of Paradise! And shall Empedocles,
Who from the perilous grim edge of life
Leaps sheer into the liquid fire and meets
Death like a lover, not be sphered and made
A virtue ministrant? All you soft orbs
By pure intelligences piloted,
Incomprehensibly their glories show
Approving.   *O ye sparkle-moving fires*
Of heaven, now silently above the flare
Of this red mountain shining, which of you
Shall be my home? Into whose stellar glow

Shall I arrive, bringing delight and life
And spiritual motion and dim fame?
Hiss, fiery serpents! Your sweet breathings warm
My face as I approach ye. Flap wild wings,
Ye dragons! flaming round this mouth of hell,
To me the mouth of heaven.

The influence of Keats soon decayed, and calmer influences supervened. He began a play on the Shakespearian model. This ambitious effort, however, was soon relinquished for a dearer, sweeter task,— the composition of a pastoral poem descriptive of the scenery surrounding his home. This subject, first suggested to him by a friend who guessed his real power, grew upon him with wondrous force, till the lines welled into perfect speech through very deepness of passion. His whole soul was occupied. The pictures that had troubled his childhood, the running river, the thymy Campsie fells, were now to live again before his spirit; and all the human sweetness and trouble, the beloved faces, the familiar human figures, stirred to the soft music of a flowing river and the distant hum of looms from cottage doors. The result was the poem entitled "The Luggie," which gives its name to the posthumous volume, and which, though it lacked the last humanizing touches of the poet, remains unique in contemporary literature.

But even while his heart was full of this exquisite utterance, this babble of green fields and silver waters, the influence of cities was growing more and more upon him, and poesy was no more the quite perfect joy that had made his boyhood happy. It was not enough to *sing* now; the thirst for applause was deepening; and it is not therefore extraordinary that even his fresh and truthful pastoral shows here and there the hectic flush of self-consciousness,—the dissatisfied glance in the direction of the public. The natural result of this was occasional merry-making, and grog-drinking, and beating the big city during the dark hours. There was high poetic pleasure in singing songs among artizans in familiar public-houses, flirting with an occasional milliner, and singing her charms in broad Scotch,—even occasionally coming to fisticuffs in obscure places, possibly owing to a hot discussion on the character of that demon of religious Scotch artizans,—the poet Shelley. I do not hesitate the least in mentioning these matters, because Gray has been too frequently represented as a morbid, unwholesome young gentleman, without natural weaknesses—a kind of aqueous Henry Kirke White, brandied faintly with ambition. He was nothing of the kind. He was a young man, as other young men are—foolish and wild in his season, though never gross or disreputable. The very excess of his sensitiveness led him into outbreaks against convention. While pouring out the sweetness of his nature in "The Luggie," he could turn aside again and again, and relieve his excitement by such doggrel as this, addressed to a companion,—

> Let olden Homer, hoary,
> Sing of wondrous deeds of glory,
> In that ever-burning story,
>   Bold and bright, friend Bob!
> *Our* theme be Pleasure, careless,
> In all stirring frolics fearless,
> In the vineyard, reckless, peerless,
>   Heroes dight, friend Bob!

Be it noted, however, that there was in Gray's nature a strange and exquisite femininity,—a perfect feminine purity and sweetness. Indeed, till the mystery of sex be medically explained, I shall ever believe that nature originally meant David Gray for a female; for besides the strangely sensitive lips and eyes, he had a woman's shape,—narrow shoulders, lissome limbs, and extraordinary breadth across the hips.

Early in his teens David had made the acquaintance of a young man of Glasgow, with whom his fortunes were destined to be intimately woven. That young man was myself. We spent year after year in intimate communion, varying the monotony of our existence by reading books together, plotting great works, writing extravagant letters to men of eminence, and wandering about the country on vagrant freaks. Whole nights and days were often passed in seclusion, in reading the great thinkers, and pondering on their lives. Full of thoughts too deep for utterance, dreaming, David would walk at a swift pace through the crowded streets, with face bent down, and eyes fixed· on the ground, taking no heed of the human beings passing to and fro. Then he would come to me crying, "I have had a dream," and would forthwith tell of visionary pictures which had haunted him in his solitary walk. This "dreaming," as he called it, consumed the greater portion of his hours of leisure.

Towards the end of the year 1859, David became convinced that he could no longer idle away the hours of his youth. His work as student and as pupil-teacher was ended, and he must seek some means of subsistence. He imagined, too, that his poor parents threw dull looks on the beggar of their bounty. Having abandoned all thoughts of entering into the Church, for which neither his taste nor his opinions fitted him, what should he do in order to earn his daily bread? His first thought was to turn schoolmaster; but no! the notion was an odious one. He next endeavoured, without success, to procure himself a situation on one of the Glasgow newspapers. Meantime, while drifting from project to project he maintained a voluminous correspondence, in the hope of persuading some eminent man to read his poem of "The Luggie."

Unfortunately, the persons to whom he wrote were too busy to pay much attention to the solici-

tations of an entire stranger. Repeated disap-
pointments only increased his self-assertion ; the
less chance there seemed of an improvement in
his position, and the less strangers seemed to
recognize his genius, the more dogged grew his
conviction that he was destined to be a great
poet. His letters were full of this conviction.
To one entire stranger he wrote : " I am a poet ;
let that be understood distinctly." Again : " I
tell you that, if I live, my name and fame shall
be second to few of any age, and to none of
my own. I speak this because I *feel* power."
Again : " I am so accustomed to compare my
own mental progress with that of such men as
Shakespeare, Goethe, and Wordsworth, that the
dream of my life will not be fulfilled, if my fame
equal not, at least, that of the latter of these
three !" This was extraordinary language, and
it is not surprising that little heed was paid to
it. Let some explanation be given here. No
man could be more humble, reverent-minded,
self-doubting, than David was in reality. Indeed, he was constitutionally timid of his own
abilities, and he was personally diffident. In

his letters only he absolutely endeavoured to wrest from his correspondents some recognition of his claim to help and sympathy. The moment sympathy came, no matter how coldly it might be expressed, he was all humility and gratitude. In this spirit, after one of his wildest flights of self-assertion, he wrote: "When I read Thomson, I despair." Again: "Being bare of all recommendations, I lied with my own conscience, deeming that if I called myself a great man you were bound to believe me." Again: "If you saw me you would wonder if the quiet, bashful, boyish-looking fellow before you was the author of all yon blood and thunder." In a lengthy correspondence with Mr. Sydney Dobell, who is also known as a writer of verse, David wrote wildly and boldly enough; but he was quite ready to plead guilty to silliness when the fits were over. But the grip of cities was on him, and he was far too conscious of outsiders. How sad and pitiable sounds the following! "Mark!" he cried, "it is not what I have done, or can now do, but what I feel myself able and born to do, that makes me so selfishly stupid. Your sentence, thrown back to me for reconsideration, would certainly seem strange to any one but myself; but the thought that I had so written to you only made me the more resolute in my actions, and the wilder in my visions. What if I sent the same sentence back to you again, with the quiet stern answer, that it is my intention to be the 'first poet of my own age,' and second only to a very few of any age. Would you think me 'mad,' 'drunk,' or an 'idiot,' or my 'self-confidence' one of the 'saddest paroxysms?' When my biography falls to be written, will not this same self-confidence be one of the most striking features of my intellectual development? Might not a poet of twenty *feel* great things? In all the stories of mental warfare that I have ever read, that mind which became of celestial clearness and godlike power did nothing for twenty years but *feel*." The hand-loom weaver's son raving about his "biography!" The youth that could babble so deliciously of green fields looking forward to the day when he would be anatomized by the small critic and chronicled by the chroniclers of small beer! It was not in this mood that he wrote his sweetest lines. The world was already too much with him.

Here, if anywhere in his career, I see signs which console me for his bitter suffering and too early death; signs that, had he lived, his fate might have been an even sadder one. Saint Beuve says, as quoted by Alfred de Musset:—

Il existe, en un mot, chez les trois quarts des hommes,
Un poëte mort jeune à qui l'homme survit !

A dead young poet whom the man survives! —and dead through that very poison which David was beginning to taste. I dare not aver that such would have been the result; I dare not say that David's poetic instinct was too weak to survive the danger. But the danger existed— clear, sparkling, deathly. Had David been hurried away to teach schools among the hills, buried among associations pure and green as those that surrounded his youth and childhood, the poetic instinct might have survived and achieved wondrous results. But he went southward,—he imbibed an atmosphere entirely unfitted for his soul at that period; and—perhaps, after all, the gods loved him and knew best.

For all at once there flashed upon David and

myself the notion of going to London, and taking the literary fortress by storm. Again and again we talked the project over, and again and again we hesitated. In the spring of 1860, we both found ourselves without an anchorage; each found it necessary to do something for daily bread. For some little time the London scheme had been in abeyance; but, on the 3rd of May, 1860, David came to me, his lips firmly compressed, his eyes full of fire, saying, " Bob, I'm off to London." " Have you funds ?" I asked. " Enough for one, not enough for two," was the reply. " If you can get the money anyhow, we'll go together." On parting, we arranged to meet on the evening of the 5th of May, in time to catch the five o'clock train. Unfortunately, however, we neglected to specify which of the two Glasgow stations was intended. At the hour appointed, David left Glasgow by one line of railway, in the belief that I had been unable to join him, but determined to try the venture alone. With the same belief and determination, I left at the same hour by the other line of railway. We arrived in different parts of London at about the same time. Had we left Glasgow in company, or had we met immediately after our arrival in London, the story of David's life might not have been so brief and sorrowful.

Though the month was May, the weather was dark, damp, cloudy. On arriving in the metropolis, David wandered about for hours, carpet-bag in hand. The magnitude of the place overwhelmed him; he was lost in that great ocean of life. He thought about Johnson and Savage, and how they wandered through London with pockets more empty than his own; but already he longed to be back in the little carpeted bedroom in the weaver's cottage. How lonely it seemed! Among all that mist of human faces there was not one to smile in welcome; and how was he to make his trembling voice heard above the roar and tumult of those streets? The very policemen seemed to look suspiciously at the stranger. To his sensitively Scottish ear the language spoken seemed quite strange and foreign; it had a painful, homeless sound about it that sank nervously on the heart-strings. As he wandered about the streets he glanced into coffee-shop after coffee-shop, seeing "beds" ticketed in each fly-blown window. His pocket contained a sovereign and a few shillings, but he would need every penny. Would not a bed be useless extravagance? he asked himself. Certainly. Where, then, should he pass the night? In Hyde Park! He had heard so much about this part of London that the name was quite familiar to him. Yes, he would pass the night in the park. Such a proceeding would save money, and be exceedingly romantic; it would be just the right sort of beginning for a poet's struggle in London! So he strolled into the great park, and wandered about its purlieus till morning. In remarking upon this foolish conduct, one must reflect that David was strong, heartsome, full of healthy youth. It was a frequent boast of his that he scarcely ever had a day's illness. Whether or not his fatal complaint was caught during this his first night in London is uncertain, but some few days afterwards David wrote thus to his father: "By-the-bye, I have had the worst *cold* I ever had in my life. I cannot get it away properly, but I feel a great deal better to-day." Alas! violent cold had settled down upon his lungs, and insidious death was already slowly approaching him. So little conscious was he of his danger, however, that I find him writing to a friend: " What brought me here? God knows, for I don't. *Alone* in such a place is a horrible thing. . . . People don't seem to understand me. . . . Westminster Abbey; I was there all day yesterday. If I live I shall be buried there — so help me God! A completely defined consciousness of *great* poetical genius is my only antidote against utter despair and despicable failure."

I suppose his purposes in coming to Babylon were about as definite as my own had been, although he had the advantage of being qualified as a pupil teacher. We tossed ourselves on the great waters as two youths who wished to learn to swim, and trusted that by diligent kicking we might escape drowning. There was the prospect of getting into a newspaper office. Again, there was the prospect of selling a few verses. Thirdly, if everything failed, there was the prospect of getting into one of the theatres as supernumeraries.*

---

* Each of the friends, indeed, unknown to each other, actually applied for such a situation; and one succeeded.

Beyond all this, there was of course the dim prospect that London would at once, and with acclamations, welcome the advent of true genius, albeit with seedy garments and a Scotch accent. It doubtless never occurred to either that besides mere "consciousness" of power, some other things were necessary for a literary struggle in London —special knowledge, capability of interesting oneself in trifles, and the pen of a ready writer. What were David's qualifications for a fight in which hundreds miserably fail year after year? Considerable knowledge of Greek, Latin, and French, great miscellaneous reading, a clerkly handwriting, and a bold purpose. Slender qualifications, doubtless, but while life lasted, there was hope.

We did not meet until upwards of a week after our arrival in London, though each had soon been apprised of the other's presence in the city. Finally we came together. David's first impulse was to describe his lodgings, situated in a by-street in the Borough. "A cold, cheerless bed-room, Bob; nothing but a blanket to cover me. For God's sake get me out of it!" We were walking side by side in the neighbourhood of the New Cut, looking about us with curious puzzled eyes, and now and then drawing each other's attention to sundry objects of interest. " Have you been well ?" I inquired. " First-rate," answered David, looking as merry as possible. Nor did he show any indications whatever of illness ; he seemed hopeful, energetic, full of health and spirits ; his sole desire was to change his lodging. It was not without qualms that he surveyed the dingy, smoky neighbourhood where I resided. The sun was shedding dismal crimson light on the chimney-pots, and the twilight was slowly thickening. We climbed up three flights of stairs to my bedroom ; dingy as it was, this apartment seemed, in David's eyes, quite a palatial sanctum ; and it was arranged that we should take up our residence together. As speedily as possible I procured David's little stock of luggage ; then, settled face to face as in old times, we made very merry.

My first idea, on questioning David about his prospects, was that my friend had had the best of luck. You see, the picture drawn on either side was a golden one; but the brightness soon melted away.   It turned out that David, on arriving in London, had sought out certain gentlemen whom he had formerly favoured with his correspondence, among others Mr. Richard Monckton Milnes, now Lord Houghton.   Though not a little astonished at the appearance of the boy-poet, Mr. Milnes had received him kindly, assisted him to the best of his power, and made some work for him in the shape of manuscript-copying.   The same gentleman had also used his influence with literary people,—to very little purpose, however.   The real truth turned out to be that David was disappointed and low-spirited.   " It's weary work, Bob ; they don't understand me ; I wish I was back in Glasgow."   It was now that David told me all about that first day and night in London, and how he had already begun a poem about " Hyde Park;" how Mr. Milnes had been good to him, had said that he was " a poet," but had insisted on his going back to Scotland and becoming a minister.   David did not at all like the notion of returning home.   He thought he had every chance of making his way in London.

About this time he was bitterly disappointed by the rejection of " The Luggie " by Mr. Thackeray, to whom Mr. Milnes had sent it, with a recommendation that it should be inserted in the " Cornhill Magazine."

Lord Houghton briefly and vividly describes his intercourse with the young poet in London. He had written to Gray strongly urging him not to make the hazardous experiment of a literary life, but to aim after a professional independence. " A few weeks afterwards," he writes, " I was told that a young man wished to see me, and when he came into the room I at once saw that it could be no other than the young Scotch Poet. It was a light, well-built, but somewhat stooping figure, with a countenance that at once brought strongly to my recollection a cast of the face of Shelley in his youth, which I had seen at Mr. Leigh Hunt's. There was the same full brow, out-looking eyes, and sensitive melancholy mouth. He told me at once that he had come to London in consequence of my letter, as from the tone of it he was sure I should befriend him. I was dismayed at this unexpected result of my advice, and could do no more than press him to return home as soon as possible. I painted as darkly as I could the chances and difficulties of a literary struggle in the crowded competition of this great city, and how strong a swimmer it required to be not to sink in such a sea of tumultuous life. 'No, he would not return.' I determined in my own mind that he should do so before I myself left town for the country, but at the same time I believed that he might derive advantage from a short personal experience of hard realities. He had confidence in his own powers, a simple certainty of his own worth, which I saw would keep him in good heart and preserve him from base temptations. He refused to take money, saying he had enough to go on with; but I gave him some light literary work, for which he was very grateful. When he came to me again, I went over some of his verse with him, and I shall not forget the passionate gratification he showed when I told him that, in my judgment, he was an undeniable poet. After this admission he was ready to submit to my criticism or correction, though he was sadly depressed at the rejection of one of his poems, over which he had evidently spent much labour and care, by the editor of a distinguished popular periodical, to whom I had sent it with a hearty recommendation. His, indeed, was not a spirit to be seriously injured by a temporary disappointment; but when he fell ill so soon afterwards, one had something of the feeling of regret that the notorious review of Keats inspires in connection with the premature loss of the author of ' Endymion.' It was only a few weeks after his arrival in London, that the poor boy came to my house apparently under the influence of violent fever. He said he had caught cold in the wet weather, having been insufficiently protected by clothing; but had delayed coming to me for fear of giving me unnecessary trouble. I at once sent him back to his lodgings, which were sufficiently comfortable, and put him under good medical superintendence. It soon became apparent that pulmonary disease had set in, but there were good hopes of arresting its progress. I visited him often, and every time with increasing interest. He had somehow found out that his lungs were affected, and the image of the destiny of Keats was ever before him."

It has been seen that Mr. Milnes was the first to perceive that the young adventurer was seriously ill. After a hurried call on his patron one day in May, David rejoined me in the near neighbourhood. "Milnes says I'm to go home and keep warm, and he'll send his own doctor to me." This was done. The doctor came, examined David's chest, said very little, and went away, leaving strict orders that the invalid should keep within doors, and take great care of himself. Neither David nor I liked the expression of the doctor's face at all.

It soon became evident that David's illness was of a most serious character. Pulmonary disease had set in; medicine, blistering, all the remedies employed in the early stages of his complaint, seemed of little avail. Just then David read the "Life of John Keats," a book which impressed him with a nervous fear of impending dissolution. He began to be filled with conceits droller than any he had imagined in health. "If I were to meet Keats in heaven," he said one day, "I wonder if I should know his face from his pictures?" Most frequently his talk was of labour uncompleted, hope deferred; and he began to pant for free country air. "If I die," he said on a certain occasion, "I shall have one consolation,—Milnes will write an introduction to the poems." At another time, with tears in his eyes, he repeated Burns's epitaph. Now and then, too, he had his fits of frolic and humour, and would laugh and joke over his unfortunate position. It cannot be said that Mr. Milnes and his friends were at all lukewarm about the case of their young friend; on the contrary, they gave him every practical assistance. Mr. Milnes himself, full of the most delicate sympathy, trudged to and fro between his own house and the invalid's lodging; his pockets laden with jelly and beef-tea, and his tongue tipped with kindly comfort. Had circumstances permitted, he would have taken the invalid into his own house. Unfortunately, however, David was compelled to remain, in company with me, in a chamber which seemed to have been constructed peculiarly for the purpose of making the occupants as uncomfortable as possible. There were draughts everywhere: through the chinks of the door, through the windows, down the chimney, and up through the flooring. When the wind blew, the whole tenement seemed on the point of crumbling to atoms; when the rain fell, the walls exuded moisture; when the sun shone, the sunshine only served to increase the characteristic dinginess of the furniture. Occasional visitors, however, could not be fully aware of these inconveniences. It was in the night-time, and in bad weather, that they were chiefly felt; and it required a few days' experience to test the superlative discomfort of what David (in a letter written afterwards) styled " the dear old ghastly bankrupt garret." His stay in these quarters was destined to be brief. Gradually, the invalid grew homesick. Nothing would content him but a speedy return to Scotland. He was carefully sent off by train, and arrived safely in his little cottage-home far north. Here all was unchanged as ever. The beloved river was flowing through the same fields, and the same familiar faces were coming and going on its banks; but the whole meaning of the pastoral pageant had changed, and the colour of all was deepening towards the final sadness.

Great, meanwhile, had been the commotion in

the handloom weaver's cottage, after the receipt
of this bulletin : " I start off to-night at five o'clock
by the Edinburgh and Glasgow Railway, right on
to London, in good health and spirits." A great
cry arose in the household. He was fairly " daft ; "
he was throwing away all his chances in the world ;
the verse-writing had turned his head. Father
and mother mourned together. The former,
though incompetent to judge literary merit of
any kind, perceived that David was hot-headed,
only half-educated, and was going to a place
where thousands of people were starving daily.
But the suspense was not to last long. The
darling son, the secret hope and pride, came
back to the old people, sick to death. All rebuke died away before the pale sad face and
the feeble tottering body ; and David was welcomed to the cottage hearth with silent prayers.

It was now placed beyond a doubt that the disease
was one of mortal danger ; yet David, surrounded
again by his old cares, busied himself with many
bright and delusive dreams of ultimate recovery.
Pictures of a pleasant dreamy convalescence in a
foreign clime floated before him morn and night,

and the fairest and dearest of the dreams was Italy. Previous to his departure for London he had concocted a wild scheme for visiting Florence, and throwing himself on the poetical sympathy of Robert Browning. He had even thought of enlisting in the English Garibaldian corps, and by that means gaining his cherished wish. "How about Italy?" he wrote to me, after returning home. "Do you still entertain its delusive notions? Pour out your soul before me; I am as a child." All at once a new dream burst upon him. A local doctor insisted that the invalid should be removed to a milder climate, and recommended Natal. In a letter full of coaxing tenderness, David besought me, for the sake of old days, to accompany him thither. I answered indecisively, but immediately made all endeavours to grant my friend's wish. Meantime I received the following :—

" Merkland, Kirkintollock,

" 10th November, 1860.

" EVER DEAR BOB,

" Your letter causes me some uneasiness; not but that your numerous objections are numerous and vital enough, but they convey the sad and firm intelligence that you cannot come with me. It is absolutely impossible for you to raise a sum sufficient! Now you know it is not necessary that I should go to Natal; nay, I have, in very fear, given up the thoughts of it; but we—or I—could go to Italy or Jamaica—this latter, as I learn, being the more preferable. Nor has there been any 'crisis' come, as you say. I would cause you much trouble (forgive me for hinting this), but I believe we could be happy as in the dear old times. Dr. —— (whose address I don't know) supposes that I shall be able to work(?) when I reach a more genial climate; and if that should prove the result, why, it is a consummation devoutly to be wished. But the matter of money bothers me. What I wrote to you was all hypothetical, i. e. things have been carried so far, but I have not heard whether or no the subscription had been gone on with. And, supposing for one instant the utterly preposterous supposition that I had money to carry us both, then comes the second objection—your dear mother! I am not so far gone, though

I fear far enough, to ignore that blessed feeling. But if it were for your good? Before God, if I thought it would in any way harm your health (that cannot be) or your hopes, I would never have mooted the proposal. On the contrary, I feel from my heart it would benefit you; and how much would it not benefit *me?* But I am baking without flour. The cash is not in my hand, and I fear never will be; the amount I would require is not so easily gathered.

"Dobell * is again laid up. He is at the Isle of Wight, at some establishment called the Victoria Baths. I am told that his friends deem his life in constant danger. He asks for your address. I shall send it only to-day; wait until you hear what he has got to say. He would prefer me to go to Brompton Hospital. *I would*

---

* Sydney Dobell, author of "Balder," "The Roman," &c. This gentleman's kindness to David, whom he never saw, is beyond all praise. Nor was the invalid ungrateful. "Poor, kind, half-immortal spirit here below," wrote David, alluding to Dobell, "shall I know thee when we meet new-born into eternal existence? . . . Dear friend Bob, did you ever know a nobler? I cannot get him out of my mind. I would write to him daily would it not pest him."

go anywhere for a change.　If I don't get money *somehow* or *somewhere* I shall die of *ennui.*　A weary desire for change, life, excitement of every, *any* kind, possesses me, and without *you* what am I?　There is no other person in the world whom I could spend a week with, and thoroughly enjoy it.　Oh, how I desire to smoke a cigar, and have a pint and a chat with you.

"By the way, how are you getting on?　Have you lots to do? and well paid for it?　Or is life a lottery with you? and the tea-caddy a vacuum? and — a snare? and — a nightmare?　Do you *dream* yet, on your old rickety sofa in the dear old ghastly bankrupt garret at No. 66?　Write to yours eternally,　　"DAVID GRAY."

The proposal to go abroad was soon abandoned, partly because the invalid began to evince a nervous home-sickness, but chiefly because it was impossible to raise a sufficient sum of money. Yet be it never said that this youth was denied the extremest loving sympathy and care.　As I look back on those days it is to me a glad wonder that so many tender faces, many of them quite strange, clustered round his sick-bed. When it is reflected that he was known only as a poor Scotch lad, that even his extraordinary lyric faculty was as yet only half-guessed, if guessed at all, the kindness of the world through his trouble is extraordinary. Milnes, Dobell, Dobell's lady-friends at Hampstead, tired never in devising plans for the salvation of the poor consumptive invalid,—goodness which sprang from the instincts of the heart itself, and not from that intellectual benevolence which invests in kind deeds with a view to a bonus from the Almighty.

The best and tenderest of people, however, cannot always agree; and in this case there was too much discussion and delay. Some recommended the long sea-voyage; one doctor recommended Brompton Hospital; Milnes suggested Torquay in Devonshire. Meantime, Gray, for the most part ignorant of the discussions that were taking place, besought his friends on all hands to come to his assistance. Late in November he addressed the editor of a local newspaper with whom he was personally acquainted, and who had taken interest in his affairs:—

" I write you in a certain commotion of mind, and may speak wrongly.   But I write to *you* because I know that it will take much to offend you when no offence is meant; and when the probable offence will proceed from youthful heat and frantic foolishness.   It may be impertinent to address you, of whom I know so little, and yet so much; but the severe circumstances *seem* to justify it.

" The medical verdict pronounced upon me is *certain and rapid death if I remain at Merkland.* That is awful enough, even to a brave man.   But there is a chance of escape; as a drowning man grasps at a straw I strive for it.   Good, kind, true Dobell writes me this morning the plans for my welfare which he has put in progress, and which most certainly meet my wishes.   They are as follows: Go *immediately*, and *as a guest* to the house of Dr. Lane, in the salubrious town of Richmond; thence, when the difficult matter of admission is overcome, to the celebrated Brompton Hospital for chest diseases; and in the Spring to Italy.   Of course, all this presupposes the conjectural problem that I will slowly recover. ' Consummation devoutly to be wished!'   Now, you think, or say, what prevents you from taking advantage of all these plans? At once, and without any squeamishness, *money for an outfit.* I did not like to ask Dobell, nor do I ask you; but hearing a 'subscription' had been *spoken of,* I urge it with all my weak force. I am not in want of an immense sum, but say £12 or £15. This would conduce to my safety as far as human means could do so. If you can aid me in getting this sum, the obligation to a sinking fellow-creature will be as indelible in his heart as the moral law.

"I hope you will not misunderstand me. My barefaced request may be summed thus: If your influence set the affair a-going, quietly and *quickly,* the thing is done, and I am off. Surely I am worth £15; and for God's sake overlook the strangeness and the freedom and the utter impertinence of this communication. I would be off for Richmond in two days, had I the money, and sitting here thinking of the fearful probabilities makes me half-mad."

It was soon found necessary, however, to act with decision. A residence in Kirkintolloch throughout the winter was, on all accounts, to be avoided. A lady, therefore, subscribed to the Brompton Hospital for chest complaints for the express purpose of procuring David admission.

One bleak wintry day, not long after the receipt of the above letter, I was gazing out of my lofty lodging-window when a startling vision presented itself, in the shape of David himself, seated with quite a gay look in an open Hansom cab. In a minute we were side by side, and one of my first impulses was to rebuke David for the folly of exposing himself during such weather, in such a vehicle. This folly, however, was on a parallel with David's general habits of thought. Sometimes, indeed, the poor boy became unusually thoughtful, as when, during his illness, he wrote thus to me: " Are you remembering that you will need clothes ? These are things you take no concern about, and so you may be seedy without knowing it. By all means hoard a few pounds if you can (I require none) for *any* emergency like this. Brush your excellent top-coat ; it is the best and warmest I ever had on my back. Mind, you have to pay ready money for a new coat. A seedy man will not get on if he requires, like you, to call personally on his employers."

David had come to London in order to go either to Brompton or to Torquay,—the hospital at which last-named place was thrown open to him by Mr. Milnes. Perceiving his dislike for the Temperance Hotel, to which he had been conducted, I consented that he should stay in the " ghastly bankrupt garret," until he should depart to one or other of the hospitals. It was finally arranged that he should accept a temporary invitation to a hydropathic establishment at Sudbrook Park, Richmond. Thither I at once conveyed him. Meanwhile, his prospects were diligently canvassed by his numerous friends. His own feelings at this time were well expressed in a letter home : " I am dreadfully afraid of Brompton; living among sallow, dolorous, dying consumptives is enough to kill me. Here I am as comfortable as can be: a fire in my room all day, plenty of meat, and good society,—nobody so ill as myself; but there, perhaps, hundreds far worse (the hospital holds 218 in all stages of the

disease ; ninety of them died last report) dying
beside me, perhaps,—it frightens me."

About the same time he sent me the following,
containing more particulars :—

> " Sudbrook Park, Richmond,
> Surrey.

" MY DEAR BOB,

" Your anxiety will be allayed by learning that I
am little worse.   The severe hours of this establishment have *not* killed me.   At 8 o'clock in
the morning a man comes into my bedroom with
a pail of cold water, and I must rise and get myself *soused*.   This *sousing* takes place three times
a day, and I'm not dead *yet*.   To-day I told the
bathman that I was utterly unable to bear it, and
refused to undress.   The doctor will hear of it;
that's the very thing I want.   The society here
is most pleasant.   No patient so bad as myself.
No wonder your father wished to go to the water
cure for a month or two; it is the most pleasant,
refreshing thing in the world.   But *I* am really
too weak to bear it.   Robert Chambers is here;
Mrs. Crowe, the authoress; Lord Brougham's

son-in-law; and at dinner and tea the literary tittle-tattle is the most wonderful you ever heard. They seem to know everything about everybody but Tennyson. Major —— (who has a *beautiful* daughter here) was crowned with a laurel-wreath for some burlesque verses he had made and read, last night. Of course you know what I am among them——a pale cadaverous young person, who sits in dark corners, and is for the most part silent; with a horrible fear of. being pounced upon by a cultivated unmarried lady, and talked to.

"Seriously, I am not better. When the novelty of my situation is gone, won't the old days at Oakfield Terrace seem pleasant? Why didn't they last for ever?

"Yours ever,

"DAVID GRAY."

All at once David began, with a delicacy peculiar to him, to consider himself an unwarrantable intruder at Sudbrook Park. In the face of all persuasion, therefore, he joined me in London, whence he shortly afterwards departed for Torquay.

He left me in good spirits, full of pleasant anticipations of Devonshire scenery. But the second day after his departure he addressed to me a wild epistle, dated from one of the Torquay hotels. He had arrived safe and sound, he said, and had been kindly received by a friend of Mr. Milnes. He had at first been delighted with the town, and everything in it.   He had gone to the hospital, had been received by " a nurse of death " (as he phrased it), and had been inducted into the privileges of the place ; but on seeing his fellow-patients, some in the last stages of disease, he had fainted away. On coming to himself he obtained an interview with the matron. To his request for a private apartment, she had answered that to favour him in that way would be to break written rules, and that he must content himself with the common privileges of the establishment. On leaving the matron, he had furtively stolen from the place, and made his way through the night to the hotel. From the hotel he addressed the following terrible letter to his parents :—

" Torquay, January 6, 1861.

" DEAR PARENTS,

" I am coming home—home-sick. I cannot

stay from home any longer. What's the good
of me being so far from home, and sick and ill?
I don't know whether I'll be *able* to come back
—sleeping none at night—crying out for my
mother, and her so far away. Oh God, I wish I
were home never to leave it more! Tell everybody that I'm coming back—no better—worse,
worse. What's about climate—about frost or
snow or cold weather when one is at home? I
wish I had never left it.

" But how am I to get back without money,
and my expenses for the journey newly paid yesterday? I came here yesterday scarcely able to
walk. O how I wish I saw my father's face—
shall I ever see it? I have no money, and I
want to get home, home, home! What shall I
do, O God? Father, I shall *steal* to see you
again, because I did not use you rightly—my
conduct to you all the time I was at home makes
me miserable, miserable, miserable! Will you
forgive me ?—do I ask that? forgiven, forgiven,
forgiven! If I can't get money to pay for my box,
I shall leave box and everything behind. I shall
try and be at home by Saturday, January 12th.

Mind the day—if I am not home—God knows where I shall be. I have come through things that would make your hearts ache for me—things which I shall never tell to anybody but you, and you shall keep them secret as the grave. Get my own little room ready, quick, quick; have it all tidy and clean and cosy against my home-coming. I wish to die there, and nobody shall nurse me, except my own dear mother, ever, ever again. O home, home, home!

"I will try and write again, but mind the day. Perhaps my father will come into Glasgow, if I *can* tell him beforehand *how, when*, and *where* I shall be. I shall try all I can to let him know.

"Mind and tell everybody that I am coming back, because I wish to be back, and cannot stay away. Tell everybody; but I shall come back in the dark, because I am so utterly unhappy. No more, no more. Mind the day.

"Yours,

"D. G.

"Don't answer—not even *think* of answering."*

---

* While lingering at Torquay, however, his mood became calmer, and he was able to relieve his overladen mind

Before I had time to comprehend the state of affairs, there came a second letter, stating that David was on the point of starting for London. "Every ring at the hotel bell makes me tremble, fancying they are coming to take me away by

---

in the composition of these lines—deeply interesting, apart from their poetic merit.

HOME SICK.

Lines written at Torquay, January, 1861.

Come to me, O my Mother! come to me,
Thine own son slowly dying far away!
Thro' the moist ways of the wide ocean, blown
By great invisible winds, come stately ships
To this calm bay for quiet anchorage;
They come, they rest awhile, they go away,
But, O my Mother, never comest thou!
The snow is round thy dwelling, the white snow,
That cold soft revelation pure as light,
And the pine-spire is mystically fringed,
Laced with encrusted silver. Here—ah me!—
The winter is decrepit, underborn,
A leper with no power but his disease.
Why am I from thee, Mother, far from thee?
Far from the frost enchantment, and the woods
Jewelled from bough to bough? Oh home, my home!
O river in the valley of my home,
With mazy-winding motion intricate,

force. *Had you seen the nurse!*   Oh! that I were back again at home—mother! mother! mother!" A few hours after I had read these lines in miserable fear, arrived Gray himself, pale, anxious, and trembling. He flung himself into my arms with a smile of sad relief. " Thank God!" he cried ; " *that's* over, and I am here !" Then his cry was for home ; he would die if he remained longer adrift ; he must depart at once. I persuaded him to wait for a few days, and in the meantime saw some of his influential friends. The skill and regimen of a medical establishment being necessary to him at this stage, it was naturally concluded that he should go to Brompton ; but David, in a high state of nervous excitement, scouted the idea. Disease had sapped the foundations of the once strong spirit. He was now bent on returning to the north, and

---

Twisting thy deathless music underneath
The polished ice-work—must I nevermore
Behold thee with familiar eyes, and watch
Thy beauty changing with the changeful day,
Thy beauty constant to the constant change?

                                        M.S.

wrote more calmly to his parents from my lodgings:—

"London, Thursday.

" MY VERY DEAR PARENTS,

" Having arrived in London last night, my friends have seized on me again, and wish me to go to Brompton. But what I saw at Torquay was enough, and I will come home, though it should freeze me to death.   You must not take literally what I wrote you in my last. I had just *ran away* from Torquay hospital, and didn't know what to do or where to go. But you see I have got to London, and surely by some means or other I shall get home. I am really home-sick. *They all tell me my life is not worth a farthing candle if I go to Scotland in this weather, but what about that.* I wish I could tell my father when to come to Glasgow, but I can't.   *If* I start to-morrow I shall be in Glasgow very late, and what am I to do if I have no cash. If he comes into Glasgow by the twelve train on Saturday, I may, if possible, see him at the train, but I would not like to say positively. Surely I'll get home somehow. I don't sleep any at night now for coughing and sweating—I am afraid to go to bed. Strongly hoping to be with you soon.

" Yours ever,

" David Gray."

" Home —home—home !" was his hourly cry. To resist these frantic appeals would have been to hasten the end of all.   In the midst of winter, I saw him into the train at Euston Square. A day afterwards, David was in the bosom of his father's household, never more to pass thence alive.   Not long after his arrival at home, he repented his rash flight. "I am not at all contented with my position. I acted like a fool; but if the hospital were the *sine qua non* again, my conduct would be the same." Further, " I lament my own foolish conduct, but what was that quotation about *impellunt in Acheron?* It was all nervous impulsion. However, I despair not, and, least of all, my dear fellow, to those whom I have deserted wrongfully."

Ere long, poor David made up his mind that he must die; and this feeling urged him to write something which would keep his memory green for ever. "I am working away at my old poem, Bob; leavening it throughout with the pure beautiful theology of Kingsley." A little later: "By-the-bye, I have about 600 lines of my poem written, but the manual labour is so weakening that I do not go on." Nor was this all. In the very shadow of the grave, he began and finished a series of sonnets on the subject of his own disease and impending death. This increased literary energy was not, as many people imagined, a sign of increased physical strength; it was merely the last flash upon the blackening brand. Gradually, but surely, life was ebbing away from the young poet.

In March, 1861, I formed the plan of visiting Scotland in the spring, and wrote to David accordingly. His delight at the prospect of a fresh meeting—perhaps a farewell one—was as great as mine. He wrote me the following, and burst out into song :*—

---

* I subjoin the poem, not only as lovely in itself, but as the last sad poetic memorial of our love and union. I find

"Merkland, March 12, 1861.

"My Dear Bob,

"I am very glad to be able to write you to-day. Rest assured to find a change in your old friend when you come down in April. And do, old fellow, let it be the end of April, when the evenings are cool and fresh, and these east-winds have howled themselves to rest. When I think of what a fair worshipful season is before you, I advise you to remove to a little room at Hampstead, where I only wish too, too much to be

---

it in his printed volume, among the sonnets entitled, " In the Shadows :"—

> Now, while the long-delaying ash assumes
> Its delicate April green, and loud and clear
> Thro' the cool, yellow, mellow twilight glooms,
> The thrush's song enchants the captive ear ;
> Now, while a shower is pleasant in the falling,
> Stirring the still perfume that shakes around ;
> Now that doves mourn, and, from the distance calling,
> The cuckoo answers, with a sovereign sound—
> Come, with thy native heart, O true and tried !
> But leave all books ; for what with converse high,
> Flavoured with Attic wit, the time shall glide
> On smoothly, as a river floweth by,
> Or as on stately pinion, through the gray
> Evening, the culver cuts his liquid way !

with you.   Don't forget to come north since you have spoken about it; it has made me very happy.   My health is no better,—not having been out of my room since I wrote, and for some time before.   The weather here is so bitterly cold and unfavourable, that I have not walked 100 yards for three weeks.   I trust your revivifying presence will electrify my weary relaxed limbs and enervated system.   The mind, you know, has a great effect on the body.   Accept the wholesome common place. . . . By-the-way, how about Dobell?   Did your mind of itself, or even against itself, recognize through the clothes *a man* —*a poet?*   Young speaks well:—

> *I never bowed but to superior worth,*
> *Nor ever failed in my allegiance there.*

Has he the modesty and make-himself-at-home manner of Milnes?"   The remainder of this letter is unfortunately lost.

In April, I saw him for the last time, and heard him speak words which showed the abandonment of hope.   "I am dying," said David, leaning back in his arm-chair in the little carpeted bedroom; "I am dying, and I've only two things to regret: that my poem is not published, and that I have not seen Italy." In the endeavour to inspire hope I spoke of the happy past, and of the happy days yet to be. David only shook his head with a sad smile. "It is the old *dream*—only a dream, Bob—but I am content." He spoke of all his friends with tenderness, and of his parents with intense and touching love. Then it was "farewell!" "After all our dreams of the future," he said, "I must leave you to fight alone; but shall there be no more ' cakes and ale ' because I die?" I returned to London; and ere long heard that David was eagerly attempting to get "The Luggie" published. Delay after delay occurred. "If my book be not immediately gone on with, I fear I may never see it. Disease presses closely on me. . . . The merit of my MSS. is very little—mere hints of better things —crude notions harshly languaged; but that must be overlooked. They are left not to the world (wild thought!), but as the simple, possible, sad, only legacy I can leave to those who have loved and love me." To a dear friend and fellow poet, William Freeland, then sub-editor of the *Glasgow Citizen*, he wrote at this time : " I feel more acutely the approach of that mystic dissolution of existence. The body is unable to perform its functions, and like rusty machinery creaks painfully to the final crash. . . . About my poem,—it troubles me like an ever present demon. Some day I'll burn all that I have ever written,— yet no ! They are all that remain of *me* as a living soul. Milnes offers £5 towards its publication. I shall have it ready by Saturday first." And to Freeland, who visited him every week, and cheered his latter moments with a true poet's converse, he wrote out a wild dedication, ending in these words : " Before I enter that nebulous uncertain land of shadowy notions and tremulous wonderings—standing on the threshold of the sun and looking back, I cry thee, O beloved ! a last farewell, lingeringly, passionately, without tears." At this period I received the following :—

" Merkland, N. S., Sunday Evening.

" Dear, dear Bob,

" By all means and instantly, ' move in this matter' of my book. Do you really and without any dream-work, think it could be gone about *immediately?* If not soon I fear I shall never behold it. *The doctors give me no hope,* and with the yellowing of the leaf 'changes' likewise 'the countenance' of your friend. Freeland is in possession of the MSS., but before I send them (I love them in so great temerity) I would like to see, and, *if at all possible,* revise them. Meanwhile, act and write. Above all, Bob, give me (and my father) no hope unless on sound foundation. Better that the rekindled desire should die than languish, bringing misery. I cannot sufficiently impress on you how important this 'book,' is to me : with what ignoble trembling I anticipate its appearance : how I shall bless you should you succeed.

" Do not tempt me with your kindness. The family have almost got over the strait, only my father being out of work. It is, indeed, a 'golden treasury' you have sent me. Many thanks. My only want is new interesting books. I shall return it soon when I get *Smith.* Do not, like a good fellow, disappoint an old friend by forgetting to send *that* work.   With what interest (thinking on my own probable volume) shall I examine the print, &c. *I am sure, sure to return it.*

" When *you* complain of physical discomfort I believe.   What is the matter ? Your letters now are a mere provoking adumbration of your condition.   I know positively nothing of you, but that you are mentally and bodily depressed, and that you will never forget Gray.   In God's name let us keep together the short time remaining.

" You tell me nothing ; write sooner too.   Recollect I have no other pleasure.   How is your mother ? and all ? Are your editorial duties oppressive ? Is life full of hope and bright faith, *yet, yet ?* Tell me, Bob, and tell me quickly.

" What a fair, sad, beautiful dream is *Italy !* Do you still entertain its delusive motions ? Pour your soul before me ; I am as a child.

" Yours for ever,

" DAVID GRAY."

Still later, in an even sweeter spirit, he wrote to an old schoolmate, Arthur Sutherland, with whom he had dreamed many a boyish dream, when they were pupil teachers together at the Normal school:—

"As my time narrows to a completion, you grow dearer. I think of you daily with quiet tears. I think of the happy, happy days we might have spent together at Maryburgh; but the vision darkens. My crown is laid in the dust for ever. Nameless too! God, how that troubles me! Had I but written one immortal poem, what a glorious consolation! But this shall be my epitaph if I have a gravestone at all,—

'Twas not a life,
'Twas but a piece of childhood thrown away.

O dear, dear Sutherland! I wish I could spend two *healthy* months with·you; we would make an effort, and do something great. But slowly, insidiously, and I fear fatally, consumption is doing its work, until I shall be only a fair odorous memory (for I have great faith in your affection for me) to you—a sad tale for your old age.

Whom the gods love, die young.

Bless the ancient Greeks for that comfort. If I was not ripe, do you think I would be gathered?

" Work for fame for my sake, dear Sutherland. Who knows but in spiritual being I may send sweet dreams to you—to advise, comfort, and command ! who knows ? At all events, when I am *mooly,* may you be fresh as the dawn.

" Yours till death, and I trust *hereafter too,*

" DAVID GRAY."

At last, chiefly through the agency of the un-wearying Dobell, the poem was placed in the hands of the printer. On the 2nd of December, 1861, a specimen-page was sent to the author. David, with the shadow of death even then dark upon him, gazed long and lingeringly at the printed page. All the mysterious past — the boyish yearnings, the flash of anticipated fame, the black surroundings of the great city—flitted across his vision like a dream. It was " good news," he said. The next day the complete silence passed over the weaver's household, for David Gray was no more. Thus, on the 3rd of December, 1861, in the twenty-fourth year of his age, he passed tran-quilly away, almost his last words being, " God has love, and I have faith." The following epitaph, written out carefully, a few months before his decease, was found among his papers :—

My Epitaph.

Below lies one whose name was traced in sand—
He died, not knowing what it was to live:
Died while the first sweet consciousness of manhood
And maiden thought electrified his soul :
Faint beatings in the calyx of the rose.
Bewildered reader, pass without a sigh
In a proud sorrow ! There is life with God,
In other kingdom of a sweeter air;
In Eden every flower is blown. Amen.

David Gray.

Sept. 27, 1861.

Draw a veil over the woe that day in the weaver's cottage, the wild broodings over the beloved face, white in the sweetness of rest after pain. A few days later, the beloved dust was shut for ever from the light, and carried a short journey, in ancient Scottish fashion, on hand-spokes, to the Auld Aisle Burial-Ground, a dull and lonely square upon an eminence, bounden by a stone wall, and deep with " the uncut hair of graves." Here, in happier seasons, had David often mused ; for here slept dust of kindred, and hither in his sight the thin black line of rude mourners often wended with new burdens. Very early, too, he blended the place with his poetic dreams, and spoke of it in a sonnet not to be found in his little printed volume :—

Old Aisle.

Aisle of the dead! your lonely bell-less tower
   Seems like a soul-less body, whence rebounds
No tones ear-sweetening, as if 'twere to embower
   The Sabbath tresses with its soothing sounds.
In pity, crumbling aisle, thou lookest o'er
   Your former sainted worshippers, whose bones
   Lie mould'ring 'neath these nettle-girded stones,
Or 'neath yon rank grave weeds! Now from afar
Is seen the sacred heavenward spire, which seems
   An intercessor for the mounds below :
And doth it not speak eloquent in dreams?
   In dreams of aged pastors who did go
Up to the hallowed mount with homely tread :
   While there, old men and simple maids and youths
   Throng lovingly to hear the sacred truths
In gentle stream poured forth. But, he is dead ;
   And in this hill of sighs he rests unknown,
   As that wild flower that by his grave hath blown.

Standing on this eminence, one can gaze round upon the scenes which it is no exaggeration to say David has immortalized in song,—the Luggie flowing, the green woods of Gartshore, the smoke curling from the little hamlet of Merkland, and the faint blue misty distance of the Campsie Fells. The place though a lonely is a gentle and happy one, fit for a poet's rest; and there, while he was sleeping sound, a quiet company gathered ere long to uncover a monument inscribed with his name. The dying voice had been heard. Over the grave now stands a plain obelisk, publicly subscribed for, and inscribed with this epitaph, written by Lord Houghton :—

THIS MONUMENT OF

AFFECTION, ADMIRATION, AND REGRET,

IS ERECTED TO

DAVID GRAY,

THE POET OF MERKLAND,

BY FRIENDS FAR AND NEAR,

DESIROUS THAT HIS GRAVE SHOULD BE REMEMBERED

AMID THE SCENES OF HIS RARE GENIUS

AND EARLY DEATH,

AND BY THE LUGGIE NOW NUMBERED WITH THE STREAMS

ILLUSTRIOUS IN SCOTTISH SONG.

BORN, 29TH JANUARY, 1838 ; DIED, 3RD DECEMBER, 1861.

Here all is said that should be said; yet perhaps the poet's own sweet epitaph, evidently prepared with a view to such a use, would have been more graceful and appropriate.

" Whom the gods love die young," is no mere pagan consolation; it has a tenderness for all forms of faith, and even when philosophically translated, as by Wordsworth, who said sweetly that " the good die first," it still possesses balm for hearts that ache over the departed. That the young soul passes away in its strength, in its prismatic dawn, with many powers undeveloped, yet no power wasted, is the beauty and the pity of the thought, the inference of tho apotheosis. The impulse has been upward, and the gods have consecrated the endeavour. The thought hovers over the death-beds of Keats and Robert Nicoll ; it is repeated even by weary old men over those poets' graves. No hope has been disappointed, no eye has seen the strong wing grow feeble and falter earthward, and the possibility of a future beyond our seeing is boundless as the aspiration of the spirit which escaped us. " Whom the gods love die young," said the Athenians ; and " bless the ancient Greeks for *that* comfort," wrote David, with the thin, tremulous, consumption-wasted hand. Beautiful, pathetically beautiful, is the halo surrounding the head of a young poet as he dies.   We scarcely mourn him,—our souls are so stirred towards the eternal.   But what comfort may abide when, from the frame that still breathes, poesy arises like an exhalation, and the man lives on.   In life as well as in death there is a Plutonian house of exiles, and they abandon all hope who enter therein; and that man inhabits the same.   How often does this horror encounter us in our daily paths?   The change is rapid and imperceptible.   Without hope, without peace, without one glimpse of the glory the young find in their own aspirations, the doomed one buffets and groans in the dark. Which of the gods may he call to his aid? None; for he believes in none.   Better for him, a thousand times better, that he slept unknown in the shadow of the village where he was born. The strong hard scholar, the energetic literary man of business has a shield against the demons of disappointment, but men like David have no such shield.   Picture the dark weary struggle for bread which must have been his lot had he lived.   He had not the power to write to order, to sell his wits for money.   He sleeps in peace.

He has taken his unchanged belief in things beautiful to the very fountain-head of all beauty, and will never know the weary strife, the poignant heartache of the unsuccessful endeavourers.

The book of poems written, and the writer laid quietly down in the auld aisle burying ground, had David Gray wholly done with earth? No; for he worked from the grave on one who loved him with a love transcending that of woman. In the weaver's cottage at Merkland subsisted tender sorrow and affectionate remembrance; but something more. The shadow lay in the cottage; a light had departed which would never again be seen on sea or land; and David Gray, the handloom-weaver, the father of the poet, felt that the meaning had departed out of his simple life. There was a great mystery. The world called his darling son a poet,—and he hardly knew what a poet was; all he *did* know was that the coming of this prodigy had given a new complexion to all the facts of existence. There was a dream-life, it appeared, beyond the work in the fields and the loom. His son, whom he had thought mad at first, was crowned and honoured for the very things which his parents had thought useless. Around him, vague, incomprehensible, floated a new atmosphere, which clever people called *poetry;* and he began to feel that it was beautiful—the more so, that it was so new and wondrous. The fountains of his nature were stirred. He sat and smoked before the fire o' nights, and found himself dreaming too! He was conscious, now, that the glory of his days was beyond that grave in the kirkyard. He was like one that walks in a mist, his eyes full of tears. But he said little of his griefs,—little, that is to say, in the way of direct complaint. "We feel very weary now David has gone!" was all the plaint I knew him to utter; he grieved so silently, wondered so speechlessly. The new life, brief and fatal, made him wise. With the eager sensitiveness of the poet himself he read the various criticisms on David's book; and so subtle was the change in him, that, though he was utterly unlearned and had hitherto had no insight whatever into the nature of poetry, he knew by instinct whether the critics were right or wrong, and felt their suggestions to the very roots of his being.

With this old man, in whom I recognized a greatness and sweetness of soul that has broadened my view of God's humblest creatures ever since, I kept up a correspondence—at first for David's sake, but latterly for my correspondent's own sake. His letters, brief and simple as they were, grew fraught with delicate and delicious meaning; I could see how he marvelled at the mysterious light he understood not, yet how fearlessly he kept his soul stirred towards the eternal silence where his son was lying. "We feel very weary now David has gone!" Ah, how weary! The long years of toil told their tale now; the thread was snapt, and labour was no longer a perfect end to the soul and satisfaction to the body. The little carpeted bedroom was a prayer-place now. The Luggie flowing, the green woods, the thymy hills, had become haunted; a voice unheard by other dwellers in the valley was calling, calling, and a hand was beckoning; and tired, more tired, dazzled, more dazzled, grew the old weaver. The very *names* of familiar scenes were now a strange trouble; for were not these names echoing in David's songs? Merkland, " the summer woods of dear Gartshire," the " fairy glen of Wooilce," Criftin, " with his host of gloomy pine-trees," all had their ghostly voices. Strange rhymes mingled with the humming of the loom. Mysterious " poetry," which he had once scorned as an idle thing, deepened and deepened in its fascination for him. All he saw and heard meant something strange in rhyme. He was drawn along by music, and he could not rest.

Beside him dwelt the mother. Her face was quite calm. She had wept bitterly, but her heart now was with other sons and daughters. David was with God, and the minister said that God was good—that was quite enough. None of the new light had troubled her eyes. She knew that her beloved had made a " heap o' rhyme,"—that was all. A good loving lad had gone to rest, but there were still bairns left, bless God !

But the old man lingered on, with hunger in his heart, wonder in his soul. This could not last for ever. In the winter of 1864, he warned me that he was growing ill; and although he attributed his illness to cold, his letters showed me the truth.   There was some physical malady, but the aggravating cause was mental.   It was my duty, however, to do all that could be done humanly to save him; and the first thing to do was to see that he had those comforts which sick men need.   I placed his case before Lord Houghton; but generous as that man is, all men are not so generous.   "It is exceedingly difficult to get people to assist a man of genius himself," wrote Lord Houghton, gloomily; "they won't assist his relations."   Lord Houghton, however, personally assisted him, and was joined by a kind colleague, Mr. Baillie Cochrane.

I felt then, and I feel now, that the condition of the old man was even more deeply affecting than the condition of David in his last moments, as deserving of sympathy, as universal in its appeal to human generosity; and I felt a yearning, moreover, to provide for the comfort of David's mother, and for the education of David's brothers. Who knew but that, among the latter, might be another bright intellect, which a little schooling might save for the world ? After puzzling myself for a plan, I at last thought that I could attain all my wishes by publishing a book to be entitled " Memorials of David Gray," and to contain contributions from all the writers of eminence whom I could enlist in the good cause.　Such a thing would *sell*, and might, moreover, be worth buying. The fine natures were not slow in responding to the appeal, and I mention some names, that they may gain honour.　Tennyson promised a poem ; Browning another ; George Eliot agreed to contribute ; Dickens, because he was too busy to write anything more, offered me an equivalent in money.　All seemed well, when one or two objections were raised on the score of propriety ; and it was even suggested, that " it looked like begging for the father on the strength of Gray's reputation." Confused and perplexed, I determined to refer the matter to one whose good sense is as great as his heart, but (luckily for his friends) a great deal harder.　" Should I or should I not, under the circumstances, go on with my scheme ? " His answer being in the negative, the book was not gone on with, and the matter dropped.

Meantime, the old man was getting worse. On the 27th April I received this letter :—

" Dear Mr. Buchanan,   " Merkland.

" We hope this will find you and Mrs. Buchanan in good health. I am not getting any better. The cough still continues. However, I rise every day a while, but it is only to sit by the fire. Weather is so cold I cannot go out, except sometimes I get out and walks round yard. *I am not looking for betterness.* I have nothing particular to say, only we thought you would be thinking us ungrateful in not writing soon.

" I remain, yours ever,

" David Gray.

" I understand there is some movement with David's stone * again."

On the 9th May, he wrote, "I have Dr. Stewart to attend me. He called on Sunday and sounded me;—he says I am a dying man, and dying fast. You cannot imagine what a weak person I am ; I am nearly bedfast." On the 16th May came the last lines I ever received from him. They are almost illegible, and their purport prevents

---

* The monument, not then erected.

me from printing them here.   A few days more,
and the old man was dead.   His green grave lies
in the shadow of the obelisk which stands over
his beloved son.   Father and child are side by
side.   A little cloud, a pathetic mystery, came
between them in life ; but that is all over.   The
old handloom-weaver, who never wrote a verse,
unconsciously reached his son's stature some time
ere he passed away. The mysterious thing called
" poetry," which operated such changes in his
simple life, became all clear at last—in that final
moment when the world's meanings become
transparent, and nothing is left but to swoon
back with closed eyes into the darkness, con-
fiding in God's mercy, content either to waken
at His footstool, or to rest painlessly for evermore.

NOTE AND ADDENDA.

A T the request of many friends, I append
to the biography of David Gray the two
poems which have reference to his life and poems,

and which are to be found scattered among my
other writings. The first poem, however, must
not be read as literally interpreting all the facts
of Gray's life. It is merely a work of imagination,
with a true experience for its groundwork.

I.

POET ANDREW.

O Loom, that loud art murmuring,
What doth he hear thee say or sing?
Thou hummest o'er the dead one's songs,
   He cannot choose but hark,
His heart with tearful rapture throngs,
   But all his face grows dark.

O cottage Fire, that burnest bright,
What pictures sees he in thy light?
A city's smoke, a white white face,
   Phantoms that fade and die,
And last, the lonely burial-place
   On the windy hill hard by.

'TIS near a year since Andrew went to sleep—
   A winter and a summer.   Yonder bed
Is where the boy was born, and where he died,
And yonder o'er the lowland is his grave:

The nook of grass and gowans where in thought
I found you standing at the set o' sun . . .
The Lord content us—'tis a weary world.
   These five-and-twenty years I've wrought and
      wrought
In this same dwelling;—hearken! you can hear
The looms that whuzzle-whazzle ben the house,
Where Jean and Mysie, lassies in their teens,
And Jamie, and a neighbour's son beside,
Work late and early. Andrew who is dead
Was our first-born; and when he crying came,
With beaded een and pale old-farrant face,
Out of the darkness, Mysie and mysel'
Were young and heartsome; and his smile, be
     sure,
Made daily toil the sweeter. Hey, his kiss
Put honey in the very porridge-pot!
His smile strung threads of sunshine on the loom!
And when he hung around his mother's neck,
He decked her out in jewels and in gold
That even ladies envied! . . . Weel! . . . in time
Came other children, newer gems and gold,
And Andrew quitted Mysie's breast for mine.
So years rolled on, like bobbins on a loom;

And Mysie and mysel' had work to do,
And Andrew took his turn among the rest,
No sweeter, dearer; till, one Sabbath day,
When Andrew was a curly-pated tot
Of sunny summers six, I had a crack
With Mister Mucklewraith the Minister,
Who put his kindly hand on Andrew's head,
Called him a clever wean, a bonnie wean,
Clever at learning, while the mannikin
Blushed red as any rose, and peeping up
Went twinkle-twinkle with his round black een;
And then, while Andrew laughed and ran awa',
The Minister went deeper in his praise,
And prophesied he would become in time
A man of mark.   This set me thinking, sir,
And watching,—and the mannock puzzled me.

  Would sit for hours upon a stool and draw
Droll faces on the slate, while other lads
Were shouting at their play; dumbly would lie
Beside the Lintock, sailing, piloting,
Navies of docken-leaves a summer day;
Had learn'd the hymns of Doctor Watts by heart,
And as for old Scots songs, could lilt them a'——

From Yarrow Braes to Bonnie Bessie Lee—
And where he learn'd them, only Heaven knew ;
And oft, although he feared to sleep his lane,
Would cowrie at the threshold in a storm
To watch the lightning,—as a birdie sits,
With fluttering fearsome heart and dripping wings,
Among the branches.   Once, I mind it weel,
In came he, running, with a bloody nose,
Part tears, part pleasure, to his fluttering heart
Holding a callow mavis golden-billed,
The thin white film of death across its een,
And told us, sobbing, how a neighbour's son
Harried the birdie's nest, and how by chance
He came upon the thief beside the burn
Throwing the birdies in to see them swim,
And how he fought him, till he yielded up
This one, the one remaining of the nest ;—
And " O the birdie's dying ! " sobbed he sore,
" The bonnie birdie's dying ! "—till it died ;
And Andrew dug a grave behind the house,
Buried his dead, and covered it with earth,
And cut, to mark the grave, a grassy turf
Where blew a bunch of gowans.   After that,
I thought and thought, and thick as bees the
        thoughts

Buzzed to the whuzzle-whazzling of the loom—
I could make naething of the mannikin !
But by-and-by, when Hope was making hay,
And web-work rose, I settled it and said
To the good wife, " 'Tis plain that yonder lad
Will never take to weaving—and at school
They say he beats the rest at all his tasks
Save figures only : I have settled it :
Andrew shall be a minister—a pride
And comfort to us, Mysie, in our age ;
He shall to college in a year or twa
(If fortune smiles as now) at Edinglass."
You guess the wife opened her een, cried " Foosh !"
And called the plan a silly senseless dream,
A hopeless, useless castle in the air ;
But ere the night was out, I talked her o'er,
And here she sat, her hands upon her knees,
Glow'ring and heark'ning, as I conjured up,
Amid the fog and reek of Edinglass,
Life's peaceful gloaming and a godly fame.
So it was broached, and after many cracks
With Mister Mucklewraith, we planned it a',
And day by day we laid a penny by
To give the lad when he should quit the bield..

And years wore on ; and year on year was cheered
By thoughts of Andrew, drest in decent black,
Throned in a Pulpit, preaching out the Word,
A house his own, and all the country-side
To touch their bonnets to him.   Weel, the lad
Grew up among us, and at seventeen
His hands were genty white, and he was tall,
And slim, and narrow-shouldered ; pale of face,
Silent, and bashful.   Then we first began
To feel how muckle more he knew than we,
To eye his knowledge in a kind of fear,
As folk might look upon a crouching beast,
Bonnie, but like enough to rise and bite.
Up came the cloud between us silly folk
And the young lad that sat among his Books
Amid the silence of the night ; and oft
It pained us sore to fancy he would learn
Enough to make him look with shame and scorn
On this old dwelling.   'Twas his _manner_, sir !
He seldom lookt his father in the face,
And when he walkt about the dwelling, seemed
Like one superior ; dumbly he would steal
To the burnside, or into Lintlin Woods,
With some new-farrant book,—and when I peeped,

Behold a book of jingling-jangling rhyme,
Fine-written nothings on a printed page;
And, pressed between the leaves, a flower per-
    chance,
Anemone or blue Forget-me-not,
Pluckt in the grassy woodland. Then I peeped
Into his drawer, among his papers there,
And found—you guess?—a heap of idle rhymes,
Big-sounding, like the worthless printed book:
Some in old copies scribbled, some on scraps.
Of writing-paper, others finely writ
With spirls and flourishes on big white sheets.
I clenched my teeth, and groaned. The beauteous
    dream
Of the good Preacher in his braw black dress,
With house and income snug, began to fade
Before the picture of a drunken loon
Bawling out songs beneath the moon and stars,—
Of poet Willie Clay, who wrote a book
About King Robert Bruce, and aye got fu',
And scattered stars in verse, and aye got fu',
Wept the world's sins, and then got fu' again,—
Of Ferguson, the feckless limb o' law,—
And Robin Burns, who gauged the whisky-casks

And brake the seventh commandment. So at once
I up and said to Andrew, " You're a fool !
You waste your time in silly senseless verse,
Lame as your own conceit: take heed ! take heed !
Or, like your betters, come to grief ere long !"
But Andrew flusht and never spake a word,
Yet eyed me sidelong with his beaded een,
And turned awa', and, as he turned, his look—
Half scorn, half sorrow—stang me.   After that,
I felt he never heeded word of ours,
And though we tried to teach him common-sense
He idled as he pleased ; and many a year,
After I spake him first, that look of his
Came dark between us, and I held my tongue,
And felt he scorned me for the poetry's sake.
This coldness grew and grew, until at last
We sat whole nights before the fire and spoke
No word to one another.   One fine day,
Says Mister Mucklewraith to me, says he,
" So ! you've a Poet in your house !" and smiled ;
" A Poet ? God forbid !" I cried ; and then
It all came out: how Andrew slyly sent
Verse to the paper ; how they printed it
In Poets' Corner ; how the printed verse

Had ca't a girdle in the callant's head;
How Mistress Mucklewraith they thought half daft
Had cut the verses out and pasted them
In albums, and had praised them to her friends.
I said but little; for my schemes and dreams
Were tumbling down like castles in the air,
And all my heart seemed hardening to stone.
But after that, in secret stealth, I bought
The papers, hunted out the printed verse,
And read it like a thief; thought some were good,
And others foolish havers, and in most
Saw naething, neither common-sense nor sound—
Words pottle-bellied, meaningless, and strange,
That strutted up and down the printed page,
Like Bailies made to bluster and look big.

'Twas useless grumbling. All my silent looks
Were lost, all Mysie's flyting fell on ears
Choke-full of other counsel; but we talked
In bed o' nights, and Mysie wept, and I
Felt stubborn, wrothful, wronged. It was to be!
But mind you, though we mourned, we ne'er forsook
The college scheme. Our sorrow, as we saw
Our Andrew growing cold to homely ways,

And scornful of the bield, but strengthened more
Our wholesome wish to educate the lad,
And do our duty by him, and help him on
With our rough hands—the Lord would do the
          rest,
The Lord would mend or mar him.   So at last,
New-clad from top to toe in home-spun cloth,
With books and linen in a muckle trunk,
He went his way to college ; and we sat,
Mysie and me, in weary darkness here ;
For though the younger bairns were still about,
It seemed our hearts had gone to Edinglass
With Andrew, and were choking in the reek
Of Edinglass town.

                    It was a gruesome fight,
Both for oursel's at home, and for the boy,
That student life at college.   Hard it was
To scrape the fees together, but beside,
The lad was young and needed meat and drink.
We sent him meal and bannocks by the train,
And country cheeses ; and with this and that,
Though sorely pushed, he throve, though now and
          then

With empty wame: spinning the siller out
By teaching grammar in a school at night.
Whiles he came home: weary old-farrant face
Pale from the midnight candle; bring home
Good news of college.   Then we shook awa'
The old sad load, began to build again
Our airy castles, and were hopeful Time
Would heal our wounds.   But, sir, they plagued
          me still—
Some of his ways! When here, he spent his time
In yonder chamber, or about the woods,
And by the waterside,—and with him books
Of poetry, as of old.   Mysel' could get
But little of his company or tongue;
And when we talkt, atweel, a kind of frost,—
My consciousness of silly ignorance,
And worse, my knowledge that the lad himsel'
Felt sorely, keenly, all my ignorant shame,
Made talk a torture out of which we crept
With burning faces.   Could you understand
One who was wild as if he found a mine
Of golden guineas, when he noticed first
The soft green streaks in a snowdrop's inner leaves?
And once again, the moonlight glimmering

Through watery transparent stalks of flax?
A flower's a flower! . . . But Andrew snooved
    about,
Aye finding wonders, mighty mysteries,
In things that ilka learless cottar kenned.
Now, 'twas the falling snow or murmuring rain;
Now, 'twas the laverock singing in the sun,
And dropping slowly to the callow young;
Now, an old tune he heard his mother lilt;
And aye those trifles made his pallid face
Flush brighter, and his cen flash keener far,
Than when he heard of yonder storm in France,
Or a King's death, or, if the like had been,
A city's downfall.

        He was born with love
For things both great and small; yet seemed to
    prize
The small things best.   To me, it seemed indeed
The callant cared for nothing for itsel',
But for some special quality it had
To set him thinking, thinking, or bestow
A tearful sense he took for luxury.
He loved us in his silent fashion weel;

But in our feckless ignorance we knew
'Twas when the humour seized him—with a sense
Of some queer power we had to waken up
The poetry—ay, and help him in his rhyme!
A kind of patronising tenderness,
A pitying pleasure in our Scottish speech
And homely ways, a love that made him note
Both ways and speech with the same curious joy
As filled him when he watched the birds and flowers.

He was as sore a puzzle to us then
As he had been before.   It puzzled us,
How a big lad, down-cheeked, almost a man,
Could pass his time in silly childish joys . . .
Until at last, a hasty letter came
From Andrew, telling he had broke awa'
From college, packed his things, and taken train
To London city, where he hoped (he said)
To make both fortune and a noble fame
Through a grand poem, carried in his trunk;
How, after struggling on with bitter heart,
He could no longer bear to fight his way
Among the common scholars; and the end
Bade us be hopeful, trusting God, and sure

The light of this old home would guide him still
Amid the reek of evil.

               Sae it was!
We twa were less amazed than you may guess,
Though we had hoped, and feared, and hoped, sae
       long!
But it was hard to bear—hard, hard, to bear!
Our castle in the clouds was gone for good;
And as for Andrew—other lads had ta'en
The same mad path, and learned the bitter task
Of poortith, cold, and tears. She grat. I sat
In silence, looking on the fuffing fire,
Where streets and ghaistly faces came and went,
And London city crumbled down to crush
Our Andrew; and my heart was sick and cold.
Ere long, the news across the country-side
Speak quickly, like the crowing of a cock
From farm to farm—the women talkt it o'er
On doorsteps, o'er the garden rails; the men
Got fu' upon it at the public-house,
And whispered it among the fields at work.
A cry was quickly raised from house to house,
That all the blame was mine, and cankered een

Lookt cold upon me, as upon a kind
Of upstart.   " Fie on pride ! " the whisper said,
The fault was Andrew's less than those who taught
His heart to look in scorn on honest work,—
Shame on them !—but the lad, poor lad, would
      learn !
O sir, the thought of this spoiled many a web
In yonder—tingling, tingling, in my ears,
Until I fairly threw my gloom aside,
Smiled like a man whose heart is light and young,
And with a future-kenning happy look
Threw up my chin, and bade them wait and see . .
But, night by night, these een lookt London ways,
And saw my laddie wandering all alone
'Mid darkness, fog, and reek, growing afar
To dark proportions and gigantic shape—
Just as a figure of a sheep-herd looms,
Awful and silent, through a mountain mist.

    Ye aiblins ken the rest.   At first, there came
Proud letters, swiftly writ, telling how folk
Now roundly called him " Poet," holding out
Bright pictures, which we smiled at wearily—
As people smile at pictures in a book,

Untrue but bonnie.   Then the letters ceased,
There came a silence cold and still as frost,—
We sat and hearkened to our beating hearts,
And prayed as we had never prayed before.
Then lastly, on the silence broke the news
That Andrew, far awa', was sick to death,
And, weary, weary of the noisy streets,
With aching head and weary hopeless heart,
Was coming home from mist and fog and noise
To grassy lowlands and the caller air.

    'Twas strange, 'twas strange!—but this, the
        weary end
Of all our bonnie biggins in the clouds,
Came like a tearful comfort.   Love sprang up
Out of the ashes of the household fire,
Where Hope was fluttering like the loose white
        film ;
And Andrew, our own boy, seemed nearer now
To this old dwelling an our aching hearts
Than he had ever been since he became
Wise with book-learning.   With an eager pain,
I met him at the train and brought him home ;
And when we met that sunny day in hairst,

The ice that long had sundered us had thawed,
We met in silence, and our een were dim.
Och, I can see that look of his this night!
Part pain, part tenderness—a weary look
Yearning for comfort such as God the Lord
Puts into parents' een.   I brought him here.
Gently we set him here beside the fire,
And spake few words, and hushed the noisy house;
Then eyed his hollow cheeks and lustrous een,
His clammy hueless brow and faded hands,
Blue veined and white like lily-flowers.   The wife
Forgot the sickness of his face, and moved
With light and happy footstep but and ben,
As though she welcomed to a merry feast
A happy guest.   In time, out came the truth:
Andrew was dying: in his lungs the dust
Of cities stole unseen, and hot as fire
Burnt—like a deil's red een that gazed at Death.
Too late for doctor's skill, though doctor's skill
We had in plenty; but the ill had ta'en
Too sure a grip.   Andrew was dying, dying:
The beauteous dream had melted like a mist
The sunlight feeds on: a' remaining now
Was Andrew, bare and barren of his pride,

Stark of conceit, a weel-belovèd child,
Helpless to help himsel', and dearer thus,
As when his yaumer*—like the corn-craik's cry
Heard in a field of wheat at dead o' night—
Brake on the hearkening darkness of the bield.

And as he nearer grew to God the Lord,
Nearer and dearer ilka day he grew
To Mysie and mysel'—our own to love,
The world's no longer.　For the first last time,
We twa, the lad and I, could sit and crack
With open hearts—free-spoken, at our ease;
I seemed to know as muckle then as he,
Because I was sae sad.

　　　　　　Thus grief, sae deep
It flowed without a murmur, brought the balm
Which blunts the edge of worldly sense and makes
Old people weans again.　In this sad time,
We never troubled at his childish ways;
We seemed to share his pleasure when he sat
List'ning to birds upon the eaves; we felt

---

* *Yaumer*, a child's cry.

Small wonder when we found him weeping o'er
His old torn books of pencilled thoughts and
      verse;
And if, outbye, I saw a bonnie flower,
I pluckt it carefully and bore it home
To my sick boy.   To me, it somehow seemed
His care for lovely earthly things had changed—
Changed from the curious love it once had been,
Grown larger, bigger, holier, peacefuller;
And though he never lost the luxury
Of loving beauteous things for poetry's sake,
His heart was God the Lord's, and he was calm.
Death came to lengthen out his solemn thoughts
Like shadows to the sunset.   So no more
We wondered.   What is folly in a lad
Healthy and heartsome, one with work to do,
Befits the freedom of a dying man. . .
Mother, who chided loud the idle lad
Of old, now sat her sadly by his side,
And read from out the Bible soft and low,
Or lilted lowly, keeking in his face,
The old Scots songs that made his een so dim.
I went about my daily work as one
Who waits to hear a knocking at the door,

Ere Death creeps in and shadows those that
          watch ;
And seated here at e'en i' the ingleside,
I watched the pictures in the fire and smoked
My pipe in silence ; for my head was fu'
Of many rhymes the lad had made of old
(Rhymes I had read in secret, as I said),
No one of which I minded till they came
Unsummoned, murmuring about my ears
Like bees among the leaves.

                    The end drew near.
Came Winter moaning, and the Doctor said
That Andrew couldna live to see the Spring ;
And day by day, while frost was hard at work,
The lad grew weaker, paler, and the blood
Came redder from the lung. One Sabbath day—
The last of winter, for the caller air
Was drawing sweetness from the barks of trees—
When down the lane, I saw to my surprise
A snowdrop blooming underneath a birk,
And gladly pluckt the flower to carry home
To Andrew.   Ere I reached the bield, the air
Was thick wi' snow, and ben in yonder room

I found him, Mysie seated at his side,
Drawn to the window in the old arm-chair,
Gazing wi' lustrous een and sickly cheek
Out on the shower, that wavered softly down
In glistening siller glamour.   Saying nought,
Into his hand I put the year's first flower,
And turned awa' to hide my face ; and he . .
. . He smiled . . and at the smile, I knew, not why,
It swam upon us, in a frosty pain,
The end was come at last, at last, and Death
Was creeping ben, his shadow on our hearts.
We gazed on Andrew, called him by his name,
And touched him softly . . and he lay awhile,
His een upon the snow, in a dark dream,
Yet neither heard nor saw ; but suddenly,
He shook awa' the vision wi' a smile,
Raised lustrous een, still smiling, to the sky,
Next upon us, then dropt them to the flower
That trembled in his hand, and murmured low,
Like one that gladly murmurs to himsel'—
" Out of the Snow, the Snowdrop—out of Death
Comes Life ;" then closed his eyes and made a
          moan,
And never spake another word again.

. . And you think weel of Andrew's book?
   You think
That folk will love him, for the poetry's sake,
Many a year to come? We take it kind
You speak so weel of Andrew!—As for me,
I can make naething of the printed book;
I am no scholar, sir, as I have said,
And Mysie there can just read print a wee.
Ay! we are feckless, ignorant of the world!
And though 'twere joy to have our boy again
And place him far above our lowly house,
We like to think of Andrew as he was
When, dumb and wee, he hung his gold and gems
Round Mysie's neck; or—as he is this night—
Lying asleep, his face to heaven—asleep,
Near to our hearts, as when he was a bairn,
Without the poetry and human pride
That came between us to our grief, langsyne.

From " Idyls and Legends of Inverburn," by
Robert Buchanan.

II.

TO DAVID IN HEAVEN.

I.

LO ! the slow moon roaming
Through fleecy mists of gloaming,
Furrowing with pearly edge the jewel-powdered
sky !
Lo, the bridge moss-laden,
Arched like foot of maiden,
And on the bridge, in silence, looking upward,
you and I !
Lo, the pleasant season
Of reaping and of mowing—
The round still moon above,—beneath, the river
duskily flowing !

II.

Violet-coloured shadows,
Blown from scented meadows,
Float o'er us to the pine-wood dark from yonder
dim corn-ridge ;
The little river gushes

Through shady sedge and rushes,
And gray gnats murmur o'er the pools, beneath
the mossy bridge ;—
And you and I stand darkly,
O'er the keystone leaning,
And watch the pale mesmeric moon, in the time
of gleaners and gleaning.

III.

Do I dream, I wonder?
As, sitting sadly under
A lonely roof in London, through the grim
square pane I gaze?
Here of you I ponder,
In a dream, and yonder
The still streets seem to stir and breathe beneath
the white moon's rays.
By the vision cherished,
By the battle bravèd,
Do I but dream a hopeless dream, in the city that
slew you, David?

IV.

Is it fancy also,
That the light which falls so

Faintly upon the stony street below me as I
      write,
      Near tall mountains passes
      Through churchyard weeds and grasses,
Barely a mower's mile away from that small
      bridge, to-night?
      And, where you are lying,—
      Grass and flowers above you—
Is mingled with your sleeping face, as calm as
      the hearts that love you?

v.

      Poet gentle-hearted,
      Are you then departed,
And have you ceased to dream the dream we loved
      of old so well?
      Has the deeply cherished
      Aspiration perished,
And are you happy, David, in that heaven where
      you dwell?
      Have you found the secret
      We, so wildly, sought for,
And is your soul enswathed, at last, in the singing
      robes you fought for?

VI.

In some heaven star-lighted,
Are you now united
Unto the poet-spirits that you loved, of English
race ?
Is Chatterton still dreaming ?
And, to give it stately seeming,
Has the music of his last strong song passed into
Keats's face ?
Is Wordsworth there ? and Spenser ?
Beyond the grave's black portals,
Can the grand eye of Milton *see* the glory he sang
to mortals ?

VII.

You at least could teach me,
Could your dear voice reach me,
Where I sit and copy out for men my soul's strange
speech,
Whether it be bootless,
Profitless, and fruitless,—
The weary aching upward strife to heights we
cannot reach,
The fame we seek in sorrow,

The agony we forego not,
The haunting singing sense that makes us climb
   —whither we know not.

VIII.

Must it last for ever,
The passionate endeavour,
Ay, have ye, there in heaven, hearts to throb and
   still aspire?
In the life you know now,
Rendered white as snow now,
Do fresher glory-heights arise, and beckon higher
   —higher?
Are you dreaming, dreaming,
Is your soul still roaming,
Still gazing upward as we gazed, of old in the
   autumn gloaming?

IX.

Lo, the book I hold here,
In the city cold here!
I hold it with a gentle hand and love it as I may;
Lo, the weary moments!
Lo, the icy comments!

And lo, false Fortune's knife of gold swift-lifted
 up to slay !
Has the strife no ending ?
Has the song no meaning ?
Linger I, idle as of old, while men are reaping or
 gleaning ?

X.

Upward my face I turn to you,
I long for you, I yearn to you,
The spectral vision trances me to utt'rance wild
 and weak ;
It is not that I mourn you,
To mourn you were to scorn you,
For you are one step nearer to the beauty singers
 seek.
But I want, and cannot see you,
I seek and cannot find you,
And, see ! I touch the book of songs you tenderly
 left behind you !

XI.

Ay, me ! I bend above it,
With tearful eyes, and love it,

With tender hand I touch the leaves, but cannot
find you there !
Mine eyes are haunted only
By that gloaming sweetly lonely,
The shadows on the mossy bridge, the glamour in
the air !
I touch the leaves, and only
See the glory they retain not—
The moon that is a lamp to Hope, who glorifies
what we gain not !

XII.

The aching and the yearning,
The hollow undiscerning,
Uplooking want I still retain, darken the leaves I
touch—
Pale promise, with much sweetness
Solemnizing incompleteness,
But ah, you knew so little then—and now you
know so much !
By the vision cherished,
By the battle bravèd,
Have you, in heaven, shamed the song, by a
loftier music, David ?

XIII.

I, who loved and knew you,
In the city that slew you,
Still hunger on, and thirst, and climb, proud-
　　hearted and alone:
Serpent-fears enfold me,
Syren-visions hold me,
And, like a wave, I gather strength, and gather-
　　ing strength, I moan;
Yea, the pale moon beckons,
Still I follow, aching,
And gather strength, only to make a louder moan,
　　in breaking!

XIV.

Though the world could turn from you,
This, at least, I learn from you:
Beauty and Truth, though never found, are worthy
　　to be sought,
The singer, upward-springing,
Is grander than his singing,
And tranquil self-sufficing joy illumes the dark of
　　thought.
This, at least, you teach me,

In a revelation :
That gods still snatch, as worthy death, the soul
    in its aspiration.

xv.

    And I think, as you thought,
    Poesy and Truth ought
Never to lie silent in the singer's heart on earth ;
    Though they be discarded,
    Slighted, unrewarded,
Though, unto vulgar seeming, they appear of little
    worth,—
    Yet tender brother-singers,
    Young or not yet born to us,
May seek there, for the singer's sake, that love
    which sweeteneth scorn to us !

xvi.

    While I sit in silence,
    Comes from mile on mile hence,
From English Keats's Roman grave, a voice that
    sweetens toil !
    Think you, no fond creatures
    Draw comfort from the features

Of Chatterton, pale Phäethon, hurled down to
    sunless soil ?
    Scorched with sunlight lying,
    Eyes of sunlight hollow,
But, see ! upon the lips a gleam of the chrism of
    Apollo !

XVII.

    Noble thought produces
    Noble ends and uses,
Noble hopes are part of Hope wherever she may
    be,
    Noble thought enhances
    Life and all its chances,
And noble self is noble song,—all this I learn
    from thee !
    And I learn, moreover,
    'Mid the city's strife too,
That such faint song as sweetens Death can sweeten
    the singer's life too !

XVIII.

    Lo, my Book !—I hold it
    In weary hands, and fold it
Unto my heart, if only as a token I aspire ;

And, by song's assistance,
Unto your dim distance,
My soul uplifted is on wings, and beckoned higher,
    nigher.
By the sweeter wisdom
You return unspeaking,
Though endless, hopeless, be the search, we exalt
    our souls in seeking.

XIX.

Higher, yet, and higher,
Ever nigher, ever nigher,
To the glory we conceive not, let us toil and strive
    and strain !——
The agonized yearning,
The imploring and the burning,
Grown awfuller, intenser, at each vista we attain,
And clearer, brighter, growing,
Up the gulfs of heaven wander,
Higher, higher yet, and higher, to the Mystery
    we ponder !

XX.

Yea, higher yet, and higher,
Ever nigher, ever nigher,

While men grow small by stooping and the reaper
        piles the grain,—
        Can it then be bootless,
        Profitless and fruitless,
The weary aching upward search for what we never
        gain ?
        Is there not awaiting
        Rest and golden weather,
Where, passionately purified, the singers may meet
        together ?

XXI.

        Up ! higher yet, and higher,
        Ever nigher, ever nigher,
Through voids that Milton and the rest beat still
        with seraph-wings ;
        Out through the great gate creeping
        Where God hath put his sleeping—
A dewy cloud detaining not the soul that soars and
        sings ;
        Up ! higher yet, and higher
        Fainting nor retreating,
Beyond the sun, beyond the stars, to the far bright
        realm of meeting !

XXII.

O Mystery! O Passion!
To sit on earth, and fashion,
What floods of music visibled may fill that fancied
place!
To think, the least that singeth,
Aspireth and upspringeth,
May weep glad tears on Keats's breast and look in
Milton's face!
When human power and failure
Are equalized for ever,
And the one great Light that haloes all is the
passionate bright endeavour!

XXIII.

But ah, that pale moon roaming
Through fleecy mists of gloaming,
Furrowing with pearly edge the jewel-powdered
sky,
And ah, the days departed
With your friendship gentle-hearted,
And ah, the dream we dreamt that night, together,
you and I!

Is it fashioned wisely,
To help us or to blind us,
That at each height we gain we turn, and behold
a heaven behind us?
Undertones, by Robert Buchanan.

III.

THE STUDENT, AND HIS VOCATION.

THE STUDENT AND HIS VOCATION.

IT is not so easy to be alone as it used to be. Fresh dropt, as it were, from the moon, and amazed at the hum and roar of innumerable mortals similarly bewildered, the mortal traveller finds it difficult now to creep into a cave or to pitch a tent in the desert. Even if beneficent Providence feed and clothe him free of trouble, the temptation to action is almost certain to be too strong for him; when everybody is fighting, he is indeed cold-blooded who does not seek a share of the blows and the glory. He is pulled into the public vortex —fights, debates, writes, studies by all means to outwrestle his neighbours and to get a head higher. Entering the city gates, greeted

by a wail as shrill and sad as if he were pene-
trating the middle circle of the Inferno, his heart is
stirred and he becomes a philanthropist. Observing the phenomena of society and the inexorable laws of trade, he turns political economist.
Marking the tendency of the race to equalization,
observing how much may be done even by tall
talk to commeasure freedom, he mounts the
rostrum and delivers political oracles. But he
is never alone. Once caught by the whirligig, he
is kept dancing round and round. He is doomed
to be a public man, big or little, one of the crowd,
—doomed in this fatal way, that once committed
to combined action with masses, no other action
contents him. With sword or with pen, in the
senate or in the pulpit, as constitution-conserver or
liberal elector, he is for ever on the move. Is it
to be wondered at that he soon loses his identity ?
The man is lost in the vocation; we know him no
longer by his face and voice, but by his badge of
office. He is a wave in the great waters. His business is public, and he is coerced by his associates.

The collective public opinion of this crowd of
travellers is what may be termed " contemporary

truth." This, of necessity, changes from generation to generation. From Hindooism to the pantheism of Greece and Rome, from that to the Catholicism of the early Church, from that to the fierce bigotry of the later Church, from that to the sour eclecticism of France, contemporary truth changes and changes. That which is true to Julius Cæsar is smiled at by Augustus; what the cowls approve the eighth Henry soon proves to be ephemeral, until Henry, in his turn, is shown to have only just begun the work of alteration. It is the same in all other movements not religious. Now contemporary truth is for monarchies, then for republics one and indivisible; now it insists upon the encyclopædia as the embodiment of all knowledge, again it indignantly tears the encyclopædia and burns the effigy of Voltaire. Noisy, vehement, dogmatic, yet earnest, beat the waters of opinion on the heavenly shore, where the sun comes and goes, and the stars keep vigil in the intervals of his coming and going; and contemporary truth is the barest froth thereof. The crowd roars, and the angels are smiling at its oracles.

Evermore, however, in all periods, in all climates and countries, there have been individuals who cared neither to lead nor to be led, who grew weary of action, however irresponsible, and who, in a supreme moment, have crept away from the mass and sought solitude.   Yet in no selfish or exclusive spirit have they sought to be alone,—in no scorn of their fellows, in no fear of blows or pain, in no wish to secure a monopoly of the grand shows which nature makes in solitary places.   Spiritual astronomers, they discovered early that it was their business to regard the heavens, not to delve in the earth, nor build cities, nor preach in the market-place.   Stargazers, they speculate from what star they and the other travellers have fallen.   The tumult, the glory, the wonder of the world electrifies, instead of disturbing, their contemplation.   These men are the Students,—pale men, with melancholy eyes, which seem to suffer from the burning light they shed on fellow-mortals.

What, then, do the Students seek, turning their eyes to these transmortal directions, troubled evermore by the passage of wondrous lights across the heavenly shore ?   They are seeking, not contemporary, but " eternal truth,"—the law beyond local law, the religion beyond creeds, the holy government beyond governments which come and go.   They are noting, in a word, not merely the phenomena which are constantly changing, but the truths which regulate such phenomena, which are evermore recurring with fresh force and novelty, and which may fairly be regarded as unchangeable. Plato, the grand great brow, gleaming divinely in the pale pure light of pagan sunset ; Spinoza, shading his wondrous eyes under heavy Jewish eyelids from a perfect glare and agony of light ; Comte, consuming a frail body in the distress of too fixed a contemplation : these, all such as these, and the host of lesser labourers, constitute the class of Students, embracing in one fine brotherhood metaphysicians, spiritualists, positivists, men of science, poets, painters, and musicians.   However much they differ in most matters, however opposite they may be in personal hopes and aspirations, they have one great point of contact :—their vocation is the study of eternal, not contemporary truth, and, to perfect that vocation, they find it imperatively necessary to live alone.

Thus, here and there, by the busy wayside, the earthly traveller catches glimpses of faint footpaths, some leading to places of nestling green, others winding up to the mountain-peaks, others conducting to the brink of waste waters peopled by the phantoms of the clouds. These paths wind to the nooks where the students dwell, hearing faintly from afar the tramp of busy feet and the cry of voices. Not always, however, do the Students remain apart. Ever and anon, at the point where the footpath joins the highway, appears a pale face, and a white hand is uplifted demanding silence. The Student has stept down with a message. Ere that message can be heard, the crowd must still itself and pause, and in that *pause* all loud cries are lost and the Student is heard saying: "Rest awhile and listen to the message I bring you! I want you just for a minute to turn with me to the infinite. Even if my words be worthless, the pause will do you good, and you will struggle along all the more freshly afterwards." In these pauses is contained the history of all literatures and all arts. In them, at intervals, the eternal calm steals strangely upon the finite unrest. Throughout all these is the whisper: " Contemporary truth is not final, and there is a light, my brothers, beyond the light of setting suns."

But the sore difficulty is how to get the crowd to pause, how to still the waters, for ever so brief a period of listening. By only one charm is the crowd won, and that charm is thorough *disinterestedness*—the very quality which is impossible to the crowd itself, or any member of the crowd. Just in so far as the Student is disinterested, will the Student fascinate his hearers. They can get stump-orators, singers for praise, fighters, German prophets, every day, but they are spell-bound at the novelty of the man who seeks no bonus. He is a kind of angelic wonder, just dropt glittering from cloudland. The sign of disinterestedness is beneficence, true love for the species; the selfish crowd never mistake unselfishness; not till that is clear will they hearken. Therefore, we never hear the true Student talk brutally of the black man, nor mock the poor temporary Philistinism of people in earnest, nor solicit attention by useless ravings and insincerities. The Student is calm. He knows he must win the crowd by disinterestedness, or by nothing. He will not bawl, though their backs are to him. If they ignore him for a time, he waits gently until they are ready. And the further proof of his disinterestedness is this,—that, however much his message is to shock the world, he will never say it brutally or conceitedly, but lovingly and reverently, always adding—" Mind, this message is not final. It is the very nature of eternal truth to evade a decisive definition; and although I have seen something in that lofty region, and wish to report what I have seen, I pretend to settle nothing by authority." The exhibition of contempt for the audience he addresses is the first fatal sign of contempt for his vocation. The fool proves himself unfit to be a messenger, by assuming the prevision of a god.

We need not go far to seek for an example of a Student who despises his vocation. The last wild utterance of Thomas Carlyle still rings in our ears.

This writer began reverently and gained hearers. He read affectionately in books and in nature, wrote nobly, aspired calmly to the contemplation of eternal truth. He secured quiet, and was recognized as a Student. Thus much, however, did not content him ; and the first signs of discontent were certain false notes in the voice — German guttural sounds, elaborate word-building, wild mannerism. Clearly hungry for more influence, he wrote privately to a friend that he would begin to " prophesy," and avowedly with a view to widening his circle of hearers — as if true prophet ever began by perceiving that there was a public, and calculating how such public might be stirred to emotion. He did prophesy. For a time, the crowd listened, till slowly and painfully his interestedness grew upon them. So thoroughly had he begun to despise his vocation, that he no longer took the trouble to utter his prophecies beautifully. So completely did he despise his public, that he deemed the grossest and least-weighed brutalities amply good enough for them. Instead of looking towards eternal truth, he gazed with the vision of a contemporary. How has this ended? The *pause* he once secured is broken. We merely hear his voice at intervals, and then always in the midst of a roar of voices. He has been whirled down into the crowd, and, though he shriek his loudest, there is no standing still to hear him.

It so happens in this case, that circumstances have so arranged themselves as to prove that Mr. Carlyle possessed very little prophetic vision. His dismal prediction of anarchy and all sorts of accompanying evils, as likely to result to England because she disagreed with him as to the mights of man, has by no means yet been realized, and the " nigger " is free. Such a man was not likely to be silenced even by the contemplation of the grand American triumph of truth and human beneficence. The more the crowd has roared around about him, the louder he has screamed. His last utterance, though uttered in a shriller and fiercer key, embodies precisely what he has been saying ever since he despised his vocation. " Ragged dung-heap of a world;" " the Almighty Maker has appointed the Nigger to be a servant;" " servantship must become a contract of permanency ;" "in a limited time, say fifty years hence, the Church, all churches and so-called religions, the Christian religion itself, shall have deliquesced into liberty of conscience, progress of opinion, progress of intellect, philanthropic movements, and other aqueous residues of a vapid badly-scented character;" "manhood suffrage,—horsehood, doghood, not yet treated of;" "universal glorious liberty—to sons of the devil in overwhelming majority, as would appear." In these sentences culminates the degradation of a Student stript of his gown. How utterly he has become swamped in the crowd, when the language he employs is that of the wildest roughs and rowdies in the swarm.

Now, if there be one true mark of the true Student it is the endeavour to express himself exquisitely. Plotinus defines the beautiful " as the splendour of the good ;" and after this beautiful —not merely good, but good glorified—the Student aims. He studies the poetic terminology, and culls all felicities of speech which secure the radiant passage of meanings to the minds of hearers. He shapes his glowing thoughts into melodious syllables, such as common men may not employ. Add to perfect disinterestedness, perfect sweetness of voice,—and the people are spell-bound. Their souls are raised, their ears delighted. Though liberalism be their watchword, they will even listen to the gospel according to the Tories,—calmly hearken, I mean, to him who wishes to show that eternal truth is on the Tory side. Had Carlyle spoken in this fashion, his own reverence for what he conceived true would have been his safeguard and his honour.

For public men are even nowadays quite ready to admit the services and honour the sincerity of the private inquirer,—especially in his capacity of reader of books. They say clearly, " We are too busy to seek precedents or study tomes—we have no time to collect learning—and we must employ you to study in our place." So while the public men are fighting keenly with a view to making some truth or seeming truth live, the Student familiarizes himself with history, philosophy, religion, science, in order to see what things have died in the past, or are dying in the present, and what things, having never been known really to die, may now be fairly assumed to be eternal. Busy people, too, are very grateful when the Student brings to them at second-hand the result of all this learned inquiry. They hearken to it, commit it to memory, even pay for it liberally; not, however, until they are perfectly satisfied of the calmness, disinterestedness, and veracity of the person who supplies it. But when the Student not only brings his message, but lards it with follies and insolencies of his own, the public retort is simple:—"The message you bring is a LIE." "Brutes! idiots!" perhaps screams the Student; "do ye dare to despise eternal truth?" And the public, justly exasperated, *lynches* the fellow, crying, "Eternal truth is all very fine, but we are now convinced of the contemporary truth that you are a humbug and a ranter."

Nor will the public men, the strugglers *en masse*, tolerate on the part of the Student any vain affectation of superiority. They know very well that the Student, from Pythagoras to Goethe, has always been a human being, however close his communication with the Olympian principalities ; and moreover, they know *this*—that mere living, even physical living, is any day as wondrous, as important, and as grand a thing as mere thinking. What right has the professor to bully the tradesman ? On what grounds does a poet scorn an alderman, a philosopher despise a member of parliament, a monk scowl at a milliner ? It is quite another thing, however, to bid the busy man, the man whose work is mean, the toiler and moiler at the tag-ends of society, pause occasionally, and inhale a sweet breath from the solitude,— to see what the stargazer is seeing, to hear what the minstrel is playing, to follow what the theorizer is proving in stately terms. But how lovingly, how reverently, does the true Student communicate with the people !—how wisely does he defer to them in matters wherein they even have their authority ! The fine affectionate love for the species is in his eyes, and every word he utters is vocal with the music of humanity. The Man's face shines radiant under the academic cowl, and the appeal at the best is an appeal from a man's heart to the heart of men. The sinner is dealt with tenderly, though the sin is never spared. The erring class is reasoned with sweetly, while the error is unmercifully turned inside out. And the contemporary strugglers, pausing to listen, feel how calm and tender a thing, how loving and how beneficent, is that eternal truth which scholiasts would lock up in their secretaries, and scientific monkeys (the true apes of Goethe's Witch's cave) seek in vain to put in a crucible.

Here, certainly, is the true clue to the wondrous influence of Mr. John Stuart Mill. Of all our Students, this one has shown himself, not the most profound, but the most reverent, the most gentle, and the most unassuming. He had the true philosophic calm,—the true rest typical of the eternal. He had no gall. Merciless in argument, he was tender and brotherly to every antagonist. All this was true of Mr. Mill, previous to his entry into parliament. The Student has since been lost in the politician—the pause difficult to secure—the influence scattered and doubtful. That a thinker so acute and thorough as this should have dreamt it possible to reconcile eternal and contemporary truth—to

be a student and a politician at the same time—
has been to me one of those mysteries which are
to be classed as insoluble.   I have watched Mr.
Mill's career with deep and grateful interest,—
and thousands, as well as myself, felt bitter when
the Light was put under the bushel of the House
of Commons.   How is it possible to connect
eternal truth with the bigotry and folly which
is represented to us by the reports in the daily
newspapers,—to think of philosophy in connection with the blatant periods of Mr. Bright
and the polished pettiness of Mr. Lowe,—and to
associate calm and intellectual repose with the
juggling insincerities of each successive Chancellor of the Exchequer?

Mr. Mill has really done what is being every
day done by inferior men.   Among the signs
which accompany the vast political crisis which is
at present agitating England, not least is the irritating attitude of the Student,—the class of man
whose business it should be to mark, accompany,
and emphasise progress, instead of muddying the
stream of controversy.   As I have suggested, the
Student is losing the fine old reverence for his

own vocation, and wasting his energies in matters over which he has really no concern. He would be an authority in the world of action as well as in the sphere of meditation,—claiming the privileges of the politician, the historian, the man of science, and the pamphleteer. He would decide great controversies by private authority, instead of calmly throwing the radiance of perfect private sight on the tendencies of his time. Dogmatism and puppyism supervene :—the Student no longer takes the trouble to express himself exquisitely ; the crudest utterance suffices ; the most listless looseness of thought, consequent on a contempt for his audience. Mr. Carlyle, as we have seen, preaches brutalism in language as harsh as the barking of Cerberus. Masters of Arts, Fellows of Colleges, and all the tribe of people who remain at school all their lives, imitate Mr. Arnold's manner, even while disagreeing with his opinions. The two sets of egotists join issue in denouncing the tendencies of their period. Some of these men might secure real and lasting influence if they reverenced and clearly pursued their own vocation. They claim double and irreconcilable privileges—the authority of the private scholar, and the authority of the public leader.

Deep philosophic repose is the air inhaled on the mountain tops, close to the stars, and must by no means be confounded with vulgar consciousness of calm. A person may step forward in an academic gown, saying : " My papa was so skilled in developing the juvenile mind as to produce out of fair materials a novelist at fourteen, a philosopher two years later, and at eighteen an authority on every question under the sun—a wondrous little Salaputium, warranted perfect, and certain never to grow any more. Oh, I am so calm, and so clever. Yet see, how admirably I hide my knowledge ; that is calm, that is restraint. I am prepared to settle all questions by means of an insect exterminator, which has never been known to fail." But how does the public receive such a person. " The Student," it replies, " evinces restraint and calm, does not talk about them ; they are, in fact, merely personal qualities. You fellows grow too quickly and stop too soon, and your calm and restraint are merely the inactivity and torpor consequent on a system of early forcing.   You have by no means *lived* enough to determine living questions, and the best proof of that is the unmanliness of your manner."   And are the public wrong ?   Do the scholastic persons show any such real love for their kind, any such ignoring of self, any such telling enthusiasm in great questions, as would soon win the confidence of men and women who live in the world outside the academy ?   I fear not. They are not Students, nor do they live alone. Brought up in classes, inoculated with the usual stuff very early, they hate solitude hugely.   They must think in bodies, or they are miserable.*

But the career of the true Student has been two-fold,—a period of probation in the world of action, previous to the period of retreat to the sphere of thought.   In that first period, no matter

---

* I must not be understood as underrating true *scholarship*,—only as noting the vicious effect of *schools*.   Why should the scholar *not* be a Student ?   Look at Clough !   He had the true calm, and his religious hunger was a real thing.   He kept his own way, without being tempted into exhibitions ;   and for this very reason he will have influence, when more pretentious and noisy schoolmen are forgotten.

how short, a man not only learns what action is and his unfitness for it, but gets such knowledge of great busy powers as makes him treat power wisely all the rest of his life. How should he know that God meant him to be a Student, until he ascertained his unfitness for aught else? Hence the misfortune of early forcing. The schoolboys are wise too soon. They begin recklessly trading without capital; evolving out of their own inner consciousness, like the German, a monster which they christen "man," and a number of little monsters which they label "facts," and going wrong in everything, because their "facts" and "man" are wrong at starting :—

> Humano capiti cervicem pictor equinam
> Jungere si velit, et varias inducere plumas
> Undique collatis membris, ut turpiter atrum
> Desinat in piscem mulier formosa superne ;
> Spectatum admissi risum teneatis, amici ?

A little actual contact with men—not merely with people teaching and people taught—would save them, too, from regarding earth as one vast seminary. They know this truth themselves in the end. We find them yearning wildly for action, writing verses of discontent, longing for the vague busy motion they have never experienced; interspersing such dissatisfied moments by putting finishing touches to their own intellectual beauty, with the complacence of a fine lady putting on powder and rouge, and praying to God as to a skilful professor passionately attached to prodigies developed by early forcing.

Too much reducing of life to system will not suit the Student. How should it, when he is growing grey in the vain search of a truth that is absolutely final. He is the man that leaves margins. He is very careful, therefore, how he deals even with contemporary superstitions, lest he may imitate the French writers, who destroyed, not only the superstitions themselves, but the noble truths underlying them. Coming on the highway, he steps among swarms of tiny lives, and he cannot step too cautiously, if he would avoid crushing something that is beautiful.

Clear on all sides of us, in the highways and the byeways, in the crowd's voices, in the Students' messages, rises one great belief, in which eternal and contemporary truth seem to unite,—that we are moving on to multiplicity. The mass is rising, rights are widening, mights are broadening. Meanwhile, some few alarmists shriek out that we lack individuals and must die. Then the reply is, " Let us die," if the vindication of eternal principles is fatal. Never, to the thinking of many, was there a time fraught with so much hope to man. The emancipation of the slave, the steps of Germany towards freedom, the extension of the suffrage, are all signs and portents. Henceforth, freedom is vindicated as a personal right, and every man is to be recognized as a responsible citizen.

And what, in the face of these things, are the cries of alarmists, the shrieks of classes,—what, in fact, is the very threat of anarchy ? Eternal truth seems saying " though ye perish, I will be vindicated." Yet in honest truth, the danger is perhaps exaggerated. When matters adjust themselves there will be no lack of leaders, no lack of Students.

If there be one truth which it behoves the Student to illustrate *now*, it is this mighty one,— God's preference of His beloved children to any one of His children. If there is one quality which seems His, and His exclusively, it seems that Divine philoprogenitiveness, that passionate love of distribution and expansion into living forms. He is exhaustless, a fountain. Every animal added seems a new ecstasy to the Maker; every life added a new embodiment of His love. He would *swarm* the earth with beings. There are never enough. Life, life, life—faces gleaming, hearts beating, must fill every cranny. Not a corner is suffered to remain empty. The whole earth breeds, and God glories. And here and everywhere, life, absolute life, is the only thing which we universally feel to be God's, and wholly sacred.

Because there is sin and misery in the world, because hearts ache and bodies die, shall we turn upon this sublimely exhaustless Being, and demand explanation? Is it not something to know how He delights in making, in endless creating, and that One who thus delights cannot be cruel. The explanation will come. Meantime, we move to multiplicity. Our selfish ascetics are no longer thought to possess god-like qualities; but it is noticed everywhere that the sublimest sign of perfect culture is divine philanthropy, and that the nearer each man seems to approach God, the more he seems to exhibit the mysterious and god-like quality of love for the species. The vocation of the Student is clear. He must aid the work of the world, but not by noise and egotistical prattling. He shall show to the crowd the nearest human approach to the perfect disinterestedness, sweetness, and exhaustless charity of God's Eternal Truth; and the people, listening at the lifting of his hand, and charmed by the sweetness of his voice, will be happier by a message sent to make still wider the activities of Law and Love.

IV.

WALT WHITMAN.

" *Cantantes, my dear Burdett, minus via lædit.*
True; but bawling out the rights of man is not
singing."—THE DIVERSIONS OF PURLEY.

WALT WHITMAN.

THE grossest abuse on the part of the majority, and the wildest panegyric on the part of a minority, have for many years been heaped on the shoulders of the man who rests his claim for judgment on the book of miscellanies noted below.* Luckily, the man is strong enough, sane enough, to take both abuse and panegyric with calmness. He believes hugely in himself, and in the part he is destined to take in American affairs. He is neither to be put down by prudes, nor tempted aside by the serenade of pipes and timbrels. A large, dispassionate, daring, and

---

* Walt Whitman's "Leaves of Grass," "Drum-Taps," etc. New York, 1867.

splendidly-proportioned animal, he remains unmoved, explanatory up to a certain point, but sphinx-like when he is questioned too closely on morality or religion. Yet when the enthusiastic and credulous, the half-formed, the inquiring, youth of a nation begin to be carried away by a man's teachings, it is time to inquire what these teachings are; for assuredly they are going to exercise extraordinary influence on life and opinion. Now, it is clear, on the best authority, that the writer in question is already exercising on the youth of America an influence similar to that exercised by Socrates over the youth of Greece, or by Raleigh over the young chivalry of England. In a word, he has become a *sacer vates* —his ministry is admitted by palpable live disciples. What the man is, and what the ministry implies, it will not take long to explain. Let it be admitted at the outset, however, that I am in concert with those who believe his to be a genuine ministry, large in its spiritual manifestations, and abundant in capability for good.

Sprung from the masses, as he himself tells us, Walt Whitman has for many years lived a vagabond life, labouring as the humour seized him, and invariably winning his bread by actual and persistent industry. He has been alternately a farmer, a carpenter, a printer. He has been a constant contributor of prose to the republican journals. He appears, moreover, at intervals, to have wandered over the North American continent, to have worked his way from city to city, and to have consorted liberally with the draff of men on bold and equal conditions. Before the outbreak of the war, he was to be found dwelling in New York, on "fish-shape Paumanok," basking there in the rays of the almost tropical sun, or sallying forth into the streets to mingle with strange companions, — from the lodging-house luminary and the omnibus-driver, down to the scowling rowdy of the wharf bars. Having written his first book, "Leaves of Grass," he set it up with his own hands, in a printing-office in Brooklyn. Some of my readers may dimly remember how the work was briefly noticed by contemporary English reviews, in a way to leave the impression that the writer was a mild maniac, with morbid developments in the region of the *os pelvis.* On the outbreak of the great rebellion, he followed in the rear of the great armies, distinguishing himself by unremitting attention to the wounded in the ambulance department, until, on receiving a clerkship in the department of the interior, he removed to Washington. Here, to the great scandal of American virtue, he continued to vagabondise as before, but without neglecting his official duties. At the street corner, at the drinking-bar, in the slums, in the hospital wards, the tall figure of Walt Whitman was encountered daily by the citizens of the capital. He knew everybody, from the president down to the crossing-sweeper.

"Well," said Abraham Lincoln, watching him as he stalked by, "*he* looks like a *man.*"

Latterly his loafing propensities appear to have grown too strong for American tolerance, and he was ejected from his clerkship, on the pretext that he had written "indecent verses," and was a "free lover." His admirers, indignant to a man at this treatment, have accumulated protest upon protest, enumerating numberless instances of his personal goodness and self-denial, and laying powerful emphasis on certain deeds, which, if truly chronicled, evince a width of sympathy and a private influence unparalleled, perhaps, in contemporary history. With all this personal business we have no concern. His admirers move for a new trial on the evidence of his written works, and to that evidence I must proceed.

In about ten thousand lines of unrhymed verse, very Biblical in form, and showing, indeed, on every page, the traces of Biblical influence, Walt Whitman professes to sow the first seeds of an indigenous literature, by putting in music the spiritual and fleshly yearnings of the cosmical man, and, more particularly, indicating the great elements which distinguish American freedom from the fabrics erected by European politicians. Starting from Paumanok, where he was born, he takes mankind in review, and sees everywhere but one wondrous life—the movement of the great masses, seeking incessantly under the sun for guarantees of personal liberty. He respects no particular creed, admits no specific morality prescribed by the civil law, but affirms

in round terms the universal equality of men,
subject to the action of particular revolutions,
and guided *en masse* by the identity of particular
leaders. The whole introduction is a reverie on
the destiny of nations, with an undertone of fore-
thought on the American future, which is to contain the surest and final triumph of the demo-
cratical man. A new race is to arise, dominating
previous ones, and grander far, with new contests,
new politics, new literatures and religions, new
inventions and arts. But how dominating? By
the perfect recognition of individual equality, by
the recognition of the personal responsibility and
spiritual significance of each being, by the abro-
gation of distinctions such as set barriers in the
way of perfect private action—action responsible
only to the being of whom it is a consequence,
and inevitably controlled, if diabolic, by the combined action of masses.

Briefly, Walt Whitman sees in the American
future the grandest realization of centuries of
idealism—equable distribution of property, lu-
minous enlargement of the spiritual horizon, perfect exercise of all the functions; no apathy, no

prudery, no shame, none of that worst absentee-
ism wherein the soul deserts its proper and ample
physical sphere, and sallies out into the regions
of the impossible and the unknown. Very finely,
indeed, does the writer set forth the divine functions of the body—the dignity and the righteous-
ness of a habitation existing only on the condition
of personal exertion ; and faintly, but truly, does
he suggest how from that personal exertion issues
spirituality, fashioning literatures, dreaming religions, and perfecting arts. "I will make," he
exclaims, "the poems of materials, for I think
they are to be the most spiritual poems; and I
will make the poems of my body and of mortality :
for I think I shall then supply myself with the
poems of my soul and of immortality."

This, I hear the reader exclaim, is rank materialism ; and, using the word in its big sense,
materialism it doubtless is. I shall observe,
further on, in what consists the peculiar value of
the present manifestation. In the meantime, let
me continue my survey of the work.

Having broadly premised, describing the great
movements of masses, Walt Whitman proceeds,

in a separate "poem" or "book," to select a
member of the great democracy, representing
typically the privileges, the immunities, the conditions, and the functions of all the rest.   He
cannot, he believes, choose a better example than
himself; so he calls this poem "Walt Whitman."
He is, for the time being, and for poetical purposes, the cosmical man, an entity, a representative of the great forces.*   He describes the delight of his own physical being, the pleasure of
the senses, the countless sensations through
which he communicates with the material universe.   All, he says, is sweet — smell, taste,
thought, the play of his limbs, the fantasies of
his mind; every attribute is welcome, and he is
ashamed of none.   He is not afraid of death; he
is content to change, if it be the nature of things
that he should change, but it is certain that he
cannot perish.   He pictures the pageant of life

---

* Let it be understood, here and elsewhere, that I shall
attach my own significance to passages in themselves sufficiently mystical.   I may misrepresent this writer; but,
apart from the present constructions, he is to me unintelligible.

in the country and in cities; all is a fine panorama, wherein mountains and valleys, nations and religions, *genre* pictures and gleams of sunlight, babes on the breast and dead men in shrouds, pyramids and brothels, deserts and populated streets, sweep wonderfully by him. To all those things he is bound:—wherever they force him, he is not wholly a free agent; but on one point he is very clear—that, so far as he is concerned, he is the most important thing of all. He has work to do; life is not merely a " suck or a sell;" nay, the whole business of ages has gone on with one object only—that he, the democrat, Walt Whitman, might have work to do. In these very strange passages, he proclaims the magnitude of the preparations for his private action :—

Who goes there? hankering, gross, mystical, nude;
How is it I extract strength from the beef I eat?

What is a man, anyhow? What am I? What are you?

All I mark as my own, you shall offset it with your own,
Else it were time lost listening to me.

I do not snivel that snivel the world over,
That months are vacuums, and the ground but wallow and
    filth;

That life is a suck and a sell, and nothing remains at the
    end but threadbare crape, and tears.

Whimpering and truckling fold with powders for invalids—
    conformity goes to the forth-removed ;
I wear my hat as I please, indoors or out.

Why should I pray ?   Why should I venerate and be cere-
    monious ?

Having pried through the strata, analysed to a hair, coun-
    sel'd with doctors, and calculated close,
I find no sweeter fat than sticks to my own bones.

In all people I see myself—none more, and not one a bar-
    leycorn less ;
And the good or bad I say of myself, I say of them.

And I know I am solid and sound ;
To me the converging objects of the universe perpetually
    flow ;
All are written to me, and I must get what the writing
    means.

I know I am deathless ;
I know this orbit of mine cannot be swept by the carpenter's
    compass ;
I know I shall not pass like a child's carlacue cut with a
    burnt stick at night.

I know I am august ;
I do not trouble my spirit to vindicate itself, or be under-
    stood ;
I see that the elementary laws never apologize ;
(I reckon I behave no prouder than the level I plant my
    house by, after all).

I exist as I am—that is enough;
If no other in the world be aware, I sit content;
And if each and all be aware, I sit content.

One world is aware, and by far the largest to me, and that
    is myself;
And whether I come to my own to-day, or in ten thousand
    or ten million years,
I can cheerfully take it now, or with equal cheerfulness I
    can wait.

My foothold is tenon'd and mortis'd in granite;
I laugh at what you call dissolution;
And I know the amplitude of time.

I am an acme of things accomplish'd, and I am an encloser
    of things to be.

My feet strike an apex of the apices of the stairs;
On every step bunches of ages, and larger bunches between
    the steps;
All below duly travel'd, and still I mount and mount.

Rise after rise bow the phantoms behind me;
Afar down I see the huge first Nothing—I know I was
    even there;
I waited unseen and always, and slept through the lethargic
    mist,
And took my time, and took no hurt from the fetid carbon.

Long I was hugg'd close—long and long.

Immense have been the preparations for me,
Faithful and friendly the arms that have help'd me.

Cycles ferried my cradle, rowing and rowing like cheerful
    boatmen;

For room to me stars kept aside in their own rings;
They sent influences to look after what was to hold me.

Before I was born out of my mother, generations guided
    me;
My embryo has never been torpid—nothing could overlay
    it.

For it the nebula cohered to an orb,
The long slow strata piled to rest it on,
Vast vegetables gave it sustenance,
Monstrous sauroids transported it in their mouths, and de-
    posited it with care.

All forces have been steadily employ'd to complete and de-
    light me;
Now on this spot I stand with my robust Soul.

It is impossible in an extract to convey an idea
of the mystic and coarse, yet living, force which
pervades the poem called " Walt Whitman."
I have chosen an extract where the utterance
is unusually clear and vivid. But more extraordinary, in their strong sympathy, are the portions describing the occupations of men. In a
few vivid touches we have striking pictures ; the
writer shifts his identity like Proteus, but breathes
the same deep undertone in every shape. He can
transfer himself into any personality, however
base. " I am the man—I suffered—I was there."

He cares for no man's pride. He holds no man unclean.

And afterwards, in the poem called " Children of Adam," he proceeds to particularise the privileges of flesh, and to assert that in his own personal living body there is no uncleanness. He sees that the beasts are not ashamed; why, therefore, should he be ashamed? Then comes passage after passage of daring animalism; the functions of the body are unhesitatingly described, and the man asserts that the basest of them is glorious. All the stuff which offended American virtue is to be found here. It is very coarse and silly, but, as we shall see, very important. It is never, however, inhuman; indeed, it is strongly masculine—unsicklied by Lesbian bestialities and Petronian abominations. It simply chronicles acts and functions which, however unfit for art, are natural, sane, and perfectly pure. I shall attempt to show, further on, that Walt Whitman is not an artist at all, not a poet, properly so called; and that this grossness, offensive in itself, is highly significant—an essential part of very imperfect work. The general question of literary immorality need not be introduced at all. No one is likely to read the book who is not intelligently chaste, or who is not familiar with numberless authors offensive to prudes — Lucretius, Virgil, Dante, Goethe, Byron, among poets; Tacitus, Rabelais, Montaigne, Cervantes, Swedenborg, among prose thinkers.

The remainder of "Leaves of Grass" is occupied with poems of democracy, and general monotonous prophecies. There is nothing more which it would serve my present purpose to describe in detail, or to interpret. The typical man continues his cry, encouraging all men, — on the open road, in the light of day, in the region of dreams. All is right with the world, he thinks. For religion he advises, "Reverence all things;" for morality, "Be not ashamed;" for political wisdom among peoples, "Resist much — obey little." He has no word for art; it is not in her temple that he burns incense. His language, as even a short extract has shown, is strong, vehement, instantaneously chosen; always forcible, and sometimes even rhythmical, like the prose of Plato. Thoughts crowd so thick upon him, that he has no time to seek their artistic equivalent; he utters his thought in any way, and his expressions gain accidental beauty from the glamour of his sympathy. As he speaks, we more than once see a man's face at white heat, and a man's hand beating down emphasis at the end of periods. He is inspired, not angry; yet as even inspiration is not infallible, he sometimes talks rank nonsense.

The second part of the volume, "Drum-Taps," is a series of poetic soliloquies on the war. It is more American and somewhat less mystical than the "Leaves of Grass;" but we have again the old cry of democracy. Here, in proportion to the absence of self-consciousness, and the presence of vivid emotion, we find absolute music, culminating once or twice in poetry. The monody on the death of Lincoln—" when lilacs last in the door-yard bloomed "—contains the three essentials of poetic art—perfect sight, supreme emotion, and true music. This, however, is unusual in Walt Whitman. Intellectual self-consciousness generally coerces emotion, insincerities and follies ensue, and instead of rising into poetry, the lines wail monotonously, and the sound drops into the circle of crabbed prose.

For there is this distinction between Walt Whitman and the poet— that Whitman is content to reiterate his truth over and over again in the same tones, with the same result; while the poet, having found a truth to utter, is coerced by his *artistic* sympathies into seeking fresh literary forms for its expression. "Bawling out the rights of man," wrote Horne Tooke, "is not singing." Artistic sympathies Walt Whitman has none; he is that curiously-crying bird—a prophet with no taste. He is careless about beautifying his truth: he is heedless of the new forms—personal, dramatic, lyrical—in which another man would clothe it, and in which his disciples will be certain to clothe it for him. He sees vividly, but he is not always so naturally moved as to sing exquisitely. He has the swagger of the prophet, not the sweetness of the musician. Hence all those crude metaphors and false notes which must shock artists, those needless bestialities which repel prudes, that general want of balance and that mental dizziness which astonish most Europeans.

But when this has been said, all blame has been said,—if, after all, a man is to incur blame for not being quite another sort of being than nature made him. Walt Whitman has arisen on the States to point the way to new literatures. He is the plain pioneer, pickaxe on shoulder, working and "roughing." The daintier gentlemen will follow, and build where he is delving.

Whitman himself would be the first to denounce those loose young gentlemen who admire him vaguely because he is loud and massive, gross and colossal, not for the sake of the truth he is teaching, and the grandeur of the result that may ensue. There are some men who can admire nothing unless it is "strong;" intellectual dram-drinkers, quite as far from the truth as sentimental tea-drinkers. Let it at once and unhesitatingly be admitted that Whitman's want of art, his grossness, his tall talk, his metaphorical word-piling are *faults* — prodigious ones; and then let us turn reverently to contemplate these signs which denote his ministry, his command of rude forces, his nationality, his manly earnestness, and, last and greatest, his wondrous sympathy with

men as men.   He emerges from the mass of un-
welded materials—in shape much like the earth-
spirit in " Faust." He is loud and coarse, like most
prophets, " sounding," as he himself phrases it,
" his barbaric yawp over the roofs of the world."
He is the voice of which America stood most in
need—a voice at which ladies scream and whipper-
snappers titter with delight, but which clearly per-
tains to a man who means to be heard. He is the
clear forerunner of the great American poets, long
yearned for, now prophesied, but not perhaps to be
beheld till the vast American democracy has sub-
sided a little from its last and grandest struggle.
Honour in his generation is, of course, his due ;
but he does not seem to solicit honour. He is too
thoroughly alive to care about being tickled into
activity, too excited already to be much moved
by finding himself that most badgered of func-
tionaries, the recognized Sir Oracle.

V.

HERRICK'S HESPERIDES:

A NOTE ON AN OLD BOOK.

Flowery rhymes that blossom free
In a tuft of greenery,
Smiled on by the sun, and bright
With the dews of lyric light.

HERRICK'S HESPERIDES.

OULD we quit Babylon, to while away an hour in Fairyland, among Titania and her maids of honour? We have only to take up the " Hesperides" of Robert Herrick. It is merely a piece of sweet and careless dissipation—the poetical epitome of a fanciful brain, and a tender, happy heart. Its author squandered all his genius in flower-painting, music-making, and sporting in the shade with Amaryllis; but his book exists, full of the author and his peccadilloes; a book to be cherished by lovers of lyrics; a pretty souvenir of a jovial verse-writer who lived and made innocent love in a cassock, who tippled " Simon the King's" canary with Ben the laureate and Selden the antiquary, and who lived a hot-headed poet's life, not the life of a philosopher, in the quiet woodland ways. It teems with that luscious physical life which abounded in the man who wrote it; it is full of his idle fancies, his naughty sayings, and his wooings of women in the abstract. A more exceptionable book than "The Complete Angler," its shortcomings spring, like the other's racy morality, from a nature which means happiness and candour.

The "Hesperides" is, perhaps, the most musical collection of occasional verses in the language. Pretty thoughts and sounds, controlled and regulated by principles of most magical harmony, wreathe magically from the quaint old book, singing and dancing, smiling and shining, perpetuating the memory of Herrick, the kindly clerical Prospero who created them. Glad verses, sad verses, mad verses, and (in a strait-laced sense) bad verses, fill these pages, melting and sighing and dying in a thousand flats and sharps of melody. A book of all moods and measures, a rainbow blended of a thousand different colours; a thing both of sable and of tinsel, of beautiful shreds and patches. It is redolent of ambrosia, nectar, and all the tipple of the gods. In short, it is a green arbour book, just as old Isaac's " Complete Angler," and Cotton's " Montaigne" are green arbour books; it is to be opened at random, in fine weather, and dreamed over. The cool flow of the syllables, the jingle and glitter of the fancies, the little hidden love-sentiments bubbling cheerily up at the ends of the stanzas, make Herrick's Hippocrene very refreshing to the parched literary Arab, the over-worn philosopher, and the lover, if not to the ambitious and metaphysical modern Alastor.

Many familiar faces—smiling up, as it were, through green leaves, daffodils, and daisies,—peep out on me as I dip into the book. One of these is the well-known " Night Piece," addressed to Mistresse Julia, his inspiration—a poem which every modern cavalier ought to have by heart. Another, also pretty generally known, is the sweet little song about " Daffodils." The following lines are also unique:—

DELIGHT IN DISORDER.

A sweet disorder in the dresse
Kindles in cloathes a wantonnesse;
A lawn about the shoulders thrown
Into a fine distraction;
An erring lace, which here and there
Enthralls a crimson stomacher;
A cuffe neglectfull, and thereby
Ribbons to flow confusedly;
A winning waves, deserving note,
In the tempestuous pettecoat;
A careless shoe-string, in whoes tye
I see a wilde civility;
Doe more bewitch me, than when art
Is too precise in every part.

The above is a fair specimen of Herrick's usual manner. It is short, pithy, and unique, characterized, like most of his verses, by quaintness of subject as well as of treatment. Few of the poems in the "Hesperides" are of much length, and the shortest are much the best. Some of the prettiest do not occupy half-a-dozen lines; but they prove the force of the hackneyed aphorism about brevity.

Her Voice.

So small, so soft, so silvery is her voice,
As, could they hear, 'twould make the damn'd rejoice,
And listen to her, walking in her chamber,
Melting melodious words to lutes of amber !

These lines are addressed to Mistresse Julia.
Who could have inspired them but a Julia or a
Sacharissa ? Who could have composed them
but a poet and a lover, unpretending though they
are ? Whenever he sings Julia's praises, all who
listen recognize a genuine singer. No matter
how slender the theme, let it be but connected
with his lady, and the poet's fine frenzy is sure
to issue forth in thoughts that breathe and words
that burn,—that burn even too brightly now and
then. Julia, in his eyes, is something to be
worshipped and adored ; she is akin to cherubim ;
her form makes music of the poet's breath, like
an Æolian harp set in the summer wind. She is
the much-belauded heroine of the " Hesperides."
She is to Herrick what the Church was to
Solomon—the maker of a sweet minstrel.

Goddess, I do love a girl
Ruby-lipped and tooth'd with pearl ;

he cries, with eyes that twinkle merrily underneath his grey hairs. Her breath is likened to " all the spices of the east," to the balm, the myrrh, and the nard; her skin is like a " lawnie firmament ;" her cheek like " cream and claret commingled," or " roses blowing." But Julia, although his favourite, was not his only lady-love. If we are to believe his own assertion, he was favourably disposed towards the whole sex— at any rate, by no means prejudiced in favour of one individual. He has scores of unpitying yet flawless " mistresses," real and ideal, whom he has transmitted to posterity under such euphonious names as Silvia, Corinna, Electra, Perinna, Perilla, and Dianeme. As a rule, he sings their praises sweetly and modestly. His sentimental morality was by no means of the dull heavy kind; on the contrary, it was brisk and easy, like the religious morality of Herbert and Wither. It was when making merry at the feet of Venus that he felt most at home—when he had nothing to do but fashion fanciful nosegays, and throw them, with a laugh, into the lap of his lady. His songs suggest the picture of a respectable British Bacchus, stout and middle-aged, lipping soft lyrics to the blushing Ariadne at his side; while, in the background of flowers and green leaves, we catch a glimpse of Oberon and Titania, walking through a stately minuet on a close-shaven lawn, to the frolicking admiration of assembled fairy-land.

Herrick's best things are his poems in praise of the country life, and his worst things are his epigrams. Whenever he sings good-humouredly, as in the former, he sings well and sweetly; whenever he sings ill-humouredly, as in the latter, he sings falsely and harshly. His gladsome, mercurial temper, had a great deal to do with the composition of his best lyrics; for the parson of Dean Prior was no philosopher, and his lightest, airiest verses are his best. What Marmontel calls " amiable ingenuity, undisguised openness," was a part of his mental as well as of his moral life; shackled by conventionalism of any sort, he lost all that happy *naïveté* which is the principal, perhaps the only, charm of his written works. His was a happy, careless nature, throwing off verses out of the fulness of a joyous heart, rioting in a pleasant, sunny element. Out of his own merry and magical circle he is stiff, stupid, and sophisticated. There was no ill-nature in him; his epigrams had no sting. The same impulse which made him err a little induced him to confess his errors honestly. Without these errors, and the few poems in which he alludes to them, neither his works nor himself can be properly understood. The epigrams I allude to are interspersed with the other poems, and are after the manner of Ben Jonson. The book would have been better without them.

One or two of his fairy poems appear to me the very perfection of musical excellence. He is coarse enough here and there, without a doubt, and now and then his elfin court entertains indiscreet notions of social propriety. But his fairies can be very engaging, very natural little people, when their creator chooses to be strict with them on the point of moral decorum; in other words, when they avoid all imitation of the fairies at St. James's, and remain the genuine little pixies of music, mischief, and moonlight. Oberon has his temple, whither he retires for devotional purposes, cleansing himself with the holy water contained in a nutshell, and bowing to the altar " in a cloud of frankincense." He has also his feasts, when mushroom tables groan with steaming dainties, when dew-wine is sweetened in goblets of " violets blew," and when the gnat, the cricket, and the grasshopper are court musicians.

The " pretty flowery and pastoral gale of fancy," which Phillips, in his " *Theatrum Poetarum*," gives Herrick credit for, was never better employed than when bruiting abroad the pleasures of a country life. The honest fellows at Dean Prior (the Devonshire parish of which he was vicar) loved their old ceremonies and customs, and kept them up right heartily; and no doubt the poet entered fully into the spirit of the local enthusiasm. He would range the woods on May morning with the maidens; sit at wakes with the old women; drink the Whitsun ale, and drain the wassail bowl on Twelfth Nights, with the men. Of all these pleasures he sang often and enthusiastically. His book is full of pictures taken from that little Devonshire vicarage. He found beauty in their old customs, however riotously conducted, however plain and homely. He tells us of the maypole, the morris-dance, the shearing feast, and the chase; singing cheerily of the " nut-browne mirth and russit wit" of such and sundry pastoral mummeries. He pictures to us, with sweet music, the merry-makings at the wake, with its creams and custards, its pageantries of Robin Hood and Maid Marian, its cudgel-plays, its rustic quarrels, " drown'd in ale or drenched in beere." He sings of St. Distaff's Day, when the flax and tow of girls who " go a-spinning" is set on fire, when plackets are scorched, and when the maidens souse the men with pails of new-drawn water. He celebrates the coming-in of the hock-cart, crowned with ears of corn, surrounded by men and women with garlands on their heads, and drawn by horses " clad in linen white as lilies." He describes both pastoral May-day, when boys and girls pluck the white-thorn boughs, when " green gowns are given," when troths are plighted; and the Christmas festivities, when the log blazes on the hearth, when " psalteries " are played, when strong beer is quaffed and mince-pies eaten. When he discourses of such homely ceremonies, in his own soft inimitable way, I know no writer of lyrics who equals him in love-liness of music, sweetness of fancy, and luscious warmth of colouring.

The greater part of the "Hesperides" was writ-ten in Devonshire, when the poet was vicar of the little parish of Dean Prior. He was preferred to the living by Charles I. in the year 1629, having been recommended by the Bishop of Exeter, to whom he more than once makes affectionate allu-sion. Herrick, then in his thirty-eighth year, had already tasted the sweets of literary society, and he did not fall in love with this same dull little Dean Prior as readily as might be antici-pated. Like Crabbe in Suffolk, and Sydney Smith on Salisbury Plain, many years afterwards, he grumbled and fretted in his solitude, de-scribing his parishioners as a "rocky genera-tion," "rude almost as rudest savages," and "churlish as the seas." Probably these words were written when the pulpit was new to him, when the cassock on his shoulders felt uncomfortable, when the boisterous young squires in the pews below him were taking his mental and moral measure.   He might have found some of the country louts suspicious and surly; for a country congregation is not always bonnet-in-hand to the new pastor; he might have been received coldly enough at first by the "wealthy nobodies."   By-and-bye, no doubt, when the awkward feeling wore off on both sides, priest and congregation fraternised.   The verses addressed to Larr prove that he felt the parting, when a Puritan was sent to take his place, and he was turned out of house and home to live on his fifths in London.   At any rate, his best verses were written in that west-country vicarage :—

> More discontents I never had,
>   Since I was born, than here ;
> Where I have been, and still am sad,
>   In this dull Devonshire.
> Yet, justly too, I must confesse,
>   I ne'r invented such
> Ennobled numbers for the presse,
>   Than where I loath'd so much.

It seems reasonable to suppose that this bilious

feeling wore off, and was absent when he wrote his sweet lyrics about rural felicity.

In reading his poems one obtains many a stray peep at the domestic life of the poet; plain allusions are thrown out, which, when patched together, may form a decently consistent picture. Although a universal lover, he never married. His little household consisted of Mistress Prudence Baldwin his housekeeper, himself, Trasy his pet spaniel, Phill his tame sparrow, a few chickens, a goose, a cat, and a pet lamb. Poor old Mistress Prew, once pretty Miss Prudence, was Robert Herrick's good angel; and many are the affectionate allusions he makes to her. Through want and sickness, through sorrow and heartache, she stood by the helpless old bachelor, taking good care of his morals, and rendering his rural home cheery and comfortable :—

> These summer birds did with their master stay
> The times of warmth, but then they fled away,
> Leaving their poet, being now grown old,
> Exposed to all the comming winter's cold.
> But thou, kind Prew, didst with my fates abide
> As well the winter's as the summer's tide.

> For which thy love, live with thy master here,
> Not one, but all the seasons of the yeare.

Herrick is fully as sincere in other matters. He is very poor, he admits the fact; but he has his cates and beer, he thanks Heaven, and his life is easy. He is not good-looking; he is mope-eyed and ungainly. He has lost a finger. He hates Oliver Cromwell. Sooner than take the Covenant against his convictions he will be thrust out of his living. He is of opinion that a king can do no wrong; that Charles I. was a martyr, and Charles II. is the very incarnation of virtue. " Robert Herrick, Vickar," says the register, " was buried on the 15th day of October, 1674." How many true singers of lyrics has England boasted since that date?

VI.

LITERARY MORALITY.

LITERARY MORALITY.

IF by morality in literature, I imply merely the moral atmosphere to be inhaled from certain written thoughts of men and women, I would not be understood as publicly pinning my faith on any particular code of society, although such and such a code may form part of the standard of my private conduct; as confounding the cardinal virtues with the maxims of a cardiphonia— "omnia dicta factaque," as Petronius says, "quasi papavere et sesamo sparsa." The conduct of life is to a great extent a private affair, about which people will never quite agree. But books are public property, and their effect is a public question. It seems, at first sight, very difficult to decide what books may be justly styled

" immoral; " in other words, what books have a pernicious effect on readers fairly qualified to read them.   Starting, however, agreed upon certain finalities—as is essential in every and any discussion—readers may come to a common understanding as to certain works.   Two points of agreement with the reader are necessary to my present purpose; and these are, briefly stated :—(1) That no book is to be judged immoral by any other rule than its effects upon the moral mind, and (2) that the moral mind, temporarily defined, is one consistent with a certain standard accepted or established by itself, and situated at a decent height above prejudice.   Bigotry is not morality.

Morality in literature is, I think, far more intimately connected with the principle of sincerity of sight than any writer has yet had the courage to point out.   Courage, indeed, is necessary, since there is no subject on which a writer is so liable to be misconceived.   The subject, however, is not a difficult one, if we take sincerity of sight into consideration.   Wherever there is insincerity in a book there can be no morality;

and wherever there is morality, but without art, there is no literature. `

Nothing, we all know, is more common than clever writing; very clever writing, in fact, is the vice of contemporary literature. Everywhere is brilliance not generally known to be Brummagem,—pasteboard marvels that glimmer like jewels down Mr. Mudie's list. It is so easy to get up a kaleidoscope; a few bits of stained glass, bright enough to catch the eye, and well contrasted, are the chief ingredients. It is so difficult to find a truth to utter; and then, when the truth is found, how hard it is to utter it beautifully! That is only a portion of the labour besetting an earnest writer. Directly he has caught his truth, and feels competent to undertake the noble task of beautifying it, he has to ask his conscience if there be not in society some deeper truth against which the new utterance may offend; and hence arise the personal demands,—" Have I a right to say these things? Do I believe in them with all my faculties of belief? Is my heart in them, and am I sure that I understand them clearly?" The moral mind must answer. If that replies in the affirmative, the minor question, of whether the truth will be palatable to society, is of no consequence. Let the words be uttered at all hazards, at all losses, and the gods will take care of the rest. It may be remarked, that what the writer believes to be a truth is in all possibility a falsehood, immoral and dangerous. The reply is, that Nature, in her wondrous wisdom for little things, regulates the immorality and the danger by a plan of her own, so delicate, so beautiful, as to have become part of the spirit of Art itself. A writer, for example, may believe with all his might that the legalisation of prostitution would be productive of good. He will do no harm by uttering his belief, founded as it is in his finest faculties, if he has weighed the matter thoroughly; and his book, though it may offend scores of respectable people, will be a moral book. If, on the other hand, the writer be hasty, insincere, writing under inadequate motives, he will be certain to betray himself, and every page of his book will offend against morality. For the conditions of expression are so occult, that no man *can* write immorally without being detected and exposed by the wise. His insincerity of sight in matters of conduct will betray itself in a hundred ways; for whatever be his mental calibre, we are in no danger of misconceiving the *temper* of his understanding. This fact, which connects the author's morality with the sincerity of his sight, is at once the cultivated reader's salvation against immoral effects from immoral books. What does not affect us as literature cannot affect our moral sensitiveness, and can therefore do no harm. So distinctly does nature work, indeed, that what is one writer's immorality, is the morality of another writer; so delicately does she work, that what shocks us in one book, plays lightly through the meaning of another, and gives us pleasure. An immoral subject, treated insincerely, leaves an immoral effect on those natures weak enough to be influenced by it at all. The same subject, treated with the power of genius and the delicacy of art, delights and exalts us; in the pure white light of the author's sincerity, and the delicate tints of literary loveliness, the immoral point just shows distinctly enough to impress purely, without paining.　All deep lovers of art must have felt this in the " Cenci."　A moral idea, on the other hand,—that is to say, an idea generally recognized as connected with morality,—disgusts us, if it be treated insincerely.　Every nerve of the reader is jarred; there is no pleasure, no ex- altation of the spirit or intellect; and the moral sense feels numbed and blunted proportionally.

The mere physical passion of man for woman is a case in point.　The description of this passion in coarse hands is abominable; yet how many poems are alive with it, and with it alone ! The early poems of Alfred de Musset are im- moral and unreal, and consequently displeasing ; some of the songs of Beranger are flooded with sensuality ; yet, just because they are sincere, they do not impress us sensually.*　In Burns

* " I find a highly remarkable contrast to this Chinese novel in the ' *Chansons de Beranger,*' which have almost every one some immoral, licentious subject for their founda- tion, which would be extremely odious to me if managed by a genius inferior to Beranger ; he, however, has succeeded in making them not only tolerable, but pleasing."—GOETHE's *Conversations*, i. p. 350.

and Beranger, even in some of their coarsest moments, the physical passion is so real, that it brings before us at once the presence of the Man; and, looking on *him*, we feel a thrill of finer human sympathy, in which the passion he is expressing cannot offend us. In the insincere writer, the passion is a gross thing; in the sincere writer, it becomes part of the life and colour of a human being. Thus finely does Nature prevent mere immorality from affecting the moral mind at all; while, in dealing with men of real genius, she makes the immoral sentiment, saturated with poetry, breathe a fine aroma, which stirs the heart not unpleasantly, and rapidly purifies itself as it mounts up to the brain.

Certain books of great worth are of course highly injurious to minds unqualified to read them. Out of Boccaccio, whom our Chaucer loved, and from whose writings our Keats drew a comb of purest honey, many young men get nothing but evil. He who has gained no standard of his own, or whose ideas of life are base and brutal, had better content himself with Messrs. Chambers's expurgated Shakespeare,

and the good books lent out of the local library.
But a true lover of books, though he be not a
mere student, may pass with clean feet through
any path of literature, as safe in the gloomy
region of Roman satire as in the bright land of
Una and the Milk-white Lamb: he knows well
that what is really shocking will not attract him,
because it is sure to be shockingly—i. e., inartis-
tically—uttered.   He feels that what is not
abominable, but somewhat removed from his own
ideas of decency, will affect him merely in proportion to the sincerity and delicacy of the revelation, and cannot hurt him, because it is subdued
or kept at a distance by the mental emotion
which the sincerity and delicacy have imparted.
It will not disconcert him, but make him love
his own standard all the better.   It is, in fact,
only on account of sensualists and fools that one
now and then wishes to throw some of his best
books in the fire.   If poor Boccaccio could only
hear what Smith and Brown say about him! If
La Fontaine only knew the moral indignation of
Gigadibs !

The list of so-called immoral books is very

numerous.   No writer, perhaps, is less spoken about, and yet has more attraction for students, than Petronius Arbiter.   What is the effect of Petronius on the moral mind?   Not, I fervently believe, an immoral effect—if we set aside certain passages which a reader " scunners " at, passes over, and obliterates from his memory.   Yet the subject is impure in the highest degree: from Gito to Trimalchio, every character in the satire is wicked.   The satire is saved from worthlessness by the sincerity of its object.   It does not carry us away as Juvenal does; but it impresses us with a picture of the times—painful, no doubt, but no more likely to shock us than the history of the reign of Charles II: then come the purer passages, irradiating and cheering us; and under all flows the deep delicious stream of the Latinity. Were the book not a satire, but a purposeless work of imagination, it might influence us otherwise, if we studied it at all.   As it is, History steps up, and makes Petronius *moral*.   We end it with a strange image of the times when it was written; but the passages which we do not forget, or try to forget, are the pure ones, such as the delicious introductory speech on eloquence, and the description of the wonderful feast of Trimalchio.

Juvenal is as gross, but he influences us far more splendidly. He carries us away, as I said above. When, as in the second satire, he launches his fierce blows at the Roman philosophers, who thinks of the coarser details? who is not full of the fiery energy which calls Vice by her name, and drags her naked through the Roman mire? When, in the sixth satire,* he vents his thunderous spleen on women, who is not hurried along to the end? and who does not feel that the cry, coming when it did, was a sincere and salutary one?

When I pass from the region of satire and come to Catullus, my feeling changes. It may sound very shocking to some of the hero-worshippers, but the " *lepidum novum libellum,*" seems to me really an immoral work, and I wish that the dry pumice-stone had rubbed out at

---

* Which Dryden, a grand specimen of literary immorality, only translated under protest.

least half of the poems. For there is sufficient
evidence in the purer portions to show that
Catullus was wholly insincere when he wrote the
fouler portions—that he was a man with splendid
instincts, and a moral sense which even repeated
indulgence in base things failed to obliterate.
Read the poems to Lesbia:

Lesbia illa,
Illa Lesbia, quam Catullus unam
Plus quam se, atque suos amavit omnes!

Lesbia, whom (if we identify her with Clodia)
Cicero himself called " *quadrantaria,*" and who
is yet immortal as Laura and Beatrice. This
one passion, expressed in marvellous numbers,
is enough to show what a heart was beating
in the poet's bosom. He who could make
infamy look so beautiful in the bright intensity
of his love was false and unreal when he stooped
to hurl filth at his contemporaries, from Cæsar
down to the Vibenii. His grossness is all purposeless, weak, insincere, adopted in imitation
of a society to which he was made immeasurably
superior by the strength of that one passion.
His love-poems to Lesbia, coarse as they are in

parts, leave on the reader an impression very different,—too pathetic, too beautiful, to be impure. Whether he bewails in half-plaintive irony the death of the sparrow, or sings in rapturous ecstasy, as in the fifth poem, or cries in agony to the gods, as in the lines beginning,—

> Si qua recordanti benefacta priora voluptas,
> Est homini, quum se cogitat esse pium,

he is in earnest, exhibiting all the depths of a misguided but noble nature.   Only intense emotion, only grand sincerity, could have made a prostitute immortal : for immortality must mean beauty.   Thus with Catullus, as with others, Nature herself delicately beautifies for the reader subjects which would otherwise offend ; and dignifies classical passion by the intensity of the emotion which she causes it to produce.

It is an easy step from Catullus to La Fontaine. Catullus was an immoral man—lived an immoral life :—

> Quisquis versibus exprimit Catullum
> Raro moribus exprimit Catonem !

But what shall we say of the charming Frenchman, the child of Nature, if ever child of Nature existed? If we want to understand him at all, we must set English notions and modern prejudice to some extent aside. Look at the man— a man, as M. Taine calls him, " peu moral, médiocrement digne, exempt de grands passions et enclin au plaisir:" " a trifler," as he is contemptuously styled by Macaulay. He sought to amuse himself, and nothing more; loved good-living, gambled, flirted, made verses, delighted in " bons vins et gentilles Gauloises." He did not even hide his infidelities from his wife. If she was indignant, he treated her remarks jocosely. He wrote to Madame de la Fontaine, that immediately on entering a place, when travelling, he inquired for the beautiful women; told of an amorous adventure in an alley; and said, speaking of the ladies of a certain town, " Si je trouve quelqu'un de ces chaperons qui couvre une jolie tête, je pourrai bien m'y assurer en passant et par curiosité seulement!" Like all gay men, he had his moments of despondency, but he was without depth. In spite of all this, he was capable of taking an independent attitude;

and his devotion to his friends was as great as his infidelity to his wife. So he left behind him his " Fables " and " Tales,"—pride and glory of the French nation. They are sincere—they are charming ; they are full of flashes of true poetry ; they are, in fact, the agreeable written *patter* of La Fontaine himself. Is their effect immoral? I think not. We are so. occupied with the manner of the teller—we are so amused with his piquancy and outspokenness, that we do not brood too long over the impure. The flashes of poetry and wit play around the " gaudriole," and purify it unconscientiously. La Fontaine sits before us in his easy chair. We see the twinkling of his merry eye, and we hear his wit tinkling against his subject—like ice tapping on the side of a beaker of champagne. We are brought up with much purer notions, but we cannot help enjoying the poet's society—he is so straightforward, so genuine. We would not like to waste precious time in his company very often ; but he is harmless. We must have a very poor opinion of ourselves if we think our moral tone can be hurt by such a shallow fellow.

It would prove no more to prolong examples of this sort. As for modern French writers of the " immoral" school, they are an imitative and inferior set—only competent to hurt schoolboys. George Sand, because she is not always sincere, has written immorally—in such trash as " Leone Levi," for example ; but where she has conferred literary splendour on illicit passion, where her words burn with the reality of a fiery nature— she has not shocked us—we have been so absorbed with the intensity of the more splendid emotion growing out of and playing over a subject deeply felt. The pleasure we have derived from her finer efforts in that direction has not been immoral in any true sense of the word ; for the sincerity of the writer has caused the revelation of the agony, and made us feel glad that our own standards are happier. Inferior writers may grovel as much as they please, but we don't heed them. We know their books are immoral, but we know also that they are not literature.

A well-meaning and conscientious man will not unfrequently disseminate immoral ideas through deficiency of insight. The late Count de Vigny did so. In his translations of Shakespeare he softened all the coarse passages, and in many cases only rendered the indelicacy more insidious. But he sinned most outrageously in his boldest original effort, the play of "Chatterton"—"An austere work," he says, "written in the silence of a labour of seventeen nights." The hero, of course, is the young English poet. The play is a plea for genius against society. The plea sounds more affective in the highflown preface than in the text which follows:—"When a man dies in this way," says De Vigny, "is he then a suicide? No; it is society that flings him into the fire! . . . There are some things which kill the ideas first and the man afterwards: hunger, for example. . . . I ask society to do no more than she is capable of doing. I do not ask her to cure the pains of the heart, and drive away unhappy ideals—to prevent Werther and Saint Preux from loving Charlotte and Julie d'Etanges. There are, I know, a thousand miscrable ideas over which society has no control. The more reason, it seems to me, to think of those which she can cure. . . . One should not suffer those whose infirmity is inspiration to perish. They are never numerous, and I cannot help thinking they possess some value, since humanity is unanimous on the subject of their grandeur, and declares their verse immortal—when they are dead. . . . Let us cease to say to them, *Despair and die.* It is for legislation to answer this plea, one of the most vital and profound that can agitate society." Unfortunately, poets starve still, and apologists like De Vigny have not made society one whit the kinder. As might have been expected, the play is full of puerilities. The "Chatterton" of De Vigny is a mere abstraction, cleverly conceived, no doubt, but no more like the real person than the real person was like a monk of the fifteenth century, or the French "Child of the Age." He has been educated with the young nobility at Oxford, has taken to literature, and has fallen in love with "Kitty Bell," who has several children by a brute of a husband. The only way he can devise to show his attachment is to give Kitty a Bible, and the first act ends with her soliloquy after receiving the same. "Why," exclaims Mrs. Bell, "why, when I

touched my husband's hand, did I reproach myself for keeping this book?   Conscience cannot
be in the wrong.   (*She stands dreaming.*)   I will
return it."   In the opinion of the French dramatists, it is exceedingly pathetic to find a married
woman and London landlady falling in love with
her lodger, and vastly probable to make certain
lords go hunting, in Chatterton's time, on Prim-
rose Hill.   Aggravated to frenzy by mingled
hunger and love, the poet determines to kill
himself; but is interrupted by the entrance of
" Le Quaker," a highly moral and sagacious person, who makes a great figure in the play..   The
two discourse on suicide.   "What!" cries the
Quaker at last, "Kitty Bell loves you!   Now,
will you kill yourself?"   Whereas, in real life,
any sensible fellow, even a Frenchman, would
have said, " Far better kill yourself, my boy,
than continue in this infatuation for an elderly
married woman."   Chatterton relents for the
time being.   He is afterwards made desperate,
however, by Lord Mayor Beckford, a personage
of whose authority De Vigny had the most exaggerated notions, and who offers the poor poet

a situation as *footman.* " O my soul, I have sold thee!" cried Chatterton, when left to himself; " I purchase thee back with this." And he thereupon drinks the opium. He then throws his manuscripts on the fire. "Go, noble thoughts written for the ungrateful!" he exclaims; "be purified in the flame, and mount to heaven with me!" At this point Kitty Bell enters the chamber, and much sweet sentiment is spoken. " Listen to me," says the marvellous boy. " You have a charming family: do you love your children?" " Assuredly—more than life." " Love your life, then, for the sake of those to whom you have given it." " Alas! 'tis not for their sakes that I love it." " What is there more beautiful in the world, Kitty Bell?" asks Chatterton; "with those angels on your knees, you resemble divine Charity." He at last tells her that he is a doomed man; whereupon she falls upon her knees, exclaiming, " Powers of heaven, spare him." He falls dead. Then again the Quaker makes his appearance, like the moral incarnated; and at his back John Bell, the brute of a husband. Kitty dies by the side of Chatterton; and the curtain falls as the Quaker cries, "In thine own kingdom, in thine own, O Lord, receive these two MARTYRS!"

It would be tedious to point out the sickliness of the story, or to show further how utterly the simplicity of truth is destroyed by the false elements introduced to add to its pathos. So utterly unreal are the circumstances, that they impress Frenchmen as ludicrously as Englishmen; they are immoral, but harmless through very silliness. The play from beginning to end, in its feebleness and falsehood, is a fair specimen of what an incompetent man may do when dealing with a subject which he does not understand. He does not feel the truth, and therefore introduces elements to make it more attractive to his sympathies. He thinks he is saying a fine thing when he is uttering what merely awakens ridicule. He pronounces Pan superior to Apollo, and gets the asses' ears for his pains; and the crown is so palpable to the eyes of all men, that nobody listens to his solemn judgments afterwards.

Wherever great sin has found truly literary expression, that expression has contained the

thrill of pain which touches and teaches. Where-
ever a gay sincere heart has chosen immoral
subjects, and succeeded in making them (as
Goethe expressed it) not only tolerable but
pleasant, Nature has stepped in with the magic
of genius to spiritualise the impure. Where
there is sin in literature and no suffering, the
description is false, because in life the moral
implication of sin is suffering; and whether a
writer expresses the truth through actual experience, or mere insight, the effect is the same.
Where immoral subjects have been treated gaily,
in levity, without the purifying literary spirituality, the result has been worthless,—it has minis-
tered neither to knowledge nor to pleasure.
And to what does all this, if admitted, lead?
To the further admission that immoral writing
proceeds primarily from insincerity of sight,
and that nothing is worthy the name of
literature which is decided on fair grounds to be
immoral.

It is easy to apply the broad test to some of
our older authors, who have certainly used language pretty freely. We shall not go very far

wrong if we pronounce many of the Elizabethan dramatists, and all the dramatists of the Restoration, to be immoral. Yet Shakespeare is occasionally as gross as any of his contemporaries; while Jonson, an inferior writer, through a straightforward and splendid nature, is singularly pure. I do not fancy, for my own part, that we should lose much if Congreve and Wycherly were thrown on the fire. It is fortunate that few females read Mrs. Behn. When we come to Swift we find a heap of coarse stuff, both in prose and verse; but is it immoral? As the bitter outpouring of a strangely little spirit, it is disagreeable, but it is real—if we except some of the worthless pieces and the worst portions of Gulliver. The descriptions in the latter part of Gulliver are immoral, because they are obviously insincere, and are therefore loathsome and injurious.

For critics should insist upon the fact that literature is meant to minister to our finer mental needs through the medium of spiritualized sensation. I do not think it possible to over-rate the moral benefit to be gained by the frequent contemplation of beautiful and ennobling literature.

But La Fontaine, as has been suggested, can awaken the sentiment of beauty—in his own little way, in his own degree. On the other hand, the moral injury we receive, from the contemplation of writings degrading and not beautiful, is also inestimable. In reading books it is easy to notice broad unrealities and indecencies, but very difficult indeed to recognize the poison coated with clean white diction. Mr. Tennyson might write a poem to-morrow which would be essentially immoral, and yet very hard to detect. In point of fact, being a man of genius, he would not do so; but if the thing were done, not many would be awake to it. It requires an occult judgment now-a-days to find out immoral books.

If an Englishman of to-day were to write like Catullus or Herrick, or to tell such tales as " La Berceau" of La Fontaine, or the ." Carpenter's Wife" of Chaucer, we should hound him from our libraries; and justly, because no Englishman, in the presence of our civilization, with the advantage of our decisive finalities as to the decencies of *language,* could say to his conscience, "I have a right to say these things; I believe in them with all my faculties of belief; my heart is in them, and I am sure that I understand them clearly." Our danger just now does not lie in that direction. There is no danger of our writers indulging in indecencies. Whatever our private life may be, our literature is singularly alive to the proprieties. As our culture has grown, as our ideas of decorum have narrowed, the immorality of books has been more and more disguised; indeed, so well is it disguised at this time, that the writers themselves often fancy they are mixing up aperients, not doses of wormwood. A shower of immoral books pours out yearly; many of them are read by religious societies and praised by bishops, and by far the larger number of them find favour with Mr. Mudie. A new public has arisen, created by new schools of writers; and now-a-days one must be careful how he throws out a hard truth, lest he hit the fretful head of the British matron. The immorality is of a different kind, but it works quite as perniciously in its own sphere as the immorality of modern French writers of the avowedly immoral school.

The immorality I complain of in modern books

is their untruth in matters affecting private conduct, their false estimates of character, the false
impressions they convey concerning modern life
in general, and especially with regard to the relations between the sexes. This immorality, of
course, shows itself mainly in our fiction; though
from our fiction it has spread into our religious
writing and our philosophy. The main purpose
of fiction is to please; and so widely is this felt,
that a novel with an avowedly didactic purpose
is very wisely avoided by the subscribers to the
circulating libraries. Scott, the greatest novelist
that ever lived, never stooped to so-called didactic
writing at all, directly or indirectly; for he knew
that to do so would have been to deny the value
of fiction altogether, because true pictures need no
dry tag to make them impress and teach. Thackeray was not quite so wise, being a so much smaller
writer and inferior artist; he worked in his own
sickening and peculiar fashion; yet he never pretended to be a didactic teacher. Didactic writing
in novels, at the best, is like a moral printed
underneath a picture, describing the things which,
it is supposed, the reader ought to infer from the

picture; or, like the commentaries bound in with
some of the French translations of Goethe's
" Faust" and Dante's "Inferno." When, therefore, we see the announcement as " A Novel with
a Purpose," we may pretty safely infer that it
will serve no wise man's purpose to read that
novel.

Life is very hard and difficult, our personal
relations with each other are complicated enough
without the intrusion of puzzles and untruths from
the circulating library. If novelists would only
paint what they are convinced they thoroughly
understand, and critics would only convict
offenders more severely, we should soon be
more comfortable. Erroneous notions of men,
drawn from books, ruin many women yearly,
paralyse the understanding, numb the faculty
of insight just as it is going to accumulate its
own wisdom, confuse the whole prospect of life
at the very outset. Vulgar Virtue (hero No. 1)
turns out a brute daily, and chills the ethereal
temper of Sentimental Suffering (heroine No. 1),
who, in an hour of adoration, has allied herself
to him. Silent Endurance (hero No. 2) bears

so much that we are suspicious; so we run a pin into his heart, and the heart bleeds—vinegar. As men and women advance in life they ascertain that happiness and beauty are not to be produced by a single faculty, but by the happy harmonious blending of all the faculties; that the hero in battle may make an atrocious husband, that vulgar virtue becomes tiresome when separated from spirituality, and that there are some things which fine natures cannot endure silently. This is not saying that a single faculty may not be remarkable and pleasing, that a hero is not a hero, that virtue is contemptible, that control over the emotions is not desirable, and even enviable. It means merely that the writers in question describe faculties and not characters; abstractions, not realities; not men and women, but peculiarities of men and women. The whole is lost in the part, and the effect is immoral in a high degree.

A well-known instance in point may be given, and then illustrations may cease. Some years ago it was the custom for every novelist to make his hero and heroine personally handsome. The appearance of " Jane Eyre" was welcomed as a salutary protest, and a revolution was the consequence. For a considerable time afterwards ugly heroes and heroines were the rage ; and the bookshop poured forth immoral books—immoral because they lived against a natural truth, that mere beauty is finer than mere ugliness, did not prove that nobility of nature is finer than mere beauty, did not tell that nobility of nature without such beauty. At present the plan of many novelists is very funny. They adopt a medium. Ugly heroes and heroines, as well as handsome ones, have gone out of fashion. A hero now is " not what would strictly be termed beautiful ; his features were faulty ; but there was—" any novel-reader will complete the sentence. In the same manner, a heroine, " although at ordinary times she attracted little attention, because, under the influence of emotion, so lovely that all the faults of feature were forgotten." I fear I hardly do the novel-writers justice in these matters of description, but their own lively paintings are so well known that my inability can cause them no injury.

Against immoral books of all kinds there is but one remedy—severe and competent criticism. If, as I have endeavoured to point out, morality in literature is dependent on sincerity of sight, and if all immoral writing betrays itself by its insincerity, feebleness, and want of verisimilitude, the work of criticism is pretty simple. To prove a work immoral in any way but one, it would be necessary to have endless discussion as to what is, and what is not morality. The one way is to apply the purely literary test, and convince the public that the question of immorality need not be discussed at all, since it is settled by the decision that the work under review is not literature.

NOTE.

The bulk of the preceding paper appeared some time since in the *Fortnightly Review*, and attracted considerable criticism. There are only a few words to be said in further defence of a "theory" which never pretended to be exhaustive. Of the kindly critic (*Spectator*) who, citing Goethe and others, alleged that sincere work is often more insidious in its immorality than inferior and insincere work, it may be asked—is he not setting up the final and arbitrary system of ethics which I disclaim at the outset,—by which Goethe's "self-love" and the like is to be adjudged "immoral?" How is a man's work to be proven immoral because it honestly clothes his natural instincts in artistic language? To another ingenious writer (*Contemporary Review*) who, in rebuking what he called my "love for the *gaudriole*," defined morality as faithfulness to the tendencies of one's time, I have nothing to reply save that a further examination of the preceding may show him that we do not disagree so thoroughly as his habit of dissecting cobwebs leads him to imagine. Other and hastier critics have merely gone over objections which had previously occurred to myself, and which are far too numerous to be mentioned here.

VII.

ON A PASSAGE IN HEINE.

" *I am a pilgrim, on the quest*
   For the City of the Blest;
   Free from sin and free from pain,
   When shall I that city gain?"

" *When suns no longer set and rise,*
   When bishops' mitres star the skies,
   When alms are dropt in all earth's streets,
   And angels nod upon their seats,

" *O pilgrim, thou shalt take thy stand*
   Within the City yet unplann'd,
   And see beneath, with sleepy shrug,
   The draff within the Pit undug."

NEW SONG TO AN OLD TUNE.

ON A PASSAGE IN HEINE.

IN the " Gestündisse " of Heinrich Heine occurs a pregnant passage concerning Hegel. " Generally," writes the bitter humourist, " Hegel's conversation was a sort of monologue, breathed forth noiselessly by fits and starts; the daily quaintness of his words often impressed me, insomuch that many of them still cling to my memory. One fine starlight evening, as we stood looking out from the window, I, a young man of twenty-five, *having just dined well and drunk my coffee*, spoke enthusiastically concerning the stars, and called them the homes of departed spirits. ' The stars, hum! hum!' muttered Hegel. ' The stars are only a brilliant leprosy in heaven's face.' ' In God's name, then, I exclaimed, ' is there no place of bliss above, where virtue meets with its reward after death?' But he, the master, glaring at me with his pale eyes, said sharply, ' So! *you want a bonus for having taken care of your sick mother, and refrained from poisoning your worthy brother!*' " It is in no profane spirit that I select this grim and terrible passage for a brief comment. The words in italics touch on the profound mystery, but only make it more hopeless.

Feeble religion, clinging with slight hands of flesh to every straw of counsel, may gain help and comfort from the prospect of rewards, may cross herself and groan at the brimstone jaws of the pit of punishments ; but out of the clear white air of theology, this doctrine of the *bonus* drops like a falling tear. There, at least, in that serene atmosphere, we cease to regard the Master merely as an Almighty Pedagogue, dealing out prizes to the good and whippings to the naughty, or as a splendid Sentimentalist, making of widows' tears and bairns' blood the rainbow of a heaven of melancholy beauty. Humbly, as in a glass, dimly, mystically, we behold something infinitely more — a Spirit abiding by the wondrous fitness of life itself, and stooping to no prevarications with the wicked or the unhappy. Life once given, the rest is easy. We are to play our little comedy or tragedy in our own fashion, and so effloresce into beauty at once, or retreat again into the phases of decay. But as for that new Jerusalem, perhaps it is not yet built, and if it indeed be fashioned, be sure that the foundation-stone of the city is not to be laid in hell. Now and henceforth, perfect bliss is a blank business, the point where man and monkey shade off into the elements. If I assassinate my father, it needs no hades to adjust the matter; and, here and elsewhere, heaven will never go by mere finite merit.

It is natural for very pious people to be afraid of theology—white light blinds quickest. But a little more theology would do our religion no harm. We find that even the tender-hearted, who will by no means believe in the Pit, are quite ready to pin their hopes on the Paradise. It is very sad. Men who, like myself, believe in the Redeemer, find it hard to follow Him beyond a beautiful halting-place. We long so wearily for sleep; yet is it not barely possible that the sleep wherewith our life is rounded may refresh us amply, so that we shall awake ready to go on and on? Waking and sleep, sleep and waking. The tired dews of one life wiped away, the pilgrim shall push forward till he is tired again. Another sleep, another waking. At every stage, the wonder deepening; at every life, the faculty for living intensifying. But eternal halt, no! God is exhaustless, and the soul thirsts everlastingly, and the path ever winds onward. Who would exchange this activity for howsoever sweet a symposium?

To the purpose, though with a far different drift, wrote Moses Mendelssohn, in his new *Phoedo*. "We may then," said Socrates, "with good grounds assume that this struggle towards completeness, this progress, this increase in inward excellence, is the destination of rational beings, and consequently, is the highest purpose of creation. We may say that this immense structure of the world was brought into being that there may be rational beings which advance from stage to stage, gradually increase in perfection, and find their happiness in their progress; that all these should be stopped in the middle of their course, not only stopped, but at once pushed back into the abyss of nothingness, and all the fruits of their efforts lost, is what the Highest Being cannot have accepted and adopted into the plan of the universe."

This world, with its infinite gulfs of sorrow and horror, its piteous lights, its ghostly sounds, merely a prelude to a Paradise beyond the sunset? How stale, flat, and unprofitable a business. If that be all, a still small voice asks how easy for Him to have abolished the preliminary agony and given us the bliss at once. What is He? The giver of a bonus. What are we? Strugglers after a bonus. Something more? Then surely that something more implies disinterestedness—contentedness to suffer a little for God's sake, when diligently assured that suffering is *in the scheme.* It may need these tears to give a zest to living; for I, at least, can conceive no life all tears, or quite without them. By all tokens around us, by the eyes of heaven over us, by the wail of the earth under us, by life, by love, by sorrow, all signs seem to imply that God by no means believes

in perfect bliss.   He has wept ere now, and bitterly; throned on the wondrous system of things,
He is not ever-smiling; why, *that* irradiate light
would wither up our eyesight, and we should
stand piteously like blind men in the sun, for the
sake of its warmth; whereas light was meant to
see by, as well as to quicken the vital principle of
pleasure. "All but philosophers," said Socrates to
his friends on that sad parting-day at Phlius, "All
but philosophers are courageous through fear and
brave through cowardice. So of men who attend
merely to decency; they are temperate through
intemperance. They abstain from some pleasures
for the love of other pleasures; they call it intemperance to be the slaves of pleasure; but it is
by serving some pleasures that they conquer
other pleasures; and so, as I have said, they are
temperate from intemperance. But this kind of
barter, my excellent Simmias, is not the true
trade of virtue; this exchange of pleasures for
pleasures, and of pains for pains, and of fears for
fears, great against small, as when you take small
change for a large coin. The only genuine
wealth for which we ought to give away all other,

is true knowledge." By knowledge Plato means Sight.

But our knowledge is not to make us vain-glorious. What are we that we are to scream up to God how virtuous we are, how wicked our neighbours! If there were heaven, and it were to go by absolute merit, perhaps the man who was hung for murder yesterday would have as good a chance as Shelley or Jeremy Bentham. Virtue is a hard matter to mete, when we imply by virtue something more than mere respect for public opinion, than mere good fortune, than mere good philosophy, than mere " ideas ;" and vice is often enough just natural shadow, which prevents you from seeing the stilly quivering depths of a brother's soul. There would be a terrible diffi-culty as to passports.

Does it need heaven and hades to make death bearable? Alas, too often. Yet death is but the glass, as it were, wherein souls may see them-selves. What says the Delphic woman on the tripod? Hark to the oracle!—

> Hark, I shadow forth to ye
> What the pure of sight will see!

Evermore, all human breath
Blows against the mirror, Death,
Evermore ye seek to know
Whence ye come, whither ye go;
Evermore the hollow sky,
Full of voices, makes reply
With the echo of your cry.

As an ever-changing mist,
Moonshine-lit or sunshine-kiss'd,
Floats before and seeks to pass,
Some huge mirror made of glass, —
Rendering, do all it will,
Its reflection dimmer still,
And the mirror's inner light
Weirder, fainter, to the sight.
Even thus all human life,
Darkening in dusky strife,
Blows with unavailing breath
On the phantom mirror, Death,
In that phantom-mirror rolls
Mist on mist of human souls,
Mist on mist whose image seems
Beautifully weird as dreams;
And among the phantasies
Few themselves can recognize,
And ye shudder, for your hearts
Know not their own counterparts.
Yet the more the mists that pass
Duskily before the glass,
Thicken into cloud and lose

Individual lights and hues,
More and more each special form
Loses shape and gathers storm,
More and more the mirror, Death,
Frights the gaze, and darkeneth.

Thus I shadow forth to ye
What the pure of sight will see!
O'er the mass rich colours roll,
When some nobler-sighted soul,
Scorning lust of pomp and pelf,
In the mirror sees himself,
Sees his face, and knows it not,
Sees sweet joy, nor questions what;
Pale with love and awe, he cries,
" Lo, the loveliness that lies
Far within the realm that we
Ever seek, yet dread to see!"
All his fellows, more or less,
Recognize that loveliness,
All around him growing bright
With a reverent delight,
All the happiness partake,
While, for that one spirit's sake,
Death itself grows unaware
Glorious and divinely fair!

Last, assure your heart that nought
Beautiful in deed or thought,
Beautiful and pure and wise,

> Ever wholly fades or dies;
> When one passionate soul in pride
> Sees Death's mirror glorified,
> Summoning his kind to see
> What is clear to such as he,
> Back to that one soul is given
> Glory he confers on heaven!

If I turn my own soul to the glass, for example, what happens?   I do not behold the heaven of the preacher,—I do not, cannot, see the blaze of a bonfire : but my eyes are troubled with deep vistas, glimpses of beautiful lands, where spirits wander to unearthly music, ever and anon turning hitherward faces sweetly troubled and strangely human. My father is there, and another whom I loved ;—the old familiar forms, the dear familiar eyes, only just a little sweetened by the light of the new knowledge.   And turning to my neighbour, I point out these things in the mirror ; but *his* face is terribly distorted, and the reflection of his poor soul yonder looks lurid, and he sees the flame at the jaws of the Pit.   "The pity of it, the pity of it, Iago!"   It is little good to compare notes with *him*.   Why should he listen, indeed ? An ordinary boyhood—a sweet friendship—a struggle for bread—more than one death-bed sorrow—what are such things that they should reverberate poetical echoes? and what interest has this man and the world at large in another memoranda of himself? Other men must answer these questions. Meanwhile let no man write indefinitely. He will have done at least something who shows how heavily the burthen of life presses, whenever our life, our love, our speculation and our faith, become too personal; that it is only out in the world mortals find any peace; that it is often in the still depths of the soul the devil sees himself best; and that, once and for all, God's business is greater than our smiles or tears.

Out of a young man's life, what a philosophy! what humour for the political economist! what mockery for the law-giver and the ready writer! Yet some of us can get no further, and see many old men who have got no further. Human suffering is inscrutable to me—my own suffering is intolerable; yet I thank God for life. I do not quite see why I should pray, or to whom I should pray; and yet pray I must. I can hope only for the best.　Men, as I see them, differ so little after all, and sin so little, and thrive so little, that an entire democritical paradise often is in my prospect.　I feel myself so paltry, and find others so paltry—I feel myself so grand, and find others so grand—that I picture only one sort of salvation, wherein kings, courtiers, pickpockets, assassins, and critics, would all get spiritualized together.

There are compensations.　Directly such things are felt with all one's might, it is astonishing how easy all life becomes.　In the pure white light of God's charity, we see our loved ones go away, and grow quite calm in time beside their grave.　In that light I tolerate myself, love myself—the being with whose unfitness for a pure heaven I have most reason to be acquainted, and with all my sins on me, I can look straight up at my Master, saying, " I am safe in Thy care for all—all will be well.　Thou didst make me, and wilt obliterate whatever is unfit in me." But it is only in my meaner moments that I solicit the *bonus !* All men are sleepy occasionally, and cowardly, and mean.　But with the wondrous world around me, with light playing sweetly on the green cheek of the earth, with men coming and going, with souls growing, rights broadening, truths purifying, I feel that life, mere life, is ample— the gift of all gifts—the finish beyond which I cannot go. If I shall *live* on, all is well. For *this* life, as I know it, the twelfth chapter of Paul's First Epistle to the Corinthians is my Gospel;— that is exhaustless; charity to men and women, and most of all to myself, is what sweetens me to myself. Charity " beareth all things, believeth all things, suffereth all things, endureth all things. Charity never faileth: but whether there be pro- phecies, they shall fail; whether there be tongues, they shall cease; whether there be knowledge, it shall vanish away." Charity is all that men lack; sin, knowledge, prayer, are nothing. All is explained in those supreme moments when a human soul irradiates a human body, and has no scorn for its abode, and can look forth and see the celestial inmates everywhere in fairer or viler bodies, and feel the breath of God lying over all, palpable, though unseen, like the air we breathe and live by.

Too much self-cogitation, I repeat, will not do; the fountain of love must be kept stirred, or it will freeze. Who can conceive any modern being, far less any modern poet, without abundant sympathetic exercise and great charity; and the finer the charity, let us hope, the clearer will be the music,—which music at least God will hear and understand. The only hope is to go forth into life and watch men and women— high or low—exactly at that point, the highest point of their spiritual life, where they contact with that ideal of perfect disinterestedness, which we call God. All contact with God somewhere. Sin is spiritualized by personal ties—human ties are invariably pathetic—and where the pathetic essence is perceptible, God is not far away. Once and for all, the danger of dangers is that of attaching too sentimental or too sleepy a construction to history or actual experience. Actual physical life is as mysterious, as progressive, as wonderful, as any of our fantastic theories or personal emotions, and the condition of perfect health is the due exercise of all the functions. Let us grow, and grow, and grow. Better annihilation

than the perfect bliss of the preacher.   God is
eternal, and can never pause:—pause is death:—
and how should God die?

THE HYMN.

 ORD, Thou hast given me life and breath,
    Sleep and foreknowledge, too, of death;
    My eyes shall close, my span pass by,
Yet, Lord, I know I shall not die.

Lord, I shall live beyond the grave,
Made happier by Thy power to save;
Yet, though I see a clime more fair,
I shall not quite cease weeping there.

Lord God, be with me day and night!
Strengthen me! give me clearer sight!
And here and there, in life and death,
Strength to despise too easy breath.

For, Lord, I am so weak and low,
So pain'd to stay, so loath to go,
And most of all I need to gain
The flower and quintessence of pain.

Lord, make me great and brave and free!
It is enough to breathe and be!
Out of the blessed need to grow
Blossoms the thirst to love and know.

And in Thy season, Master blest,
Grant me a little sleep and rest;
Then, wakening,—in a sweeter place,
Thy sunlight pouring on my face.

Lord, let me breathe! Lord, let me be!
Give me Thy light, and let me see!
And now and then, to make me strong,
A little sleep, but not too long.

Thus, Lord, for ever let me range
Through pain, through tears, through strife, through change,
Make me full blessed in Thy light,
But never at the price of Sight!

VIII.

ON MY OWN TENTATIVES.

" Hard hand, hold mine ! deep eyes, look into these !
Strong soul, befriend a troubled modern's song !
Thou poor man, beaten on by rain and breeze,
Thou who shalt rule the nations, make me strong."

AN INVOCATION TO LAZARUS.

ON MY OWN TENTATIVES.

I SHALL offer no apology for now entering upon the discussion of so personal a matter as the purport of my own poetical writings. If I am self-conscious and interested here (and I by no means hope wholly to escape misconstruction) I have been so all along; for while discussing the poetic character, describing the Student's vocation, inquiring what is and what is not Literary Morality, and finally bringing the whole matter to the test of spiritual and theological light, I have been steadily proceeding in this direction. Whom should these thoughts guide, if they are not to be as lamps to my own feet? Whom should I dare

to rebuke, if I were fearful of setting an example ?
I must utter my message at any cost—believing,
as I do, that, although I may utterly fail to
clothe my aspirations or opinions in artistic or
permanent forms, yet that those aspirations and
opinions are fraught with the deepest importance,—are destined sooner or later to bear fruit
that will make art nobler, and deeply gladden the
spirits of men.

In three volumes of ambitious verse,* consisting chiefly of tentative attempts to picture
contemporary scenes, I have been doing my best
to show that actual life, independent of accessories,
is the true material for poetic art; that, further,
actual national life is the perfectly approven
material for every British poet; and that, in a
word, the further the poet finds it necessary to
recede from his own time, the less trustworthy is
his imagination, the more constrained his sympathy, and the smaller his chance of creating true
and durable types for human contemplation. The

---

* I do not here include " Undertones," which belongs to
a totally different category.

success of my writings with simple people may be no sign of their possessing durable poetic worth, but it at least implies that I have been labouring in the right direction. On reviewing the history of my three books I find that I have every reason to congratulate myself on the sympathy of the great body of public writers. My greatest opponents have been found among men of what is called "literary culture"—an epithet implying excellent education, vast reading, real intelligence, and much respect for tradition. "You have evidently gone to the life for your subjects," writes a distinguished living critic, "but still I would have you remember that if one, while going to the life, chooses a subject which is naturally poetical, one's chances of the best poetical success will be increased tenfold." A gifted young contemporary, who seems fond of throwing stones in my direction, fiercely upbraids me for writing "Idyls of the gallows and the gutter," and singing songs of "costermongers and their trulls." Gentlemen from the universities shake their heads over me sadly, and complain, somewhat irrelevantly, I think, that I am not Greek. Now, I am quite ready to credit all these gentlemen with perfect sincerity, and, so far as taste is founded on tradition, with perfect good taste.   Whether from too elaborate a collegiate education, or from class pride, or from actual deficiency of imagination, they do really associate vulgarity with a certain class of subjects, they do really feel that contemporary life is not naturally poetic, they do really breathe more freely under the masks of the old drama, than when face to face with the terrific commonplaces and sub-lime vulgarities of great cities.   Views of contem-porary life, to please them, must be greatly ideal-ized or subdued to the repose of Greek sculpture ; but, for the most part, they would consign con-temporary material to the comic writer, and re-serve our ordinary daily surroundings for the use of the manufacturers of Adelphi farces.   In " Pin-dar and Poets unrivalled," they confine their sympathy to tradition, and care most for sta-tuesque woes and nude intellectualities moving on a background of antique landscape.   If they are to find a poetic theme on the soil, they must go very far back in the chronicle—say, as far as Boadicea. The more misty the figures, the less their vulgarity, in the eyes of those who wish to build colleges on Parnassus, and who learn Greek in order to address the Muses, forgetting that the nine ladies now favour the moderns, and have almost entirely forgotten their beautiful native tongue.

However, the mania for false refinement, which distinguishes educated vulgarity, must not blind us to the truth that a large portion of the public, and these highly intellectual people, are quite incapable of perceiving the poetry existing close to their own thresholds. The little world in which they move is so vulgar and sordid, or so artificial, that the further they escape from its suggestions they feel the freer. What they cannot feel in the office or the drawing-room they try to feel in the garden of Academus. Their daily life, their daily knowledge and duty, is not earnest enough to supply their spiritual needs, and they very naturally conclude that the experience of their neighbours is as mean as theirs. In the ranks of such men we not seldom find the lost Student; but the majority call themselves cultured, as their neighbours call themselves virtuous,—just for want of some other spicier peculiarity to distinguish them from their fellows.

Let it be at once conceded that our modern life is complex and irritating, and, at a superficial glance, sadly deficient in picturesqueness. Streets are not beautiful, and this is the age of streets; trade seems selfish and common, and this is the age of trade; railways, educational establishments, poor houses, debating societies, are not romantic, and this is the age of all these. But if we strip off the hard outer crust of these things, if we pass from the unpicturesqueness of externals to the currents which flow beneath, who then shall say that this life is barren of poetry? Never, I think, did such strange lights and shades glimmer on the soul's depths, never was suffering more heroic, or courage more sublime, never was the reticence of deep emotion woven in so closely with the mystery and the wonder of the world. Yet a very brief glance at recent poetry will show how blind our poets have been to this most legitimate material. Of the poets of the last generation, Wordsworth and Crabbe depicted actual life as they beheld it; Wordsworth dissecting silent endurance with iron pathos, and Crabbe protruding unpoetic details with the art of the parish clerk. While Crabbe's pictures are nearly worthless, poetically speaking, and have done much to deepen the prejudice against the poetic treatment of contemporary life, Wordsworth's are really poetic, but are often too cold and academic in the outline, too little disinterested, except where they deal in mere emotions, to be quite satisfactory. Hood, alone, once or twice caught the throb of the great heart of modern time; had his sympathies been closelier concentrated, had his necessities been less urgent, I believe this wonderful and totally misunderstood genius might have done much to revolutionize English poetry; for he more than once evinced glimmers of sympathy, sanity, insight, and single-hearted beneficence, which it is difficult to discover even in Wordsworth. Among contemporaries there has been shown a more earnest craving to do justice to the present. Tennyson has given us a garden philosopher's group of modern idyls, often significant, sometimes deep, and always finely representative of English elegance. "The Gardener's

Daughter," " The Miller's Daughter," and " The Brook," * are exquisite attempts to paint English landscape, with the addition of a few delicate figures; but if we wish to perceive the full amount of Tennyson's apprehensiveness towards modern life, we must turn to " Maud," which is full of interest, in spite of its inferiority as a poem. On the whole Tennyson does not, and cannot, sympathise much with life not ornate, though he has nobly striven to educate his eye and heart. Clough endeavoured, with some success, to express in verse much of the unsatisfied longing of middle-class culture, but his instincts were scholastic, not humanitarian. Mr. Arnold no sooner touches the solid ground of contemporary thought, than all his grace forsakes him, and his utterance becomes the merest prose. Mr. Browning, of whose

---

* Of these three poems, the last is infinitely the highest, because it draws its most touching force from a *universal* spiritual chord—the contrast of the changefulness of human life with the durability of natural objects. The " Grandmother" is fine for a similar reason. I confess, however, that I am blind to the poetic merit of the " Northern Farmer," however conscious of its force as a photograph.

moral and mental greatness there can be no question, has only once or twice attempted essentially English themes; and, although this writer's human sympathy is wondrously deep and beautiful, it is often overcast by intellectualities that deaden the sense of life. Mrs. Browning, alone, of all the recent poets, reached the deep significance of her century. "Aurora Leigh" is too wild and diffuse, too morbidly female, to be called a great work of art, but it contains passages newer, truer, and profounder than any other modern poem. England has lost her greatest modern light in Mrs. Browning. She has left little behind her to represent her mighty sympathy and capacity for apprehending, but she stands unique in these days—specifically a *poet*—one troubled by the great mystery of life, and finding no speech adequate but song. Had she survived, and been open to English influences, she would have written her name on the forehead of her time, and forced the stream of English poetry into a newer and a deeper channel.

But it is at least clear, from these examples, that the poetry of humanity is newly dawning.

To the preacher, to the poet, to the philosopher, the people must look more constantly than heretofore for guidance. Religion and science have their spheres defined for them: our singers are but learning to define theirs. Genius, as much as liberty, is the nation's birthright, and it misses its aim when it confines its ministrations to any section of the state. Poetic art has been tacitly regarded, like music and painting, as an accomplishment for the refined, and it has suffered immeasurably as an art, from its ridiculous fetters. It has dealt with life in a fragmentary form, and with the least earnest and least picturesque phases of life. Yet the intensity of being (for example) among those who daily face peril, who are never beyond want, who have constant presentiments of danger, who wallow in sin and trouble, ought to bring to the poet, as to the painter, as lofty an inspiration as may be gained from those living in comfort, who make lamentation a luxury and invent futilities to mourn over. The world is full of these voices, and the poet has to set them into perfect speech. But this truth has been little understood, and but partially acted upon. Our earliest English poets had some leanings towards the heroism of fate-stricken men; and Chaucer could dwell on the love of a hind with the same affection as upon the devotion of a knight. The old poet had a wholesome regard for merit unbiassed by accessories; but the broad light he wrote in has suffered a long eclipse.

The risk of appearing self-credulous shall not prevent me from explicitly expressing, in the interests of art and artists, the principles which have regulated my own tentative attempts at this poetry of humanity. They may be briefly enumerated. That the whole significance and harmony of life is never to be lost sight of in depicting any fragmentary form of life, and that, therefore, the poet should free himself entirely from all arbitrary systems of ethics and codes of opinion, aiming, in a word, at that thorough disinterestedness which is our only means to the true perception of God's creatures. That every fragmentary form of life is not fit for song, but that every form is so fit which can be spiritualized without the introduction of false elements to the final literary form of harmonious numbers. That, failing the heroic statue and the noble features, almost every human figure becomes idealized whenever we take into consideration the background of life, or picture, or sentiment on which it moves; and that it is to this background a poet must often look for the means of casting over his picture the refluent colours of poetic harmony. That the true clue to poetic success in this kind is the intensity of the poet's own insight, whereby a dramatic situation, however undignified, however vulgar to the unimaginative, is made to intersect through the medium of lyrical emotion with the entire mystery of human life, and thus to appeal with more or less force to every heart that has felt the world.

Truth, then, to hit the sense of hearers, was to be strangely spiritualized—spiritual truth being truth seen through the peculiar medium of a man's own individual soul. The poet's first task was to purify the *medium* as much as possible, to drain it of all prejudices in favour of special virtue, or knowledge, or culture. It was the poet's business, not to preach morality, not to inculcate intellectuality, not to describe this or that form of life as finally and significantly holy, but to be just without judgment to the pathos and power of all he saw or apprehended. The accessories must be laid aside, the conventionalities disregarded, and the deep human heart laid bare. The only bond incumbent on the poet was the *artistic* one. It was not enough merely to represent life,—it was necessary that the representatives should be beautiful. It was not enough to mirror truth,— the truth must be spiritualized. It was not enough to catch the speech of man or woman,—that speech must be subtly set to music.

With these views, still faint, but strengthening upon me, I wrote the poems of "Inverburn,"—a series of dramatic soliloquies put into the mouths of certain poor folk, figures seen on the background of a familiar Scottish village,—

> The clachan, with its humming sound of looms,
> The quaint old gables, roofs of turf and thatch,
> The glimmering spire that peeps above the firs,
> The waggons in the lanes, the waterfall
> With cool sound plunging in its wood-nest wild,
> The stream whose soft blue arms encircle all,—
> And in the background heathery norland hills,

> Hued like the azure of the dew-berrie,
> And mingling with the regions of the Rain!

I cannot, of course, say where I have perfectly succeeded in realizing my own ideal in these poems; but I am at least conscious to some extent where I have failed. In "Willie Baird" and "Poet Andrew," the speech, respectively, of an old schoolmaster and a village weaver, I attempt a perfect ideal background, the power and dreamy influence of nature in the one case, and the intense glow of great human emotion in the other. The "English Housewife's Gossip" lacks the background, touches nowhere on the great universal chords of sympathy, and is insomuch unsuccessful as a poem. The "Two Babes" is, even from my own favourable stand-point, a mixed business, of whose poetic merit I am by no means confident. It is on poems like "Willie Baird" and "Poet Andrew," and a few of the shorter pieces, that I should take my stand if I were forced to point to any of these poems as poetic successes, from the lofty modern point of view that I am at present taking.

In "London Poems," I was at least a great

deal juster to the rude forces of life, my sympathy was bolder and more confident, my soul clearer and more trustworthy as a medium, however poor might be my power of perfect artistic spiritualization. As common life was approached more closely, as the danger of vulgarity threatened more and more to interfere with the reader's sense of beauty, the stronger and tenderer was the lyrical note needed.

> —— Even in the unsung city's streets,
> Seem'd quiet wonders meet for serious song,
> Truth hard to phrase and render musical.
> For ah! the weariness and weight of tears,
> The crying out to God, the wish for slumber,
> They lay so deep, so deep! God heard them all;
> He set them unto music of His own;
> But easier far the task to sing of kings,
> Or weave weird ballads where the moon-dew glistens,
> Than body forth this life in beauteous sound.

In writing such poems as "Liz" and "Nell," the intensest dramatic care was necessary to escape vulgarity on the one hand, and false refinement on the other. "Liz," although the offspring of the very lowest social deposits, possesses great natural intelligence, and speaks more than once with a refinement consequent on strange purity of thought. Moreover, she has been under spiritual influences. She is a beautiful living soul, just conscious of the unfitness of the atmosphere she is breathing ; but, above all, she is a large-hearted woman, with wonderful capacity for loving. She is on the whole quite an exceptional study, although in many of her moods typical of a class. " Nell " is not so exceptional, and since it is harder to create types than eccentricities, her utterance was far more difficult to spiritualize into music. She is a woman quite without refined instincts, coarse, uncultured, impulsive. Her love, though profound, is insufficient to escape mere commonplace ; and it was necessary to breathe around her the fascination of a tragic subject, the lurid light of an ever-deepening terror.

In the *language* of both these poems I followed nature as closely as possible ; so far as poetic speech can follow ordinary speech. I had to add nothing, but merely (as a sympathetic critic happily expressed it) to " deduct whatever hid, instead of expressing, the natural meaning of the speakers;" for to obtrude slips of grammar, mis-spellings, and other meaningless blotches, in short, to lay undue emphasis on the mere language employed, would have been wilfully to destroy the artistic verisimilitude of such poems. Every stronger stress, every more noticeable trick of style, added after the speech was sufficient to hint the quality of the speakers, was so much over-truth, offending against the truth's harmony. The object was, while clearly conveying the caste of the speakers, to afford an artistic insight into their souls, and to blend them with the great universal mysteries of life and death. Vulgarity obtruded is not truth spiritualized and made clear, but truth still hooded and masked, and little likely to reveal anything to the vision of its contemplators.

By at least one critic I have been charged with idealizing the speech a little too much. Both "Liz" and "Nell," it is averred, occasionally speak in a strain very uncommon in their class. In reply to this I may observe how much mis-pronunciations, vulgarisms, and the like, have blinded educated people to the wonderful force and picturesqueness of the language of the lower classes. They know nothing of the educated luxury of using language in order to conceal thought, but speak because they have something to say, and try to explain themselves as forcibly as possible. Take the talk of sailors, for example, even of the common smacks-men who live precarious lives upon our coasts. How full of picture, emphasis, fervour—everything but circumlocution. "There was a star i' the old moon's weather horn this morning; nor I didn't much like the coppery clouds this dog-watch." The speech of the lower classes in cities is not much less powerful and uncommon. Metaphor. abounds to an extraordinary degree, and words are often chosen with a singular sense of sound. "And then," said an old Irish apple-woman to me, speaking of the death of her half-starved baby, "God's hand gript me round the heart, and sure I couldn't breathe or see." This, however, is a subject too elaborate for discussion here, and must be reserved for a separate paper.

It is difficult to satisfy all critics. By some my language has been thought over-refined ; by others, it has been condemned as vulgar and inharmonious. The style of the ornate school of writers, where the melody of sweet syllables is essayed without constant reference to emotion or thought, has, I confess, but little fascination for me. I have usually, and perhaps too implicitly, trusted to the character of the emotion in order to produce poetic harmony. I have preferred the simplicity of truth, the vigor of simple speech, to all habitual finesse or fantastic elaboration. Words have been valuable to me purely as a means of expressing meaning, nor have I often introduced epithets or tricks of style, merely to satisfy the vulgarity of schoolmen.

A far more serious charge than that concerning any mere question of style has been brought by genteel critics against poems such as those I have been discussing. It has been said that, under the form of dramatic soliloquy, the writer's own subjective spectacles have been sometimes put on the eyes of common-place people, thus crediting the speakers with sentimentalisms which have no existence out of the sphere of blind poetic sympathy. The sensations of Liz during her one memorable visit to the country, the intense loving tenderness of the coarse woman Nell towards her brutal paramour, the exquisite delicacy and fine spiritual vision of the old village schoolmaster, the yearning for pastoral light and music in the heart of the old ballad-maker, all these, it is suggested, are over-elaborate sentimentalisms, too tender emotions accorded to people who, in reality, have very little sentiment or emotion to boast of.　Thus, in a strain of critical gentility, writes the editor of the "Pall Mall Gazette," criticising the "Ballad-maker:" " Our present author would have us imagine that an exterior of squalor and rudeness is inevitably and incessantly accompanied by an abject and querulous frame of mind.　He is unwilling even to believe that a Londoner can for a moment forget or cease to be sick of the smoke and the strange faces that surround him.　His imaginary sufferers moreover have a childish and literally lack-a-daisy longing to meet with the simplest country objects." Now, of all the city poems I have written, there are four only which, from this profound point of view, can be considered querulous and lack-a-daisy. Two of

these, "The Starling" and "The Linnet," are
what I may call "bird poems," companion pieces,
where, by natural laws of association, and in very
different ways, a caged starling and a caged
linnet are made to flash upon their owners
wild or bright glimpses of the outlying dis-
tricts from which they come. The third poem,
"The Ballad Maker," is clearly and avowedly
the story of a man translated from the country
to the town ; and naturally, being of a poetic and
dreamy turn of mind, strangely impressed with
the contrast. He is querulous: and why not?
But where is the querulousness, where the
childish longing for country objects in Liz. Liz
breathes happily only in the deep miasma of the
city: a being possible only there ; knowing nothing of light or sunshine, and caring to know
nothing of these. She tries the country once,
because she thinks that life is easier there ; but
far from moving her to joy, the light and colour
trouble her to intensest pain.

> I would not stay out yonder if I could,
> For one feels dead, and all looks pure and good :
> I could not bear a light so bright and still.

With these four poems the catalogue of such "sentimentalities" may be brought to a close. In what, for instance, consists the sorrow of the Little Milliner who, far from drooping in the city, found there a constant round of joy from day to day :—

And London streets, with all their noise and stir,
Had many a pleasant sight to pleasure her.
There were the shops, where wonders ever new,
As in a garden, changed the whole year through.
Oft would she stand, and watch, with laughter sweet,
The punch and judy in the quiet street;
Or look and listen while soft minuets
Play'd the street organ with the marionettes.
Or join the motley group of merry folks
Round the street huckster, with his wares and jokes.
Fearless and glad, she joined the crowd that flows
Along the streets at festivals and shows.
In summer time she loved the parks and squares,
Where fine folk drive their carriages and pairs.
In winter time her blood was in a glow,
At the white coming of the pleasant snow.
And in the stormy nights, when dark rain pours,
She found it pleasant, too, to sit in-doors,
And sing, and sew, and listen to the gales,
Or read the penny journal with the tales.

It was clearly my endeavour, in this poem, to

evolve the fine Arcadian feeling out of the dullest obscurity, to show how even brick walls and stone houses may be made to blossom, as it were, into blooms and flowers ;—to produce by delicate passion and sweet emotion an effect similar to that which pastoral poets have produced by means of greenery and bright sunshine. In close connection with all that is dark and solitary in London life, the little milliner was to walk in a light such as lies on country fields, exhibiting, as a critic happily phrases it, "all the passion of youth, modulated by all the innocence of a naked baby."

But my wish to vindicate certain artistic principles must not betray me further into detailed expositions of separate poems. I wish to offer a general explanation, not special panegyrics. One more word here, however, on the kind of dramatic soliloquy I have adopted in these pieces. In such individual utterance there *is* clearly a danger of one-sidedness, of crediting the world with the poet's own emotion, the more so as that emotion must interpenetrate more or less consciously with the actual emotion of the speaker, so as to result in a conscientious and moving picture, with a faint though audible tone of lyric harmony. The reader must not only see the truth, but see it through the novel medium of a poetic individuality. It may be a truth old as the hills, hoary with the snows of century after century, but it is only a *poetic* truth so far as the new mental light irradiates and transfigures it. If the world sees such figures as Liz, Nell, Poet Andrew, Meg Blanc, through the troubled atmosphere of the writer's soul, let not the world complain that it sees them no longer under the dark loveless shadow in which they were previously perceived, if perceived at all. One cannot so clear that atmosphere as to bring it to the ambient purity and perfect veracity of God's own air. The poet, be he great dramatist, like Sophocles, or morbid dreamer, like Blake, cannot free himself wholly from the disturbing forces of his own heart. He has but one clue to the mystery, and that is his own individuality. "It is astonishing," says a loose but occasionally felicitous writer, "how large a harvest of new truths would be reaped simply through the accident of a man's feeling, or being made to feel more *deeply* than other men.   He sees the same objects, neither more nor fewer, but he sees them engraved in lines far stronger, and more determinate, and the difference in the strength makes the whole difference between consciousness and sub-consciousness.   And in questions of the mere understanding, we see the same fact illustrated.   The author who wins notice the most, is not he that perplexes men by truths drawn from fountains of absolute novelty—truths as yet unsunned—and from that cause obscure; but he that awakens into illuminated consciousness, ancient lineaments of truth long slumbering in the mind, although too faint to have extorted attention."*   And here is an explanation why, through all truly good and sane poetic art, runs that strange personal light which fascinates as music or style, and is the invariable characteristic of the true singer.

I must not be understood as insisting that *humble* cotemporary life is the only legitimate

---

* De Quincey on Wordsworth's Poetry, page 260.

material of the modern poet.   Strongly as I am convinced that the mighty reserve force, the ardent strength and sanity of this people, lies little acknowledged in the ranks of that class which is only just emerging into political power, firmly as I would indicate how exotic teachers have emasculated the youth and the flower of our schools and universities, I would yet be just to all cotemporary life, social, political, moral.   " Religion," says Goëthe, " stands in the same relation to art as any other of the higher interests of life.   It is a subject, and its rights are those of all other subjects."   Yet how scantily are morality and religion represented in modern art.   Why, for instance, is our Christianity forgotten as a *subject?*   Where is the great poem, where the noble music built on that wondrous theme ?   Milton, with all his power, is academic, not modern; and, with the exception of a few faint utterances of Wordsworth, all our other religious poetry is conventional and inartistic.

We hear, indeed, the metallic periods of the didactic teacher, and the feeble wail of the religious enthusiast, but seldom indeed are our nobler intellectual and spiritual strivings phrased into perfect song. The reticence of false culture steals over the lips of many who might instruct us deeply by their experience, who, if they do speak, are moved by the retrograde spirit of another civilization, and use the formal periods of an alien tongue. Why, in the name of our new gods, are we still to be bound by the fetters of Prometheus. We are, if not quite *Celts*, more Celts than Greeks, and, thank heaven, not altogether an intellectual nation. We have nothing in common with the Athenian civilization. In the same spirit that we demolished their monuments, to transport them piecemeal to our museums, we mutilate their language to carry it into our schools. In our clumsy attempts to imitate ancient art and literature, we seek in vain to hide the gait of the barbarian. Even our strongest natures fail at this task. They might be very admirable Englishmen if they did not aspire to be very intellectual Greeks.

There is reason to apprehend that this traditional intellectuality is melting away, and that clearer and nobler forces are beginning to operate upon our young minds. " Off, off, ye lendings ! " We are a modern people, slightly barbaric in matters of art; but our natures have a glow of emotion quite unknown to the frigid spirit of Athenian inquiry. There is a great emotional and spiritual life yet unrepresented, there are rude forces not yet brought into play, but all of which must sooner or later have their place in art; and the indigenous product of our experience, however inferior to other civilizations, is yet vastly superior to all exotics grafted on the weathered trunk of what was once a noble tree.

In answer to thoughts like this, I have heard it urged that Art is not local but cosmopolitan, and that the artist should aim, as all great artists have aimed, at universality. It is true that the highest art owes its permanence to its universality, but it is also true that the intensity of the local insight, the keenness of the artist's apprehension of his own time, is the very *cause* that his work compasses universal truth; since each man's spiritual experience, if rightly depicted, must correspond in numberless soul-touching particulars, with the combined experience of the world. There is no catholicity, no universality, no true art, to be got by chill aiming at these things; they are the product of individual natures, acted upon by the great forces of the world and the period. , It is nonsense to point to Greek art, especially Greek sculpture, as "universal" in the sense of non-nationality. Nothing can be more Greek, and that is why nothing can be more great.

But I must draw these remarks to the close. The conclusion of the whole matter, as affecting poets and poetry, is this, that although there may be high and good poetry moving in a limited range of sympathy, the very highest and best poetry is the poetry which appeals to most classes of the state, through those universal chords which communicate with all' hearts alike. (Shakespeare, Chaucer, Burns). A true poem of this sort has a side for the uncultivated, another for the refined; a body and soul that reach down to the heart's beatings, and up to the very heaven of mysteries. It is virtually inexhaustible—large, typical, human. I can congratulate myself on having attempted, however humbly, to touch this poetry of humanity; but the appreciation of my own mere tentatives in this direction is of far less importance to me than the welfare of English art generally, and the vindication of its place in European progress.

 Cætera, quæ vacuas tenuissent carmina mentis,
Omnia jam vulgata. Quis aut Eurysthea durum,
Aut illaudati nescit Busiridis aras?
Cui non dictus Hylas puer, Latonia Delos?
 Hippodaméque, humeróque Pelops insignis eburno,
Acer equis? *Tentanda via est, qua me quoque possim
Tollere humo, victórque virûm volitare per ora!*
Vir. Georg. III. 3.

THE END.

CHISWICK PRESS:—PRINTED BY WHITTINGHAM AND WILKINS,
TOOKS COURT, CHANCERY LANE.

A List of Books

PUBLISHING BY

SAMPSON LOW, SON, AND MARSTON,

MILTON HOUSE, LUDGATE HILL, LONDON.

**** *Where the price is not given, the work was not ready at the time of issuing this list.*

[*November,* 1867.

NEW ILLUSTRATED WORKS.

CHRISTIAN LYRICS. Chiefly selected from Modern Authors. 138 Poems, illustrated with upwards of 150 Engravings, under the superintendence of J. D. Cooper. Small 4to. cloth extra, 10s. 6d.; morocco, 21s.

**** This Work forms Messrs Low and Co.'s Annual Christmas Presentation Volume for 1868.

THE STORY WITHOUT AN END. From the German of Carové. By Sarah Austin. Illustrated with Sixteen Original Water-Colour Drawings by E. V. B., printed in Fac-simile and numerous Illustrations on wood. Small 4to. cloth extra, 12s.; with ivory tablet, 15s.; morocco, 21s.

**** Also a Large Paper Edition, with the Plates mounted, only 250 copies of which are printed. In morocco, 31s. 6d.

LIST OF THE COLOURED ILLUSTRATIONS:

Title Page.	8. Two Worldly People.
1. In the Hut there was only a Bed,—	9. Between the Real and the Unreal.
2. And a Neglected Looking-glass.	10. Kindred Spirits.
3. After Breakfast.	11. Starlight.
4. Wandering Stars.	12. Hazel Nuts.
5. Dreams.	13. Love and Hate.
6. A Palm-tree Grove.	14. The Joy of Spring.
7. The Garden.	15. Death but a Sleep.

"*Nowhere will he find the Book of Nature more freshly and beautifully opened for him than in ' The Story without an End,' of its kind one of the best that was ever written.*"—Quarterly Review, Feb. 1867.

No effort has been spared to render this volume the most perfect specimen of colour-printing yet produced; and it is believed that it will form one of the most charmingly illustrated books of the season.

THE POETRY OF NATURE. Selected and Illustrated with Thirty-six Engravings by Harrison Weir. Crown 8vo. handsomely bound in cloth, gilt edges, 5s.; morocco, 10s. 6d.

**** Forming the new volume of Low's Choice Editions of Choice Books.

THE PYRENEES; a Description of Summer Life at French Watering Places. By Henry Blackburn, author of "Travelling in Spain in the Present Day." With upwards of 100 Illustrations by Gustave Doré. Royal 8vo, cloth, 18s.; morocco, 25s.

TWO CENTURIES OF SONG; or, Melodies, Madrigals, Sonnets, and other Occasional Verse of the English Poets of the last 200 years. With Critical and Biographical Notes by Walter Thornbury. Illustrated by Original Pictures of Eminent Artists, Drawn and Engraved especially for this work. Printed on toned paper, with coloured borders, designed by Henry Shaw, F.S.A. Very handsomely bound. Cloth extra, 21s.; morocco, 42s.

Choice Editions of Choice Books. New Editions. Illustrated by C. W. Cope, R.A., T. Creswick, R.A., Edward Duncan, Birket Foster, J. C. Horsley, A. R. A., George Hicks, R. Redgrave, R.A., C. Stonehouse, F. Tayler, George Thomas, H. J. Townshend, E. H. Wehnert, Harrison Weir, &c. Crown 8vo. cloth, 5s. each; mor. 10s. 6d.

Bloomfield's Farmer's Boy.	Keat's Eve of St. Agnes.
Campbell's Pleasures of Hope.	Milton's l'Allegro.
Cundall's Elizabethan Poetry.	Poetry of Nature.
Coleridge's Ancient Mariner.	Roger's Pleasures of Memory.
Goldsmith's Deserted Village.	Shakespeare's Songs and Sonnets.
Goldsmith's Vicar of Wakefield.	Tennyson's May Queen.
Gray's Elegy in a Churchyard.	Wordsworth's Pastoral Poems.

"*Such works are a glorious beatification for a poet. Such works as these educate townsmen, who, surrounded by dead and artificial things, as country people are by life and nature, scarcely learn to look at nature till taught by these concentrated specimens of her beauty.*"—Athenæum.

Bishop Heber's Hymns. An Illustrated Edition, with upwards of one hundred Designs. Engraved, in the first style of Art under the superintendence of J. D. Cooper. Small 4to. handsomely bound, price Half a Guinea; morocco, 21s.

The Divine and Moral Songs of Dr. Watts: a New and very choice Edition. Illustrated with One Hundred Woodcuts in the first style of the Art, from Original Designs by Eminent Artists; engraved by J. D. Cooper. Small 4to. cloth extra, price 7s. 6d.; morocco, 15s.

Milton's Paradise Lost. With the original Steel Engravings of John Martin. Printed on large paper, royal 4to. handsomely bound, 3l. 13s. 6d.; morocco extra, 5l. 15s. 6d.

Light after Darkness: Religious Poems by Harriet Beecher Stowe. With Illustrations. Small post 8vo. cloth, 3s. 6d.

Pictures of English Life; illustrated by Ten folio page Illustrations on wood, by J. D. Cooper, after Drawings by R. Barnes and E. M. Whimperis, with appropriate descriptive Poems, printed in floreated borders. Imperial folio, cloth extra, 14s.

Favourite English Poems. *Complete Edition.* Comprising a Collection of the most celebrated Poems in the English Language, with but one or two exceptions unabridged, from Chaucer to Tennyson. With 300 Illustrations by the first Artists. Two vols. royal 8vo. half bound top gilt, Roxburgh style, 1l. 18s.; antique calf, 3l. 3s.

. Either Volume sold separately as distinct works. 1. " Early English Poems, Chaucer to Dyer." 2. " Favourite English Poems, Thomson to Tennyson." Each handsomely bound in cloth, 1l. 1s.

"*One of the choicest gift-books of the year, " Favourite English Poems" is not a toy book, to be laid for a week on the Christmas table and then thrown aside with the sparkling trifles of the Christmas tree, but an honest book, to be admired in the season of pleasant remembrances for its artistic beauty; and, when the holydays are over, to be placed for frequent and affectionate consultation on a favourite shelf.*"—Athenæum.

Schiller's Lay of the Bell. Sir E. Bulwer Lytton's translation; beautifully illustrated by forty-two wood Engravings, drawn by Thomas Scott, and engraved by J. D. Cooper, after the Etchings by Retzsch. Oblong 4to. cloth extra, 14s.; morocco, 25s.

Pictures of Society, Grave and Gay; comprising One Hundred Engravings on Wood. Handsomely bound in cloth, with an elaborate and novel Design, by Messrs. Leighton and Co. Royal 8vo. price 21s.

An Entirely New Edition of Edgar A. Poe's Poems. Illustrated by Eminent Artists. Small 4to. cloth extra, price 10s. 6d.

A History of Lace, from the Earliest Period; with upwards of One Hundred Illustrations and Coloured Designs. By Mrs. Bury Palliser. One volume, 8vo. choicely bound in cloth. 31s. 6d.

The Bayard Series.

CHOICE COMPANIONABLE BOOKS
FOR HOME AND ABROAD,

COMPRISING

HISTORY, BIOGRAPHY, TRAVEL, ESSAYS, NOVELETTES, ETC.

Which, under an Editor of known taste and ability, will be very choicely printed at the Chiswick Press; with Vignette Title-page, Notes, and Index; the aim being to insure permanent value, as well as present attractiveness, and to render each volume an acquisition to the libraries of a new generation of readers. Size, a handsome 16mo. bound flexible in cloth extra, gilt edges, averaging about 220 pages.

Each Volume, complete in itself, price Half-a-crown.

The earlier Volumes consist of

THE STORY OF THE CHEVALIER BAYARD. From the French of the Loyal Servant, M. de Berville, and others. By E. Walford. With Introduction and Notes by the Editor.

> " Praise of him must walk the earth
> For ever, and to noble deeds give birth.
> This is the happy warrior; this is he
> That every man in arms would wish to be."—*Wordsworth.*

THE ESSAYS OF ABRAHAM COWLEY. Comprising all his Prose Works; the Celebrated Character of Cromwell, Cutter of Coleman Street, &c. &c. With Life, Notes, and Illustrations by Dr. Hurd and others. Newly edited.

> " *Cowley's prose stamps him as a man of genius, and an improver of the English language.*"—Thos. Campbell.

ABDALLAH AND THE FOUR-LEAVED SHAMROCK. By Edouard Laboullaye, of the French Academy. Translated by Mary L. Booth.

> *One of the noblest and purest French stories ever written.*

SAINT LOUIS, KING OF FRANCE. The curious and characteristic Life of this Monarch by De Joinville. Translated by James Hutton.

> " *A king, a hero, and a man.*"—Gibbon.

TABLE-TALK AND OPINIONS OF NAPOLEON THE GREAT. A compilation from the best sources of this great man's shrewd and often prophetic thoughts, forming the best inner life of the most extraordinary man of modern times.

The Gentle Life Series.

Printed in Elzevir, on Toned Paper, and handsomely bound,
forming suitable Volumes for Presents.

Price 6s. each; or in calf extra, price 10s. 6d.

I.

THE GENTLE LIFE. Essays in Aid of the Formation of
Character of Gentlemen and Gentlewomen. Seventh Edition.

*" His notion of a gentleman is of the noblest and truest order. . . . . .
The volume is a capital specimen of what may be done by honest reason,
high feeling, and cultivated intellect. . . . A little compendium of
cheerful philosophy."*—Daily News.

*" Deserves to be printed in letters of gold, and circulated in every
house."*—Chambers's Journal.

*" The writer's object is to teach people to be truthful, sincere, generous;
to be humble-minded, but bold in thought and action."*—Spectator.

*" Full of truth and persuasiveness, the book is a valuable composition
and one to which the reader will often turn for companionship."*—Morning
Post.

*" It is with the more satisfaction that we meet with a new essayist who
delights without the smallest pedantry to quote the choicest wisdom of our
forefathers, and who abides by those old-fashioned Christian ideas of duty
which Steele and Addison, wits and men of the world, were not ashamed to
set before the young Englishmen of 1713."*—London Review.

*" Altogether the book is sterling; admirable both for its sound sense,
freedom from sentimentality, and yet thoroughly Christian in feeling as
well as principle."*—Literary Churchman.

II.

ABOUT IN THE WORLD. Essays by the Author of " The
Gentle Life."

" It is not easy to open it at any page without finding some happy idea."
Morning Post.

*" Another characteristic merit of these essays is, that they make it their
business, gently but firmly, to apply the qualifications and the corrections,
which all philanthropic theories, all general rules or maxims, or principles,
stand in need of before you can make them work."*—Literary Churchman.

*" More exquisite and finished writing, deeper and more subtle thought,
calmer and more comprehensive judgments have been reserved to produce
' About in the World.' "*—Public Opinion.

III.

FAMILIAR WORDS. An Index Verborum, or Quotation
Handook. Affording an immediate Reference to Phrases and Sentences
that have become embedded in the English language. Second and enlarged Edition.

" The most extensive dictionary of quotation we have met with."—Notes
and Queries.

" Should be on every library table, by the side of ' Roget's Thesaurus.' "
—Daily News.

" Will add to the author's credit with all honest workers."—Examiner.

" A valuable book."—London Review.

*" Almost every familiar quotation is to be found in this work, which
forms a book of reference absolutely indispensable to the literary man, and
of interest and service to the public generally. Mr. Friswell has our best
thanks for his painstaking, laborious, and conscientious work."*—City Press.

IV.

LIKE UNTO CHRIST. A new translation of the " De Imitatione Christi," usually ascribed to Thomas à Kempis. With a Vignette from an Original Drawing by Sir Thomas Lawrence.

> " *Think of the little work of Thomas à Kempis, translated into a hundred languages, and sold by millions of copies, and which, in inmost moments of deep thought, men make the guide of their hearts, and the friend of their closets.*"—Archbishop of York, at the Literary Fund, 1865.
>
> " *Could not be presented in a more exquisite form, for a more sightly volume was never seen.*"—Illustrated London News.
>
> " *An admirable version of an excellent book. Not only is the translation a thoroughly idiomatic one, but the volume itself is a specimen of beautiful typography. The foot-notes contain numerous and useful references to authorities, and interesting examples of various readings.*"—Reader.
>
> " *The preliminary essay is well-written, good, and interesting.*"—Saturday Review.
>
> " *Evinces independent scholarship, a profound feeling for the original, and a minute attention to delicate shades of expression, which may well make it acceptable even to those who can enjoy the work without a translator's aid.*"—Nonconformist.

V.

ESSAYS BY MONTAIGNE. Edited, Compared, Revised, and Annotated by the Author of " The Gentle Life." With Vignette Portrait.

> " *The present edition of Montaigne is a charming specimen of typography, and does great credit to its publishers. Such an edition of Montaigne has long been wanting.*"—Press.
>
> " *The reader really gets in a compact form all of the charming, chatty Montaigne that he needs to know.*"—Observer.
>
> "*This edition is pure of questionable matter, and its perusal is calculated to enrich without corrupting the mind of the reader.*"—Daily News.
>
> " *We should be glad if any words of ours could help to bespeak a large circulation for this handsome attractive book; and who can refuse his homage to the good-humoured industry of the editor.*"—Illustrated Times

VI.

THE COUNTESS OF PEMBROKE'S ARCADIA. Written by Sir Philip Sidney. Edited, with Notes, by the Author of " The Gentle Life." Dedicated, by permission, to the Earl of Derby. 7s. 6d.

> *"All the best things in the Arcadia are retained intact in Mr. Friswell's edition, and even brought into greater prominence than in the original, by the curtailment of some of its inferior portions, and the omission of most of its eclogues and other metrical digressions.*"—Examiner.
>
> " *The book is now presented to the modern reader in a shape the most likely to be acceptable in these days of much literature and fastidious taste.*"—Daily News.
>
> " *It is a good work, therefore, to have republished the Arcadia in the elegant form in which it now lies before us, and our acknowledgments are due both to publisher and editor;—to the publisher for the extremely graceful form in which the book appears;—to the editor for the care he has bestowed upon the text and its literary illustration. The subsequent additions to the Arcadia by Sir W. Alexander, by W. B., and by Mr. Johnstone, are all rejected. Other interpolations have been cut down, if not entirely cut out. Obsolete words and usages are commented on in succinct notes, and there is an alphabetical index to all such explanations, so as to give the edition as much philological value as possible.*"—Literary Churchman.
>
> " *It was in itself a thing so interesting as a development of English literature, that we are thankful to Mr. Friswell for reproducing, in a very elegant volume, the chief work of the gallant and chivalrous, the gay yet learned knight, who patronized the muse of Spenser, and fell upon the bloody field of Zutphen, leaving behind him a light of heroism and humane compassion which would shed an eternal glory on his name, though all he ever wrote had perished with himself.*"—London Review.

VI.

THE GENTLE LIFE. Second Series.

*" There is not a single thought in the volume that does not contribute in
some measure to the formation of a true gentleman."*—Daily News.

*" Will refresh the purest soul, and do much to inform the general
reader."*—Press.

" These charming collection of essays."—London Review.

*" There is the same mingled power and simplicity which makes the
author so emphatically a first-rate essayist, giving a fascination in each
essay which will make this volume at least as popular as its elder brother."*
—Star.

" These essays are amongst the best in our language."—Public Opinion.

VIII.

VARIA : Readings from Rare Books. Reprinted, by permission, from the *Saturday Review, Spectator,* &c. Crown 8vo. 6s.

CONTENTS:—The Angelic Doctor, Nostradamus, Thomas à Kempis,
Dr. John Faustus, Quevedo, Mad. Guyon, Paracelsus, Howell the
Traveller, Michael Scott, Lodowick Muggleton, Sir Thomas Browne
George Psalmanazar, The Highwaymen, The Spirit World.

*" An extremely pretty and agreeable volume. We can strongly recom-
mend it to any one who has a fancy for the bye-ways of literature."*—
Guardian.

*" The books discussed in this volume are no less valuable than they are
rare, but life is not long enough to allow a reader to wade through such thick
folios, and therefore the compiler is entitled to the gratitude of the public
for having sifted their contents, and thereby rendered their treasures available to the general reader."*—Observer.

*" The same scholarly style which distinguished the earlier volumes is
clearly distinguishable here. The author has the excellent gift of uniting,
in a very high degree, the charm which interests with the power which in-
structs."*—Observer.

IX.

A CONCORDANCE OR VERBAL INDEX to the whole of Milton's Poetical Works. Comprising upwards of 20,000 References. By Charles D. Cleveland, LL.D. With Vignette Portrait of Milton. 1 vol. small post, printed on toned paper, at the Chiswick Press. 6s.

*** This work affords an immediate reference to any passage in any
edition of Milton's Poems, to which it may be justly termed an indispensable Appendix.

*" An elegant volume, and, so far as a short use of it gives one a right to
pronounce, fully to be depended upon."*—Illustrated Times.

*" An invaluable Index, which the publishers have done a public service
in reprinting."*—Notes and Queries.

*" By the admirers of Milton the book will be highly appreciated, but its
chief value will, if we mistake not, be found in the fact that it is a compact
word-book of the English language."*—Record.

*" Answers honestly to its title, and is well-printed, portable, and con-
venient."*—Guardian.

THE SILENT HOUR. Essays for Sunday Reading, Original and Selected. By the Author of " The Gentle Life."

LITERATURE, WORKS OF REFERENCE AND EDUCATION.

DAVID GRAY, and other Essays on Poetry and Poets. By Robert Buchanan. Small post 8vo.

The Book of the Sonnet: being Selections, with an Essay on Sonnets and Sonneteers, by the late Leigh Hunt. Edited, from the original MS., with additions, by S. Adams Lee. 2 vols. 18s.

Poems of the Inner Life. Selected chiefly from modern Authors, by permission. Small post 8vo. 6s.; gilt edges, 6s. 6d.

Life Portraits of Shakspeare; with an Examination of the Authenticity, and a History of the various Representations of the Poet. Illustrated by Photographs of authentic and received Portraits. Square 8vo. 21s.; or with Photograph of the Will, 25s.

Richmond and its Inhabitants, from the Olden Time. With Memoirs and Notes by Richard Crisp. With Illustrations. Post 8vo. 10s. 6d.

The Complete Poetical Works of John Milton, with a Life of the Author: and a Verbal Index containing upwards of 20,000 references to all the Poems. By Charles Dexter Cleveland. New Edition. 8vo. 12s.

Her Majesty's Mails: a History of the Post Office, and an Industrial Account of its Present Condition. By Wm. Lewins, of the General Post Office. 2nd edition, revised, and enlarged, with a Photographic Portrait of Sir Rowland Hill. Small post 8vo. 6s.

" Will take its stand as a really useful book of reference on the history of the Post. We heartily recommend it as a thoroughly careful performance."—Saturday Review.

" In conclusion, we have only to say that Mr. Lewins's book is a most useful and complete one—one that should be put into the hands of every young Englishman and foreigner desiring to know how our institutions grow."—Reader.

The Origin and History of the English Language, and of the early literature it embodies. By the Hon. George P. Marsh, U. S. Minister at Turin, Author of " Lectures on the English Language." 8vo. cloth extra, 16s.

Lectures on the English Language; forming the Introductory Series to the foregoing Work. By the same Author. 8vo. Cloth, 16s. This is the only author's edition.

Man and Nature; or, Physical Geography as Modified by Human Action. By George P. Marsh, Author of " Lectures on the English Language," &c. 8vo. cloth, 14s.

" Mr. Marsh, well known as the author of two of the most scholarly works yet published on the English language, sets himself in excellent spirit, and with immense learning, to indicate the character, and, approximately, the extent of the changes produced by human action in the physical condition of the globe we inhabit. In four divisions of his work, Mr. Marsh traces the history of human industry as shown in the extensive modification and extirpation of animal and vegetable life in the woods, the waters, and the sands; and, in a concluding chapter, he discusses the probable and possible geographical changes yet to be wrought. The whole of Mr. Marsh's book is an eloquent showing of the duty of care in the establishment of harmony between man's life and the forces of nature, so as to bring to their highest points the fertility of the soil, the vigour of the animal life, and the salubrity of the climate, on which we have to depend for the physical well-being of mankind."—Examiner.

A History of Banks for Savings; including a full account of the origin and progress of Mr. Gladstone's recent prudential measures. By William Lewins, Author of " Her Majesty's Mails." 8vo. cloth. 12s.

English and Scotch Ballads, &c. An extensive Collection. Designed as a Complement to the Works of the British Poets, and embracing nearly all the Ancient and Traditionary Ballads both of England and Scotland, in all the important varieties of form in which they are extant, with Notices of the kindred Ballads of other Nations. Edited by F. J. Child, new Edition, revised by the Editor. 8 vols. fcap. cloth, 3s. 6d. each.

The English Catalogue of Books: giving the date of publication of every book published from 1835 to 1863, in addition to the title, size, price, and publisher, in one alphabet. An entirely new work, combining the Copyrights of the " London Catalogue" and the " British Catalogue." One thick volume of 900 pages, half morocco, 45s.

Index to the Subjects of Books published in the United Kingdom during the last Twenty Years—1837-1857. Containing as many as 74,000 references, under subjects, so as to ensure immediate reference to the books on the subject required, each giving title, price, publisher, and date. Two valuable Appendices are also given—A, containing full lists of all Libraries, Collections, Series, and Miscellanies—and B, a List of Literary Societies, Printing Societies, and their Issues. One vol. royal 8vo. Morocco, 1l. 6s.

The Handy-book of Patent and Copyright Law, English and Foreign. By James Fraser, Esq. Post 8vo. cloth, 4s. 6d.

A Concise Summary of the Law of English and French Copyright Law and International Law, by Peter Burke. 12mo. 5s.

The American Catalogue, or English Guide to American Literature; giving the full title of original Works published in the United States of America since the year 1800, with especial reference to the works of interest to Great Britain, with the size, price, place, date of publication, and London prices. With comprehensive Index. 8vo. 2s. 6d. Also Supplement, 1837-60. 8vo. 6d.

Dr. Worcester's New and Greatly Enlarged Dictionary of the English Language. Adapted for Library or College Reference, comprising 40,000 Words more than Johnson's Dictionary, and 250 pages more than the Quarto Edition of Webster's Dictionary. In one Volume, royal 4to. cloth, 1,834 pp. price 31s. 6d. Half russia, 2l. 2s. The Cheapest Book ever published.

" The volumes before us show a vast amount of diligence; but with Webster it is diligence in combination with fancifulness,—with Worcester in combination with good sense and judgment. Worcester's is the soberer and safer book, and may be pronounced the best existing English Lexicon."—*Athenæum*.

The Publishers' Circular, and General Record of British and Foreign Literature; giving a transcript of the title-page of every work published in Great Britain, and every work of interest published abroad, with lists of all the publishing houses.

Published regularly on the 1st and 15th of every Month, and forwarded post free to all parts of the world on payment of 8s. per annum.

The Ladies' Reader : with some Plain and Simple Rules and Instructions for a good style of Reading aloud, and a variety of Selections for Exercise. By George Vandenhoff, M.A., Author of " The Art of Elocution." Fcap. 8vo. Cloth, 5s.

The Clerical Assistant: an Elocutionary Guide to the Reading
of the Scriptures and the Liturgy, several passages being marked for
Pitch and Emphasis: with some Observations on Clerical Bronchitus.
By George Vandenhoff, M.A. Fcap. 8vo. Cloth, 3s. 6d.

The Art of Elocution as an essential part of Rhetoric, with instructions in Gesture, and an Appendix of Oratorical, Poetical and Dramatic extracts. By George Vandenhoff, M A. Third Edition. 5s.

An English Grammar. By Matthew Green. New edition revised. 12mo. cloth, 1s. 6d.

Latin-English Lexicon, by Dr. Andrews. New Edition. 8vo. 18s.
The superiority of this justly-famed Lexicon is retained over all others
by the fulness of its quotations, the including in the vocabulary proper
names, the distinguishing whether the derivative is classical or otherwise,
the exactness of the references to the original authors, and in the price.
" *Every page bears the impress of industry and care.*"—Athenæum.
" *The best Latin Dictionary, whether for the scholar or advanced student.*"—Spectator.
" *We never saw such a book published at such a price.*"—Examiner.

The Farm and Fruit of Old. From Virgil. By a Market Gardener. 1s.

Usque ad Cælum ; or, the Dwellings of the People. By Thomas
Hare, Esq., Barrister-at-Law. Fcap. 1s.

A Few Hints on proving Wills, &c, without professional assistance. By a Probate-Court Official. Fcap. cloth, 6d.

A Handbook to the Charities of London. By Sampson Low,
Jun. Comprising an Account of upwards of 800 Institutions chiefly in
London and its Vicinity. A Guide to the Benevolent and to the Unfor-
tunate. Cloth limp, 1s. 6d.

The Charities of London : an Account of the Origin, Operations,
and general Condition of the Charitable, Educational, and Religious
Institutions of London. By Sampson Low, Jun. 8th publication (com-
menced 1836). With an Alphabetical Summary of the whole corrected
to April, 1867. Cloth, 5s.

Prince Albert's Golden Precepts. *Second Edition,* with Photograph. A Memorial of the Prince Consort; comprising Maxims and
Extracts from Addresses of His late Royal Highness. Many now for
the first time collected and carefully arranged. With an Index. Royal
16mo. beautifully printed on toned paper, cloth, gilt edges, 2s. 6d.

Our Little Ones in Heaven : Thoughts in Prose and Verse, selected from the Writings of favourite Authors; with Frontispiece after
Sir Joshua Reynolds. Fcap. 8vo. cloth extra, 3s. 6d.

Six Essays on Commons Preservation. Written in Competition
for Prizes offered by Henry W. Peek, Esq.
By John M. Maidlow, M.D. Lincoln's Inn, Barrister at Law, (to whom the
first Prize was awarded).
William Phipson Beale, Lincoln's Inn, (to whom the second Prize was
awarded).
F. Octavius Crump, Middle Temple.
Henry Hicks Hocking, St. John's College, Oxford.
Robert Hunter, M.A. London University.
Edgar H. Lockhart, M.A. Lincoln's Inn.

Rural Essays. With Practical Hints on Farming and Agricultural Architecture. By Ik. Marvel, Author of " Reveries of a Bachelor." 1 vol. post 8vo. with numerous Illustrations. 8s.

The Book of the Hand; or, the Science of Modern Palmistry. Chiefly according to the Systems of D'Arpentigny and Desbarolles. By A. R. Craig, M.A. Crown 8vo. 7s. 6d.

NEW BOOKS FOR YOUNG PEOPLE.

TORIES of the Gorilla Country. By P. Du Chaillu, Author of " Explorations in Equatorial Africa;" with Illustrations. [*Just ready.*

Last Rambles amongst the Indians beyond the Rocky Mountains and the Andes. By George Catlin; with numerous Illustrations by the Author. Crown 8vo. 5s.

Life amongst the Indians. An entirely New Edition, by the same Author. Crown 8vo. 5s.

Alwyn Morton; his School and Schoolfellows. A Story of St. Nicholas' Grammar School. Crown 8vo. with Illustrations. 5s.

Queer Little People. By Harriet Beecher Stowe, Author of " Uncle Tom's Cabin." Fcap. Popular Edition. price 1s.

A Bushel of Merry Thoughts. By William Busch. Described and Ofnamented by Harry Rogers, with upwards of 100 Humerous Illustrations. Oblong, price 2s. 6d.

The Story without an End. From the German of Carové, by Sarah Austin. Illustrated with 16 Original Drawings by E. V. B. printed in colours by Messrs. Leighton Brothers. Fcap. 4to. cloth extra. [*Shortly.*

Also, Cheap Edition. Illustrated by Harvey. Fcap. 16mo. cloth extra, 2s. 6d.

● " Of its kind one of the best books that was ever written." *Quarterly Review*, Jan. 1867.

The Marvels of Optics. By F. Marion. Translated and edited by C. W. Quin. With 60 Illustrations. Small post 8vo. cloth extra. [*Shortly.*

Thunder and Lightning. Translated from the French of De Fonvielle, by Dr. T. L. Phipson. With 38 full-page Woodcuts. Small post 8vo. cloth extra. [*Shortly*

The Silver Skates; a Story of Holland Life. Edited by W. H. G. Kingston. Illustrated, small post 8vo. cloth extra, 3s. 6d.

The Boy's Own Book of Boats. By W. H. G. Kingston. Illustrations by E. Weedon, engraved by W. J. Linton. An Entirely New Edition. Fcap. 8vo. cloth, 3s. 6d.
" *This well-written, well-wrought book.*"—Athenæum.

Also by the same Author,

Ernest Bracebridge: or, Boy's Own Book of Sports. 3s. 6d.
The Fire Ships. A Story of the Days of Lord Cochrane. 5s.
The Cruise of the Frolic. 5s.
Jack Buntline: the Life of a Sailor Boy. 2s.

The Voyage of the Constance; a tale of the Polar Seas. By Mary Gillies. New Edition, with 8 Illustrations by Charles Keene. Fcap. 3s. 6d.

The True History of Dame Perkins and her Grey Mare. Told for the Countryside and the Fireside. By Lindon Meadows. With Eight Coloured Illustrations by Phiz. Small 4to. cloth, 5*s.*

Great Fun Stories. Told by Thomas Hood and Thomas Archer to 48 coloured pictures of Edward Wehnert. Beautifully printed in colours, 10*s.* 6*d.* Plain, 6*s.* well bound in cloth, gilt edges.

Or in Eight separate books, 1*s. each, coloured.* 6*d. plain.*

The Cherry-coloured Cat. The Live Rocking-Horse. Master Mischief. Cousin Nellie. Harry High-Stepper. Grandmamma's Spectacles. How the House was Built. Dog Toby.

Great Fun and More Fun for our Little Friends. By Harriet Myrtle. With Edward Wehnert's Pictures. 2 vols. each 5*s.*

Under the Waves; or the Hermit Crab in Society. By Annie E. Ridley. Impl. 16mo. cloth extra, with coloured illustration Cloth, 4*s.*; gilt edges, 4*s.* 6*d.*

Also beautifully Illustrated:—

Little Bird Red and Little Bird Blue. Coloured, 5*s.*
Snow-Flakes, and what they told the Children. Coloured, 5*s.*
Child's Book of the Sagacity of Animals. 5*s.*; or coloured, 7*s.* 6*d.*
Child's Picture Fable Book. 5*s.*; or coloured, 7*s.* 6*d.*
Child's Treasury of Story Books. 5*s.*; or coloured, 7*s.* 6*d.*
The Nursery Playmate. 200 Pictures. 5*s.*; or coloured, 9*s.*

How to Make Miniature Pumps and a Fire-Engine: a Book for Boys. With Seven Illustrations. Fcap. 8vo. 1*s.*

Emily's Choice; an Australian Tale. By Maud Jeanne Franc, Author of " Vermont Vale," &c. Small post 8vo. 5*s.*

Vermont Vale; or, Home Pictures in Australia. By Maud Jeanne Franc. Small post 8vo, with a frontispiece, cloth extra, 5*s.*

Marian; or, the Light of some one's Home. By Maud Jeanne Franc. Small post 8vo. 5*s.*

Golden Hair; a Story for Young People. By Sir Lascelles Wraxall, Bart. With Eight full page Illustrations, 5*s.*

Also, same price, full of Illustrations:—

Black Panther; a Boy's Adventures among the Red Skins.
Stanton Grange; or, Boy's Life at a Private Tutor's. By the Rev. C. J. Atkinson.

Paul Duncan's Little by Little; a Tale for Boys. Edited by Frank Freeman. With an Illustration by Charles Keene. Fcap. 8vo. cloth 2*s.*; gilt edges, 2*s.* 6*d.* Also, same price,

Boy Missionary; a Tale for Young People. By Mrs. J. M. Parker.
Difficulties Overcome. By Miss Brightwell.
The Babes in the Basket: a Tale in the West Indian Insurrection.
Jack Buntline: the Life of a Sailor Boy. By W. H. G. Kingston.

The Swiss Family Robinson; or, the Adventures of a Father and Mother and Four Sons on a Desert Island. With Explanatory Notes and Illustrations. First and Second Series. New Edition, complete in one volume, 3*s.* 6*d.*

Geography for my Children. By Mrs. Harriet Beecher Stowe. Author of "Uncle Tom's Cabin," &c. Arranged and Edited by an English Lady, under the Direction of the Authoress. With upwards of Fifty Illustrations. Cloth extra, 4s. 6d.

Stories of the Woods ; or, the Adventures of Leather-Stocking : A Book for Boys, compiled from Cooper's Series of "Leather-Stocking Tales." Fcap. cloth, Illustrated, 5s.

Child's Play. Illustrated with Sixteen Coloured Drawings by E. V. B., printed in fac-simile by W. Dickes' process, and ornamented with Initial Letters. New edition, with India paper tints, royal 8vo. cloth extra, bevelled cloth, 7s. 6d. The Original Edition of this work was published at One Guinea.

Child's Delight. Forty-two Songs for the Little Ones, with forty-two Pictures. 1s. ; coloured, 2s. 6d.

Goody Platts, and her Two Cats. By Thomas Miller. Fcap. 8vo. cloth, 1s.

Little Blue Hood : a Story for Little People. By Thomas Miller, with coloured frontispiece. Fcap. 8vo. cloth, 2s. 6d.

Mark Willson's First Reader. By the Author of " The Picture Alphabet" and "The Picture Primer." With 120 Pictures. 1s.

The Picture Alphabet; or Child's First Letter Book. With new and original Designs. 6d.

The Picture Primer. 6d.

HISTORY AND BIOGRAPHY.

THE Life of John James Audubon, the Naturalist, including his Romantic Adventures in the back woods of America, Correspondence with celebrated Europeans, &c. Edited, from materials supplied by his widow, by Robert Buchanan. 8vo. [*Shortly*.

Madame Recamier, Memoirs and Correspondence of. Translated from the French and edited by J. M. Luyster. With Portrait. Crown 8vo. 7s. 6d.

The Conspiracy of Count Fieschi : an Episode in Italian History. By M. De Celesia. Translated by David Hilton, Esq., Author of a "History of Brigandage." With Portrait. 8vo. 12s.

 " *This work will be read with great interest, and will assist in a comprehensive study of Italian history.*"—Observer.

 " *As an epitome of Genoese history for thirty years it is exceedingly interesting, as well as exceedingly able. The English public are greatly indebted to Mr. Wheeler for introducing to them a historian so full of verve, so expert, and so graceful in the manipulation of facts.*"—London Review.

 " *This vigorous Memoir of Count Gianluigi Fieschi, written in excellent Italian, is here reproduced in capital English.*"—Examiner.

Christian Heroes in the Army and Navy. By Charles Rogers, LL.D. Author of "Lyra Britannica." Crown 8vo. 3s. 6d.

The Navy of the United States during the Rebellion; comprising
the origin and increase of the Ironclad Fleet. By Charles B. Boynton,
D.D. 2 vols. 8vo. Illustrated with numerous plain and coloured Engravings of the more celebrated vessels. Vol. I. now ready. 20s.

A History of America, from the Declaration of Independence of
the thirteen United States, to the close of the campaign of 1778. By
George Bancroft; forming the third volume of the History of the American Revolution. 8vo. cloth, 12s.

A History of Brigandage in Italy; with Adventures of the
more celebrated Brigands. By David Hilton, Esq. 2 vols. post 8vo.
cloth, 16s.

A History of the Gipsies, with Specimens of the Gipsy Language.
By Walter Simson. Post 8vo, 10s. 6d.

A History of West Point, the United States Military Academy
and its Military Importance. By Capt. E. C. Boynton, A.M. With
Plans and Illustrations. 8vo. 21s.

The Twelve Great Battles of England, from Hastings to Waterloo.
With Plans, fcap. 8vo. cloth extra, 3s. 6d.

George Washington's Life, by Washington Irving. 5 vols.
royal 8vo. 12s. each   Library Illustrated Edition. 5 vols. Imp. 8vo. 4l. 4s.

Plutarch's Lives. An entirely new Library Edition, carefully
revised and corrected, with some Original Translations by the Editor.
Edited by A. H. Clough, Esq. sometime Fellow of Oriel College, Oxford,
and late Professor of English Language and Literature at University
College. 5 vols. 8vo. cloth. 2l. 10s.

   " ' *Plutarch's Lives* ' *will be read by thousands, and in the version of Mr.
Clough.*"—Quarterly Review.
   " *Mr. Clough's work is worthy of all praise, and we hope that it will
tend to revive the study of Plutarch.*"—Times.

Life of John Adams, 2nd President of the United States, by C.
F. Adams. 8vo. 14s. Life and Works complete, 10 vols. 14s. each.

Life and Administration of Abraham Lincoln. Fcap. 8vo.
stiff cover, 1s.; with map, speeches, &c. crown 8vo. 3s. 6d.

The Prison Life of Jefferson Davis; embracing Details and
Incidents in his Captivity, together with Conversations on Topics of
great Public Interest. By John J. Craven, M.D., Physician of the
Prisoner during his Confinement. 1 vol. post 8vo. price 8s.

The Life and Correspondence of Benjamin Silliman, M.D.,
LL.D., late Professor of Chemistry, Mineralogy, and Geology in Yale
College, U.S.A. Chiefly from his own MSS. and Diary. By George
Fisher. With Portrait. 2 vols. post 8vo. price 24s.

Six Months at the White House with Abraham Lincoln: the
Story of a Picture. By F. B. Carpenter. 12mo; 7s. 6d.

TRAVEL AND ADVENTURE.

SOCIAL Life of the Chinese: a Daguerreotype of Daily Life in China. Condensed from the Work of the Rev. J. Doolittle, by the Rev. Paxton Hood. With above 100 Illustrations. Post 8vo. 　　　　　　　　　　　　　|*Nearly ready.*

" The book before us supplies a large quantity of minute and valuable information concerning a country of high commercial and national importance, and as to which the amount of popular information is even more than ordinarily scanty. The author speaks with the authority of an eye-witness; and the minuteness of detail which his work exhibits will, to most readers, go far to establish its trustworthiness."—Saturday Review.

" We have no hesitation in saying that from these pages may be gathered more information about the social life of the Chinese than can be obtained from any other source. The importance of the work as a key to a right understanding of the character of so vast a portion of the human race ought to insure it an extensive circulation."—Athenæum.

The Open Polar Sea: a Narrative of a Voyage of Discovery towards the North Pole. By Dr. Isaac I. Hayes. An entirely new and cheaper edition. With Illustrations. Small post 8vo. 6s.

" The story of this last Arctic enterprise is most stirring, and it is well for Dr. Hayes's literary venture that this is the case, for it must be conceded that the great number of works on Arctic voyages has somewhat dulled the edge of curiosity with which they were formerly received by the public; but a spell of fascination will ever cling to the narrative of brave and adventurous travel, and Dr. Hayes's heroism and endurance are of no common order. . . . This was the crowning feat of Dr. Hayes's enterprise. He set up a cairn, within which he deposited a record, stating that after a toilsome march of forty-six days from his winter harbour, he stood on the shores of the Polar basin, on the most northerly land ever reached by man. The latitude attained was 81 deg. 35 min.; that reached by Parry over the ice was 82 deg. 45 min. . . . What we have said of Dr. Hayes's book will, we trust, send many readers to its pages." —Athenæum.

LETTERS ON ENGLAND. By M. Louis Blanc. Two Series, each 2 vols. 16s.

" These sparkling letters written on and within ' Old England' by a wit, a scholar, and a gentleman."—Athenæum.

" Letters full of epigram, and of singular clearness and sense."—Spectator.

" The author is very fair in his opinions of English habits, English institutions, and English public men; his eulogy is discriminating, and his censures are for the most part such as Englishmen themselves must acknowledge to be just."—Saturday Review.

" Perhaps the very cleverest sketches in this clever and amusing book are his short, pithy, graphic summaries of persons and characters. His contrasts especially are very effectively done. The book is well worth reading, and is full of suggestive thought and pointed writing."—Guardian.

" He never conceals his admiration for the all-pervading liberty of Britain, and he points out with incisive distinctness our failure to realize its great fruits, as well as otherwise to fulfil our national destiny. Whatever he touches, whether it be to us a glory or a disgrace, he illuminates it, and brings it distinctly before the gaze, that we and others may cherish it or flee from it."—Daily News.

Brazil and the Brazilians. Pourtrayed in Historical and Descriptive Sketches by the Rev. James C. Fletcher and the Rev. D. P. Kidder, D. D. An enlargement of the original work, presenting the Material and Moral Progress of the Empire during the last Ten Years, and the results of the Authors' recent Explorations on the Amazon to the verge of Peru. With 150 Illustrations. 8vo. cloth extra. 18s.

The Old Country. Its Scenery, Art, and People. By James M. Hoppin. 1 vol. small post 8vo. 7s. 6d.

The Black Country and its Green Border Land; or, Expeditions and Explorations round Birmingham, Wolverhampton, &c. By Elihu Burritt. [*Nearly ready.*

A Walk from London to the Land's End. By Elihu Burritt, Author of "A Walk from London to John O'Groats:" with several Illustrations. Small post 8vo. 6s. Uniform with the cheaper edition of "John O'Groats."

A Walk from London to John O'Groats. With Notes by the Way. By Elihu Burritt. Second and cheaper edition. With Photographic Portrait of the Author. Small post 8vo. 6s.

New Paris Guide. Paris. Par les Principaux Ecrivains et Artistes de la France. Première Partie—Le Science, l'Art. 2 vols. 10s. each. Sold separately.

"It appears to be such a Guide as no other capital can boast; the intellect of Paris employed in the faithful illustration of the form and spirit of the town, and the chief things that are in it; an encyclopædia of Paris, by the most competent hands, free from encyclopædic dullness, readable as a romance, instructive as a dictionary, full of good pictures, and so cheap that little less than the great sale it deserves can pay what must have been the cost of its production."—*Examiner.*

The Diamond Guide to Paris. 320 pages, with a Map and upwards of 100 Illustrations. Cloth, 2s. 6d.

Travelling in Spain in the Present Day. By Henry Blackburn. With numerous illustrations. Square post 8vo, cloth extra, 16s.

The Voyage Alone; a Sail in the "Yawl, Rob Roy." By John M'Gregor, Author of "A Thousand Miles in the Rob Roy Canoe. With Illustrations. [*Shortly.*

A Thousand Miles in the Rob Roy Canoe, on Rivers and Lakes of Europe. By John Macgregor, M.A. Fifth edition. With a map, and numerous Illustrations. Fcap. 8vo. cloth, 5s.

The Rob Roy on the Baltic. A Canoe Voyage in Norway, Sweden, &c. By John Macgregor, M.A. With a Map and numerous Illustrations. Fcap. 8vo. 5s.

Description of the New Rob Roy Canoe, built for a Voyage through Norway, Sweden, and the Baltic. Dedicated to the Canoe Club by the Captain. With Illustrations. Price 1s.

Captain Hall's Life with the Esquimaux. New and cheaper Edition, with Coloured Engravings and upwards of 100 Woodcuts. With a Map. Price 7s. 6d. cloth extra. Forming the cheapest and most popular Edition of a work on Arctic Life and Exploration ever published.

"*This is a very remarkable book, and unless we very much misunderstand both him and his book, the author is one of those men of whom great nations do well to be proud.*"—Spectator.

A Winter in Algeria, 1863-4. By Mrs. George Albert Rogers. With illustrations. 8vo. cloth, 12s.

Turkey. By J. Lewis Farley, F.S.S., Author of "Two Years in Syria." With Illustrations in Chromo-lithography, and a Portrait of His Highness Fuad Pasha. 8vo. 12s.

Wild Scenes in South America; or, Life in the Llanos of Venezuela. By Don Ramon Paez. Numerous Illustrations. Post 8vo. cl. 10s. 6d.

The Land of Thor. By J. Rosse Browne. With upwards of 100 Illustrations. Cloth, 8s. 6d.

The Story of the Great March : a Diary of General Sherman's
Campaign through Georgia and the Carolinas. By Brevet-Major G. W.
Nichols, Aide-de-Camp to General Sherman. With a coloured Map and
numerous Illustrations. 12mo. cloth, price 7*s.* 6*d.*

The Prairie and Overland Traveller; a Companion for Emigrants,
Traders, Travellers, Hunters, and Soldiers, traversing great Plains and
Prairies. By Capt. R. B. Marcey. Illustrated. Fcap. 8vo. cloth, 2*s.* 6*d.*

Home and Abroad (*Second Series*). A Sketch-book of Life, Men,
and Travel, by Bayard Taylor. With Illustrations, post 8vo. cloth,
8*s.* 6*d.*

Northern Travel.   Summer and Winter Pictures of Sweden,
Lapland, and Norway, by Bayard Taylor. 1 vol. post 8vo., cloth, 8*s.* 6*d.*
Also by the same Author, each complete in 1 vol., with Illustrations.
Central Africa ; Egypt and the White Nile. 7*s.* 6*d.*
India, China, and Japan. 7*s.* 6*d.*
Palestine, Asia Minor, Sicily, and Spain. 7*s.* 6*d.*
Travels in Greece and Russia. With an Excursion to Crete. 7*s.* 6*d.*
Colorado. A Summer Trip. 7*s.* 6*d.*

After the War : a Southern Tour extending from May, 1865,
to May, 1866. By Whitlaw Reid, Librarian to the House of Representatives. Illustrated. Post 8vo. price 10*s.* 6*d.*

Thirty Years of Army Life on the Border. By Colonel R. B.
Marcy, U.S.A., Author of " The Prairie Traveller." With numerous
Illustrations. 8vo. price 12*s.*

INDIA, AMERICA, AND THE COLONIES.

THE Great West. Guide and Hand-Book for Travellers,
Miners, and Emigrants to the Western and Pacific States of
America; with a new Map. By Edward H. Hall. 1*s.*
Appleton's Hand-Book of American Travel — The
Northern Tour; with Maps of Routes of Travel and the principal
Cities. By Edward H. Hall. New Edition. 1 vol. post 8vo. 12*s.*

Twelve Years in Canterbury, New Zealand; with Visits to the
other Provinces, and Reminiscences of the Route Home through Australia. By Mrs. Charles Thomson. Fcap. 8vo. cloth, 3*s.* 6*d.*

Life's Work as it is; or, the Emigrant's Home in Australia. By
a Colonist. Small post 8vo. 3*s.* 6*d.*.

Canada in 1864; a Hand-book for Settlers. By Henry T. N.
Chesshyre. Fcap. 8vo. 2*s.* 6*d.*
" *When a man has something to say he can convey a good deal of matter
in a few words. This book is but a small book, yet it leaves nothing untold
that requires telling. The author is himself a settler, and knows what
information is most necessary for those who are about to become settlers.*"
—Athenæum.

A History of the Discovery and Exploration of Australia ; or,
an Account of the Progress of Geographical Discovery in that Continent, from the Earliest Period to the Present Day. By the Rev. Julian
E. Tenison Woods, F.R.G.S., &c., &c. 2 vols. demy 8vo. cloth, 28*s.*

South Australia : its Progress and Prosperity. By A. Forster, Esq. Demy 8vo. cloth, with Map, 15s.

Jamaica and the Colonial Office : Who caused the Crisis ? By George Price, Esq. late Member of the Executive Committees of Governors. 8vo. cloth, with a Plan, 5s.

The Colony of Victoria : its History, Commerce, and Gold Mining: its Social and Political Institutions, down to the End of 1863. With Remarks, Incidental and Comparative, upon the other Australian Colonies. By William Westgarth, Author of " Victoria and the Gold Mines," &c. 8vo. with a Map, cloth, 16s.

Tracks of McKinlay and Party across Australia. By John Davis, one of the Expedition. With an Introductory View of recent Explorations. By Wm. Westgarth. With numerous Illustrations in chromolithography, and Map. 8vo. cloth, 16s.

The Progress and Present State of British India ; a Manual of Indian History, Geography, and Finance, for general use : based upon Official Documents, furnished under the authority of Her Majesty's Secretary of State for India. By Montgomery Martin, Esq., Author of a " History of the British Colonies," &c. Post 8vo. cloth, 10s. 6d.

The Cotton Kingdom : a Traveller's Observations on Cotton and Slavery in America, based upon three former volumes of Travels and Explorations. By Frederick Law Olmsted. With Map. 2 vols. post 8vo. 1l. 1s.

A History of the Origin, Formation, and Adoption of the Constitution of the United States of America, with Notices of its Principal Framers. By George Ticknor Curtis, Esq. 2 vols. 8vo. Cloth, 1l. 4s.

The Principles of Political Economy applied to the Condition, the Resources, and Institutions of the American People. By Francis Bowen. 8vo. Cloth, 14s.

A History of New South Wales from the Discovery of New Holland in 1616 to the present time. By the late Roderick Flanagan, Esq., Member of the Philosophical Society of New South Wales. 2 vols. 8vo. 24s.

Canada and its Resources. Two Prize Essays, by Hogan and Morris. 7s., or separately, 1s. 6d. each, and Map, 3s.

SCIENCE AND DISCOVERY.

DICTIONARY of Photography, on the Basis of Sutton's Dictionary. Rewritten by Professor Dawson, of King's College, Editor of the " Journal of Photography ;" and Thomas Sutton, B.A., Editor of " Photograph Notes." 8vo. with numerous Illustrations. 8s. 6d.

A History of the Atlantic Telegraph. By Henry M. Field. 12mo. 7s. 6d.

The Structure of Animal Life. By Louis Agassiz. With 46 Diagrams. 8vo. cloth, 10s. 6d.

The Physical Geography of the Sea and its Meteorology ; or, the
Economy of the Sea and its Adaptations, its Salts, its Waters, its Climates,
its Inhabitants, and whatever there may be of general interest in its Commercial Uses or Industrial Pursuits. By Commander M. F. Maury, LL.D.
Tenth Edition. With Charts. Post 8vo. cloth extra, 5s.

*" To Captain Maury we are indebted for much information—indeed, for
all that mankind possesses—of the crust of the earth beneath the blue
waters of the Atlantic and Pacific oceans. Hopelessly scientific would
these subjects be in the hands of most men, yet upon each and all of them
Captain Maury enlists our attention, or charms us with explanations and
theories, replete with originality and genius. His is indeed a nautical
manual, a hand-book of the sea, investing with fresh interest every wave
that beats upon our shores; and it cannot fail to awaken in both sailors
and landsmen a craving to know more intimately the secrets of that wonderful element. The good that Maury has done in awakening the powers
of observation of the Royal and Mercantile Navies of England and America
is incalculable."*—Blackwood's Magazine.

The Kedge Anchor ; or, Young Sailor's Assistant, by William
Brady. Seventy Illustrations. 8vo. 16s.

Archaia ; or, Studies of the Cosmogony and Natural History of
the Hebrew Scriptures. By Professor Dawson, Principal of McGill
College, Canada. Post 8vo. cloth, cheaper edition, 6s.

Ichnographs, from the Sandstone of the Connecticut River,
Massachusetts, U. S. A. By James Dean, M.D. One volume, 4to. with
Forty-six Plates, cloth, 27s.

The Recent Progress of Astronomy, by Elias Loomis, LL.D.
3rd Edition. Post 8vo. 7s. 6d.

An Introduction to Practical Astronomy, by the Same. 8vo.
cloth. 8s.

Manual of Mineralogy, including Observations on Mines, Rocks,
Reduction of Ores, and the Application of the Science to the Arts, with
260 Illustrations. Designed for the Use of Schools and Colleges. By·
James D. Dana, A.M., Author of a " System of Mineralogy." New Edition, revised and enlarged. 12mo. Half bound, 7s. 6d.

Cyclopædia of Mathematical Science, by Davies and Peck. 8vo.
Sheep. 18s.

TRADE, AGRICULTURE, DOMESTIC ECONOMY, ETC.

THE Book of Farm Implements, and their Construction;
by John L. Thomas. With 200 Illustrations. 12mo. 6s. 6d.

The Practical Surveyor's Guide; by A. Duncan. Fcp.
8vo. 4s. 6d.

Villas and Cottages; by Calvert Vaux, Architect. 300 Illustrations. 8vo. cloth. 12s.

Bee-Keeping. By "The Times" Bee-master. Small post 8vo.
numerous Illustrations, cloth, 5s.

The English and Australian Cookery Book. Small post 8vo.
Coloured Illustrations, cloth extra, 4s. 6d.

The Bubbles of Finance : the Revelations of a City Man. Fcap. 8vo. fancy boards, price 2s. 6d.

The Profits of Panics. By the Author of " The Bubbles of Finance." 12mo. boards. 1s.

Coffee : A Treatise on its Nature and Cultivation. With some remarks on the management and purchase of Coffee Estates. By Arthur R. W. Lascelles. Post 8vo. cloth, 2s. 6d.

The Railway Freighter's Guide. Defining mutual liabilities of Carriers and Freighters, and explaining system of rates, accounts, invoices, checks, booking, and permits, and all other details pertaining to traffic management, as sanctioned by Acts of Parliament, Bye-laws, and General Usage. By J. S. Martin. 12mo. Cloth, 2s. 6d.

THEOLOGY.

THE Origin and History of the Books of the New Testament, Canonical and Apocryphal. Designed to show what the Bible is not, what it is, and how to use it. By Professor C. E. Stowe. 8vo. 8s. 6d. With plates, 10s. 6d.

" *The work exhibits in every page the stamp of untiring industry, personal research, and sound method. There is such a tone of hearty earnestness, vigorous thought, and clear decisive expression about the book, that one is cordially disposed to welcome a theological work which is neither unitarian in doctrine, sensational in style, nor destructive in spirit.*"—London Review.

" *The author brings out forcibly the overwhelming manuscript evidence for the books of the New Testament as compared with the like evidence for the best attested of the profane writers. . . . He adds these remarks :* ' *I insert these extracts here because the Fathers had ways of looking at the books of the Bible which in our day have nearly become obsolete, and which ought, in some measure at least, to be revived. The incredulity of our own times in regard to the Bible is due, not so much to the want of evidence as to the want of that reverence, and affection, and admiration of the Scriptures, which so distinguished the Christians of the early ages,*' *words in which we can heartily concur.*"—Churchman.

" *Without making ourselves responsible for all the writer's opinions, particularly on the question of inspiration, we have no hesitation in recording our judgment that this is one of the most useful books which our times have produced.*"—Watchman.

" *The book is very ably written, and will be read with pleasure by all those who wish to find fresh arguments to confirm them in their faith.*"—Observer.

The Vicarious Sacrifice ; grounded on Principles of Universal Obligation. By Horace Bushnell, D.D., Author of " Nature and the Supernatural, &c. Crown 8vo. 7s. 6d.

" *An important contribution to theological literature, whether we regard the amount of thought which it contains, the systematic nature of the treatise, or the practical effect of its teaching. . . . No one can rise from the study of his book without having his mind enlarged by its profound speculation, his devotion stirred by its piety, and his faith established on a broader basis of thought and knowledge.*"—Guardian.

Also by the same Author.

Christ and His Salvation. 6s.

Nature and the Supernatural. 3s. 6d

Christian Nurture. 1s. 6d.

Character of Jesus. 6d.

New Life. 1s. 6d.

Work and Play. 3s. 6d.

The Land and the Book, or Biblical Illustrations drawn from the Manners and Customs, the Scenes and the Scenery of the Holy Land, by W. M. Thomson, M.D., twenty-five years a Missionary in Syria and Palestine. With 3 Maps and several hundred Illustrations. 2 vols. Post 8vo. cloth. 1*l.* 1*s.*

Missionary Geography for the use of Teachers and Missionary Collectors. Fcap. 8vo. with numerous maps and illustrations, 3*s.* 6*d.*

A Topographical Picture of Ancient Jerusalem; beautifully coloured. Nine feet by six feet, on rollers, varnished. 3*l.* 3*s.*

The Light of the World: a most True Relation of a Pilgrimess travelling towards Eternity. Divided into Three Parts: which deserve to be read, understood, and considered by all who desire to be saved. Reprinted from the edition of 1696. Beautifully printed by Clay on toned paper. Crown 8vo. pp. 593, bevelled boards, 10*s.* 6*d.*

The Life of the late Dr. Mountain, Bishop of Quebec. 8vo. cloth, price 10*s.* 6*d.*

The Mission of Great Sufferings. By Elihu Burritt. 12mo. 5*s.*

> "*Mr. Burritt strikes this chord of sympathy with suffering in tones that make the reader's heart thrill within him. But the tales he tells of the present age must not be allowed to leave the impression that we have sailed into an Utopian period of a living and universal love, both of God and man. They do prove—and it is a precious and cheering thing, although not the most precious—that the present generation is promptly pitiful at any cost of self-sacrifice towards evils that it really feels to be evils, disease and hunger, and cold and nakedness. The book is a specimen of powerful, heart-stirring writing.*"—Guardian.
>
> "*This is a most valuable work on a subject of deep importance. The object is to show the aim and action of great sufferings in the development of Christian faith and of spiritual life.*"—Observer.

Faith's Work Perfected. The Rise and Progress of the Orphan Houses of Halle. From the German of Francke. By William L. Gage. Fcap. 2*s.* 6*d.*

A Short Method of Prayer; an Analysis of a Work so entitled by Madame de la Mothe-Guyon; by Thomas C. Upham, Professor of Mental and Moral Philosophy in Bowdoin College, U.S. America. Printed by Whittingham. 12mo. cloth. 1*s.*

Christian Believing and Living. By F. D. Huntington, D.D. Crown 8vo. cloth, 3*s.* 6*d.*

Life Thoughts. By the Rev. Henry Ward Beecher. Two Series, complete in one volume, well printed and well bound. 2*s.* 6*d.* Superior edition, illustrated with ornamented borders. Sm. 4to. cloth extra. 7*s.* 6*d.*

Dr. Beecher's Life and Correspondence: an Autobiography. Edited by his Son. 2 vols. post 8vo. with Illustrations, price 21*s.*

Life and Experience of Madame de la Mothe Guyon. By Professor Upham. Edited by an English Clergyman. Crown 8vo. cloth, with Portrait. Third Edition, 7*s.* 6*d.*

By the same Author.

Life of Madame Catherine Adorna; 12mo. cloth. 4*s.* 6*d.*
The Life of Faith, and Interior Life. 2 vols. 5*s.* 6*d.* each.
The Divine Union. 7*s.* 6*d.*

LAW AND JURISPRUDENCE.

WHEATON'S Elements of International Law. An entirely new edition, edited by R. E. Dana, Author of "Two Years before the Mast," &c. Royal 8vo. cloth extra, 30s.

History of the Law of Nations; by Henry Wheaton. LL.D. author of the "Elements of International Law." Roy. 8vo. cloth, 31s. 6d.

Commentaries on American Law; by Chancellor Kent. Ninth and entirely New Edition. 4 vols. 8vo. calf. 5l. 5s.; cloth, 4l. 10s.

Treatise on the Law of Evidence; by Simon Greenleaf, LL.D. 3 vols. 8vo. calf. 4l. 4s.

Treatise on the Measure of Damages; or, An Enquiry into the Principles which govern the Amount of Compensation in Courts of Justice. By Theodore Sedgwick. Third revised Edition, enlarged. Imperial 8vo. cloth. 31s. 6d.

Justice Story's Commentaries on the Constitution of the United States. 2 vols. 36s.

Justice Story's Commentaries on the Laws, viz. Bailments—Agency—Bills of Exchange—Promissory Notes—Partnership—and Conflict of Laws. 6 vols. 8vo. cloth, each 28s.

Justice Story's Equity Jurisprudence. 2 vols. 8vo. 63s.; and Equity Pleadings. 1 vol. 8vo. 31s. 6d.

W. W. Story's Treatise on the Law of Contracts. Fourth Edition, greatly enlarged and revised. 2 vols. 8vo. cloth, 63s.

MEDICAL.

HUMAN Physiology, Statical and Dynamical; by Dr. Draper. 300 Illustrations. 8vo. 25s.

A Treatise on the Practice of Medicine; by Dr. George B. Wood. Fourth Edition. 2 vols. 36s.

A Treatise on Fractures, by J. F. Malgaigne, Chirurgien de l'Hôpital Saint Louis, Translated, with Notes and Additions, by John H. Packard, M.D. With 106 Illustrations. 8vo. sheep. 1l. 1s.

Elements of Chemical Physics; with numerous Illustrations. By Josiah P. Cooke. 8vo. cloth. 16s.
  "*As an introduction to Chemical Physics, this is by far the most comprehensive work in our language.*"—Athenæum.

A History of Medicine, from its Origin to the Nineteenth Century. By Dr. P. V. Renouard. 8vo. 18s.

Letters to a Young Physician just entering upon Practice; by James Jackson, M.D. Fcp. 8vo. 5s.

Lectures on the Diseases of Women and Children. By Dr. G. S. Bedford. 4th Edition. 8vo. 18s.

The Principles and Practice of Obstetrics. By Gunning S.
Bedford, A.M., M.D. With Engravings. 8vo. Cloth, 1*l.* 1*s.*

Principles and Practice of Dental Surgery; by C. A. Harris. 6th
Edition. 8vo. 24*s.*

Chemical and Pharmaceutical Manipulations; by C. and C. Morfit.
Royal 8vo. Second Edition enlarged. 21*s.*

FICTION AND MISCELLANEOUS.

 NEW Novel. By Mrs. H. B. Stowe. 3 vols.
                                         [*Immediately.*
Anne Judge, Spinster. By F. W. Robinson, Author of
" Grandmother's Money." 3 vols. 24*s.*

Norwood. By Henry Ward Beecher. 3 vols. crown 8vo.
                                         [*Shortly.*

Other People's Windows. By J. Hain Friswell. 2 vols. post 8vo.
                                         [*Shortly.*

The Hunchback's Charge. By W. Clark Russell. 3 vols. post
8vo. 24*s.*

The Guardian Angel: a Romance. By the Author of " The
Autocrat of the Breakfast Table." 2 vols.   [*Shortly.*

Humphrey Dyot. By James Greenwood, Author of " A Night
in a Workhouse," &c. 3 vols.

Toilers of the Sea. By Victor Hugo. Translated by W. Moy
Thomas. Cheap edition. With engravings from original pictures by
Gustave Doré. Crown 8vo. 6*s.*

A Casual Acquaintance. By Mrs. Duffus Hardy. 2 vols.
post 8vo, 16*s.*

The Story of Kennett. By Bayard Taylor. 2 vols. post 8vo, 16*s.*

Mr. Charles Reade's celebrated Romance, Hard Cash. A new
and cheap Standard Edition. Price 6*s.* handsomely bound in cloth.

Passing the Time. By Blanchard Jerrold. 2 vols. post 8vo. 16*s.*

Marian Rooke. By Henry Sedley. 3 vols. 24*s.*

Sir Felix Foy, Bart. By Dutton Cook. 3 vols. post 8vo. 24*s.*
The Trials of the Tredgolds. By the same. 3 vols. 24*s.*
Hobson's Choice, by the same Author. 2*s.*

Selvaggio. By the Author of " Mary Powell." One vol. 8*s.*
Also, by the same Author.
Miss Biddy Frobisher. 1 vol. 8*s.*
The Masque at Ludlow, and other Romanesques. 8*s.*

A Mere Story. By the Author of " Twice Lost." 3 vols. 24*s.*

John Godfrey's Fortunes. By Bayard Taylor. 3 vols. 24*s.*
Hannah Thurston. By the same Author. 3 vols. 24*s.*

A Splendid Fortune. By J. Hain Friswell. 3 vols. post 8vo. 24*s.*

Lion-Hearted; a Novel. By Mrs. Grey. 2 vols. post 8vo. 16*s.*

A Dangerous Secret. By Annie Thomas. 2 vols. 16*s.*

St. Agnes Bay; or, Love at First Sight. Post 8vo. cloth, 7*s.*

The White Favour. By H. Holl. 3 vols. 24*s.*
> The Old House in Crosby Square. By the same Author. 2 vols. 16*s.*
> More Secrets than One. By the same Author. 3 vols. 24*s.*

Strathcairn. By Charles Allston Collins. 2 vols. post 8vo. 16*s.*

A Good Fight in the Battle of Life: a Prize Story founded on
Facts. Reprinted by permission from "Cassell's Family Paper."
Crown 8vo. cloth, 7*s. 6d.*

Female Life in Prison. By a Prison Matron. Fourth and
cheaper edition: with a Photograph, by permission, from the engraving
of Mrs. Fry reading to the Prisoners in 1816. 1 vol. crown 8vo., 5*s.*

Myself and My Relatives. *Second Thousand.* With Frontispiece on Steel from a Drawing by John E. Millais, A.R.A. Cr. 8vo. 5*s.*

Tales for the Marines. By Walter Thornbury. 2 vols. post
8vo. 16*s.*
> "*Who would not wish to be a Marine, if that would secure a succession*
> *of tales like these?*"—Athenæum.

Helen Felton's Question: a Book for Girls By Agnes Wylde.
Cheaper Edition, with Frontispiece. Crown 8vo. 3*s. 6d.*

Faith Gartney's Girlhood. By Mrs. D. T. Whitney. Fcap.
8vo. with coloured Frontispiece, cloth, price 3*s. 6d.*

The Gayworthys. By the same Author. Third Edition, with
coloured Frontispiece. Cloth, 3*s. 6d.*

A Summer in Leslie Goldthwaite's Life. By the same Author.
With Illustrations. Fcap. 8vo. 2*s. 6d.*

The Professor at the Breakfast Table. By Oliver W. Holmes,
Author of the "Autocrat of the Breakfast Table." Fcap. 3*s. 6d.*

The Rooks' Garden, and other Papers. By Cuthbert Bede,
Author of "The Adventures of Mr. Verdant Green." Post 8vo. 7*s. 6d.*

The Journal of a Waiting Gentlewoman. Edited by Beatrice
A. Jourdan. Post 8vo. 8*s.*

The White Wife; with other stories, Supernatural, Romantic
and Legendary. Collected and Illustrated by Cuthbert Bede. Post 8vo.
cloth, 6*s.*

Wayside Warbles. By Edward Capern, Rural Postman, Bide-
ford, Devon. Fcap. 8vo. cloth, 5*s.*

House and Home Papers. By Mrs. H B. Stowe. 12mo. boards,
1*s.*; cloth extra, 2*s. 6d.*

Little Foxes. By Mrs. H. B. Stowe. Cloth extra, 3*s. 6d.*
Popular Edition, fancy boards, 1*s.*

The Pearl of Orr's Island. A Story of the Coast of Maine. By Mrs. Harriet Beecher Stowe. Author of " Uncle Tom's Cabin," " Minister's Wooing." In popular form, Part I. 1s. 6d.; Part II. 2s.; or, complete in one volume, with engraving on steel from water-colour by John Gilbert. Handsomely bound in cloth, 5s.

The Minister's Wooing: a Tale of New England. By the Author of " Uncle Tom's Cabin." Two Editions:—1. In post 8vo. cloth, with Thirteen Illustrations by Hablot K. Browne. 5s.—2. Popular Edition, crown 8vo cloth, with a Design by the same Artist. 2s. 6d.

Nothing to Wear, and Two Millions, by William Allen Butler. 1s.

Railway Editions of Popular Fiction. On good paper, well-printed and bound, fancy boards.

Paul Foster's Daughter. 2s.	Faith Gartney's Girlhood. 1s. 6d.
The Lost Sir Massingberd. 2s.	Mrs. Stowe's Little Foxes. 1s.
The Bubbles of Finance. 2s.	—————— House and Home. 1s.
Profits of Panics. 1s.	Footsteps Behind Him, 2s.
The Gayworthys. 1s. 6d.	Right at Last. By Mrs. Gaskell. 2s.
The Autocrat of the Breakfast Table. 1s.	Hobson's Choice. By Dutton Cook. 2s.
The King's Mail. 2s.	Mattins and Muttons; or, the Beauty of Brighton. 2s.
My Lady Ludlow. 2s.	
When the Snow Falls, 2s.	

Tauchnitz's New Series of Copyright German Authors.

Auerbach's On the Heights. Translated by F. E. Bunnett. 3 vols. limp cloth, 6s.

Reuter's In the Year '13. Translated by C. L. Lewes. Limp cloth, 2s.

Goethe's Faust. Translated by John Auster, LL.D. Limp cloth, 2s.

Fouqué's Undine; and other Tales. Translated by F. E. Bunnett. Limp cloth, 2s.

Heyse (Paul), L'Arrabiata.

Princess of Brunswick, and other Tales. By Zschokke.

LONDON: SAMPSON LOW, SON, AND MARSTON.

MILTON HOUSE, LUDGATE HILL.

English, American, and Colonial Booksellers and Publishers.

Chiswick Press:—Whittingham and Wilkins, Tooks Court, Chancery Lane.

www.ingramcontent.com/pod-product-compliance
Lightning Source LLC
Chambersburg PA
CBHW021759110726
47902CB00006B/1578